"You were in my house yesterday."

Jonna's voice shook.

"What makes you think so?" She felt Sam's deadly stillness.

"Magic was out. She was inside when I left."

"Magic?"

"The cat."

"Yeah, I know. I just don't understand what that has to do with me."

"She couldn't have opened the door herself." Was Magic the only reason she had thought he'd been in her house? She couldn't remember.

But she did remember the hair standing up on the back of her neck as she toured the rooms, looking for a hint of something out of place. And she had felt his *presence*....

Dear Reader,

'Tis the season when all things weird and wonderful walk the earth, and in that spirit, we have two terrifying tales to tempt you over to the dark side of love.

Start with Marilyn Tracy's *Memory's Lamp* and share heroine Sandy Rush's terror as the impossible becomes possible, as another woman's memories invade her mind and fill her with fear of the one man she needs— longs—to trust. Then accompany Premiere author Val Daniels to that eerie space *Between Dusk and Dawn*, where nothing is what it seems, and where Sam Barton may not be the protector Jonna Sanders hopes for but instead the very danger from which she should be fleeing.

In months to come, we'll be bringing you more eerily romantic stories by more of your favorite authors, but until then, be careful. After all, you never know what will be waiting in the shadows—Silhouette Shadows.

Yours,

Leslie J. Wainger
Senior Editor and Editorial Coordinator

Please address questions and book requests to:
Silhouette Reader Service
U.S.: 3010 Walden Ave., P.O. Box 1325, Buffalo, NY 14269
Canadian: P.O. Box 609, Fort Erie, Ont. L2A 5X3

VAL DANIELS

BETWEEN DUSK AND DAWN

Published by Silhouette Books
America's Publisher of Contemporary Romance

To Danedri, my all grown-up, spectacular baby girl.
May you always be able to tell the good guys from
the bad—especially now that I'm not with you to
point them out.

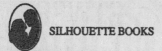 SILHOUETTE BOOKS

ISBN 0-373-27042-9

BETWEEN DUSK AND DAWN

Copyright © 1994 by Vivian A. Thompson

VAL DANIELS

wrote her first romance in the sixth grade, when her teacher told the class to transform a short story about a bear attack into a play. Val changed it to a romance in the process by bringing a neighboring family to visit the isolated farm. Saving the neighbor's daughter from the bear gave the shy son, the main character in the original story, the courage to declare his affection for her. In Val's current stories, the heroes and heroines are older and wiser, and their problems are not bears, but the romantic ending remains the same.

Val lives in Kansas with her husband, Dan, their teenagers, Danedri and Drew, and a Murphy dog.

Dear Reader,

I've loved romances since my grandmother began sharing hers with me when I was twelve years old. My addiction to horror/suspense came later, as I discovered Dean Koontz, Mary Higgins Clark, Thomas Harris, Robert R. McCammon, Stephen King—the list continues to grow. (And I know I'm not the only romance reader who is an avid fan of these books.)

I searched for stories that combined the two—Koontz's *Lightning* came close, but when the guy who had loved so dramatically throughout the book didn't get the girl in the end, I cried. So when I heard Silhouette planned to marry my two favorite genres into "romantic stories from the dark side of love," I went right to my computer and started typing. It took about four pages to figure out that writing such an unusual combination was really tough. How do you blend edge-of-your-seat suspense with the ecstasy of falling in love? What did the two kinds of stories have in common? Emotion. I went for that.

I can't begin to describe the emotions I felt when Mary Theresa Hussey called to say Silhouette wanted to publish *Between Dusk and Dawn*. Let's just say I still smile a lot, knowing some of those magic feelings I tried so hard to capture must have come through.

I hope my story gives you a suspenseful, heart-stopping chill or two and a romantic, heartwarming high. Enjoy!

Sincerely,

Val Daniels

PROLOGUE

He'd always liked his hands. Always. But lately, they were more expressive, even more artistic than ever. He flexed them, held them up to the light, admired the beautiful strength of them as he paused in his task. His hands reflected his growing power, his competence, what he was destined to be.

He could hardly wait until he could face *her* with his accomplishments. He would lay the meticulously prepared book in front of her, watch her face fill with surprise, with pride at the quality of his work. And when his mother's surprise turned to dismay as she comprehended his true talent, his real genius, he would snicker and add her to the pages he had reserved for her.

His attention returned to the record. *The Record,* he revised in italics in his mind. He closed the leather-covered book, letting his thumb mark the page he had just completed. Perhaps he would have the words *The Record* engraved here in gold leaf. Certainly such a chronicle deserved that dignity.

Yes. That was what he would do.

With that decision made, he resumed his work, pausing to study his neat block lettering across the top of the last finished page. He had framed the clipping with a lightweight mat and carefully centered it on the page. He double-checked the margins he'd left around the edges. Perfect. Each one exactly the same. Setting the ruler aside, he reread the obituary.

Leah Thurston Darcy

Leah Thurston Darcy, 37, formerly of Keysbrook, Kentucky, died April 6 at home. Born in Ohio and raised in Kentucky, she received a bachelor's degree in journalism at North East Texas State University. She moved to Colorado after her marriage to Steven E. Darcy. She worked for the Denver *Chronicle* until her death. Mrs. Darcy was a member of the First Christian Church of Denver and the National Association of Women Communicators. She recently received the prestigious National Communicators Award for Excellence in Government/Political Reporting.

Survivors include her husband of sixteen years; two daughters, Regan and Cynthia; her parents, Mr. and Mrs. Donald Thurston, Keysbrook, KY.; and her sister, Amy Thurston Collins, Keysbrook, KY.

Burial took place at Woodlawn Memorial Cemetery, Denver, Colorado.

He sighed with satisfaction. Lovingly turning to the next unblemished page, he took the yearbook photo from its protective sandwich bag. A thrill gripped him as he anticipated his next project. He'd been fortunate enough this time to find a color photo. "Fortunate, indeed," he murmured, handling the glossy print with ritualistic care. He didn't want to mar it with fingerprints.

Too bad it isn't bigger, he thought, moving the picture from one spot to another. Only when he had found its proper position on the creamy page would he begin the tedious process of lettering.

"There," he said finally, marking each corner where the picture would fit with a barely discernible dot. He set the picture aside to pick up the specially nibbed pen.

This was the crucial part. The lettering must be right, especially since he did it freehand: names in flowing script, everything else in block style.

His brow grew damp with intense concentration, his tongue dipped out of the corner of his mouth with each downward stroke of the pen. At last, he laid the photo inside the precisely placed marks and stood to view his labors from a wider perspective.

"Yes." He praised his meticulous work with a pleased nod, then lifted his small glass in a toast. "Congratulations on winning my award, Jonna Sanders," he said softly. "You're the best so far. You'll get only *my* best. I promise."

CHAPTER ONE

He came with the dusk, blending with the lengthening shadows beneath the cottonwoods that stood sentry along the road leading to the farmstead. Jonna sensed his presence before she heard him; heard him long before she saw him. She peered over her shoulder into the gloom as a twig snapped. She rose from where she'd been kneeling to paint the bottom of the screen door as a footstep scraped against the hard dirt of the rutted drive. A shiver rippled through her as he appeared, taking several purposeful steps into the unshaded yard and what was left of the light.

He was dressed in black, his long dark coat open and flowing behind him in the ceaseless Kansas wind. He stopped, watching as she dropped her paintbrush into the drip-decorated can. She grabbed a rag from beside her tools and forced herself to come forward to greet him.

"Hi," she called tentatively. She struggled to see his eyes as she sensed them on her.

He moved another step or two.

She suddenly felt isolated and vulnerable, reluctant to have him close in on her. She squared her shoulders and edged toward the porch steps, trying all the while to give her uneasiness a name. By nature, she was open, too trusting for her own good her friends said—and she'd proved this over and over again. But something about this man made her feel wary.

Her farm was far away from the beaten path, so maybe it was simply that strangers, even salesmen, rarely stopped here. Perhaps it was the time of day or that someone had been asking questions about her in town. Maybe the fine hair on her neck stood on end because darkness was closer than she had realized, and he, like the night, had crept quietly upon her.

Or maybe, she realized, it was the stranger himself. He was tall, muscular, yet he came on cat's feet—silent, graceful. The incongruity seemed menacing.

And where was his car? She was nine miles from anywhere so no one came to visit on foot.

Car trouble. Of course! He must have walked in from the highway. Jonna felt herself breathe a little easier, but not much. After all, she never knew who might be traveling the stretch of Highway 50, which ran for two miles through the middle of her land.

She nervously rubbed at the gray paint splotches bruising her hands and finally saw his midnight-dark eyes as they followed the motion.

She descended to the lowest step and immediately wished she'd kept her vigil from the top of the porch. His height left her at a disadvantage and his intense wordless stare pinned and paralyzed her, like a fly trapped in a web. His nearness seemed to force the air from her lungs.

She mentally shook herself. Her apprehension was ridiculous, uncalled for. She refused to give it credence.

"Can I help you?" Her voice, friendly yet controlled, was near its normal tone, only a fraction higher than usual.

"Jonna Sanders?" It was a question but his voice was sure. He knew exactly whom he was talking to.

"Yes?" she answered cautiously. *Who wants to know?* The cooling autumn wind whipped around the corner of the house, layering her response beneath its low moan, and a premonition of inevitable change gripped her. Jonna dismissed the thought that he had brought the dusk and the chill in the wind with him.

"Winter's coming," he said softly, as if in answer to her unspoken thought. He studied the landscape around him as if trying to decide what that season would do to it.

Jonna's brow wrinkled impatiently. "Can I help you, mister? If you came to speculate about the weather—" she waved vaguely toward the half-painted screen door "—I'm afraid I need to get back to work."

One corner of the man's mouth attempted a smile, but whatever motivated it didn't reach his troubled eyes. "I came about the job," he said. "I hear you need a hired hand?"

"Moss sent you?" She released a long sigh she hadn't known was building. "I wasn't expecting you until Friday."

He opened his mouth, then obviously changed his mind about explaining why he was early. "Then the position hasn't been filled?" he asked.

"No." As far as she knew, he was the only person interested. "But quite frankly, the more I think about it, the more I think I should just lease out all the grazing land and quit trying to keep things going myself." She'd been mulling the whole issue again just before he arrived, so the thought came easily, but she wasn't sure why she told him. Probably because she wanted something to fall back on if she told him she couldn't hire him.

"Why don't you?"

His question seemed odd, since he wanted the job himself. Jonna busied her fingers with the rag. "You mean why don't I lease the land?" She felt him nod and shrugged. "I guess because my father would roll over in his grave at the thought," she admitted. "And I don't have the nerve to face his ghost if he came back to haunt me."

Her attempt at humor did nothing to relax the tension between them.

"How much did Moss tell you about what I'm looking for?" she asked, grasping for her common sense. It wasn't exactly the corporate world, but this was a job interview, for heaven's sake. And certainly nothing for *her* to be nervous about. Especially since the determined set of his lean face and his powerful body said he really wanted this job.

"Not much," the man admitted.

"Did he tell you I wasn't going to be able to pay much right now?"

"No, ma'am." His nose lifted slightly. "But I don't have much experience either so it will probably be about what I'm worth."

He had a slight drawl. An Okie, perhaps? "At least you're honest." Again, his gaze whipped away and Jonna couldn't help but ask, "Aren't you?"

He stared off toward the hills that rose behind the house. "Honest as the day is long—most of the time," he added quietly, and his gaze returned to capture and hold hers.

"And when aren't you honest, Mr. . . . ?"

"Barton. Sam Barton," he filled in for her.

"When aren't you honest, Mr. Barton?"

His hesitation was infinitesimal. "Some people can't deal with the truth."

"Does that include you?"

She almost hoped he would say yes so she could be rid of him, but she couldn't doubt his honesty at the moment.

His jaw tightened. His eyes were fierce. "You can't protect yourself from the truth."

She cringed under his intensity. "No, you can't, Mr. Barton," she agreed, drawn to him in spite of herself.

"Why don't you tell me a little about the experience you do have," she invited, more out of curiosity than because it mattered.

She *wanted* to hire him. His reluctant honesty drew her in much the same way she imagined a June bug was drawn to yard light. And she had to get someone established in the job before she left for L.A. in a little more than a week, didn't she? She wanted it to be him.

He said he'd grown up around horses, though he had never worked with cattle. "But I can learn anything," he assured her solemnly.

And she believed. Looking at him, at the tightly controlled power he exuded, at his square, determined face, at his long capable fingers, she didn't doubt for a second that he could do anything he set his mind to.

"What does the job entail?"

A muscle tightened in his jaw and she realized that it was the second time he'd asked.

She'd been staring. "For the next few months anyway, what I need is pretty simple," she said. "I need someone to take care of the horses every day—there are two of them," she began, then gave him an abbreviated list of the daily routine of raising range-fed cattle.

From time to time he muttered, "I see." But of course, he didn't. He was peering past her, watching the night overcome the last bit of light.

She sighed wistfully. "Then, my next priority this fall is mending fences. First, of course, we have to see exactly what needs fixing. You'll need to use Murphy—the sorrel with white-stockinged forelegs—and ride the fences, repairing the minor things, making notes of the bigger problems so you can take the truck out to them with the equipment and necessary supplies later.

"That reminds me," she added, "my truck is inside the front end of the barn, but it needs to be repaired before anyone will get much use out of it so—except when I need it—you'll have to use my little pickup. But as long as the weather holds, you'll be doing yourself a favor to take one of the horses when you're out and about. At least until you get acquainted with the uneven terrain, a vehicle can be a drawback." She was rambling.

"I see." This time he did. He was actually looking at her. Some of the tension in his stance was gone and she realized that somewhere in the middle of the last statement, she'd pretty much said he was hired.

She smiled at him hopefully. He still had not answered a single one of her smiles with anything more than a weary twist of his lips.

He did now.

"I don't suppose you're mechanically inclined?" she said breathlessly.

"I'm not bad."

Lord, what an understatement! The subtle grin spread from his mouth to his eyes, warming them momentarily, sparking the same warmth in her veins.

"I've had a lot more experience with engines than with cattle," he continued.

She couldn't seem to take her gaze from his lips, even though the smile had disappeared. "I think the truck might need a new starter."

"I'll take a look at it first chance I get," he promised.

Now that she had his attention, she contrarily wished he would become engrossed in their surroundings again. She licked her lips nervously. "Anyway. That gives you some idea of what you'll be doing for the next month or two. Next spring the real work begins, but we'll put on an extra hand for that."

"I doubt I'll be here by then."

She laughed in nervous surprise. "Then why am I hiring you?"

"You need me," he said, his voice a quiet rasp, as if the smile had been so rusty it caused everything else to creak. "And I need to be here."

His words brought the shiver back and centered it in Jonna's bones. "Why?"

"I need the job," he answered simply. Something elemental in his tone reached her soul and a need of her own simmered to life.

"And the house," he added, looking at the front door of the house she'd been preparing for its new occupant. "I understand it comes with the job."

"That's how I get by with paying as little as I do," she admitted. "And it's warm in the winter and solid and partially furnished. Hopefully, it makes up some for the low pay. And you're right about me needing you," she said lightly. "I haven't exactly been bombarded with applicants." She held out her hand. "Glad to have you, Sam Barton."

His fingers closed around hers and something flashed between them. The danger she had sensed even before she saw him was real, so real it displaced the air around her and made breathing impossible. It was in his grip, his eyes, and evident in the very deliberate way he immediately let her go.

She suppressed a shiver. She shouldn't have hired him, but she had. She shouldn't have touched him, but she had. Somehow, none of it could be undone.

Sam watched her stammer through a few sentences more, then went to get his car. He'd left it in her driveway by the house on top of the hill and walked down when he'd seen the porch light come on at the farmhouse below.

He drew a deep breath and closed his eyes for a second, letting the peacefulness of his surroundings wash over him. He supposed it was too much to hope that it would also settle the pace of his heart.

He hadn't expected to feel so damn disturbed by her. She'd been a name, and the image the name had conjured had been somewhat mixed with the image of the other one. The one in Colorado. He'd expected Jonna to be tall, plumped slightly by the years she'd accumulated since college, perhaps with glasses and a piercing, suspicious gaze.

He hadn't expected her to be full of life, with a permanent, sparkling challenge in her eyes. He hadn't expected her warmth. He hadn't expected a petite and very shapely body with long legs stretching beneath the sexy, tight cut-offs, or the mass of golden brown hair that looked like the wind had had a wonderful time playing and pulling delicate strands from the restricting band that held it back.

He hadn't expected her flawless, delicately featured face to have retained the innocence her yearbook picture showed; or hazel eyes that were wide and trusting, even though she had tried so hard to be wary.

He definitely hadn't anticipated his reaction to her—hadn't anticipated, and wouldn't tolerate it. He refused to let his body distract him from why he was here.

It was night now, though too early for stars. Unbroken by the evenly spaced lights of civilization and city planners, night here was a vast, quiet black that swallowed everything. It seemed so physical, he had the feeling he could fist his hand and punch a hole in it, opening a crack that would leak bright light.

The thought was a whimsical one, the first he'd had in months, and a bitter smile twisted the corners of his mouth.

He'd been right to come, he knew. This sojourn with Jonna Sanders would be either his salvation or his ruination.

Grateful for the chance to reexamine the lay of the land in the dark, he paused in the middle of the rough track that lurched upward from the tree-sheltered main drive. From this vantage point, just above the tree line, he could see forever.

In the distance, tiny headlights weaved in and out, up and down the barren hills. One set would disappear; another would appear much farther away. The previous ones would suddenly spark into view, much closer than they had been. It was like a fairy show, as fascinating as any laser-light display he'd seen.

He couldn't have created a better place for his stand if he were God.

Behind him, to the right down the path he'd just climbed, the two-story white farmhouse waited like a warm welcome at the end of a long day. Jonna had said the house wasn't ready yet to be occupied and he'd told her he didn't mind. She must be trying anyway, he decided. He watched as one light after another brightened the many windows.

Her silhouette twisted and posed on the shade in one of the upstairs corners. Her arms lifted gracefully above her head and a shape billowed from her hands as if she could throw fluid motion from her fingertips. Then, the lean, gently curved line of her body bent and became an indecipherable shadow and he turned away, denying himself his need to watch.

She was making up a bed, he decided, and shook his head at her bother. He'd have to change it, of course. Bed or no bed, the room on the opposite side was probably the only one with a clear view of the modern house on the crest of the stark hill. Her house.

That house, a triangular, modified A-frame, loomed like a grounded bat above him.

The flat side facing him was nothing more than a vast expanse of smoky glass. The sides of the house swept back at angles, the roof slanted down from its peak of about two and a half stories until they converged to barely the height of a single story at the other end. A covered walkway separated a double garage from the house. His car was parked in front of the duplicate door on the opposite side of the point.

Sam surveyed the ground around her house as he settled into his car. He'd covered the area completely when he'd arrived a little while ago. It would be hard to take her by surprise, he'd decided then. His opinion didn't change with the night. It was an almost perfect fortress if she wanted it to be.

But she didn't lock her doors.

Did she relax her guard only when she was working somewhere on the property, or was that a habit she also practiced at night or when she went into town?

There were ways to find out without raising her suspicions, he supposed, and he had time—plenty of time, now that he had a reason to be here.

He grinned with satisfaction, started the car and rounded the circular drive past the garage. Perched on the summit of the rough path, he marveled again at the terrain before him.

A few stars were out now and night had softened the hills' rough and raw edges.

Denise had always had an affinity for great drama, and this was as dramatic as you could get. And she'd always wanted to learn to fly. If she were here, she would have wished for a pair of wings. "Look, Sam," he could hear his sister saying, "I could spread them and soar for miles and miles without a single bit of effort."

Sam felt the familiar guilt clutch his stomach as bile rose in his throat. "You would have loved this wild place, Denise," he whispered. The wind groaned softly, speaking the same language as the torn and ragged edges of his soul, and he wondered for the millionth time in this past year and a half if he was crazy.

They thought so at the college. Even Barry, his sworn and faithful friend, doubted Sam's sanity. Thank heavens, that hadn't kept Barry from promising his help. Sam would have to call Barry first thing in the morning, he remembered. He'd promised to touch base often.

Sam reviewed his mental to-do list as he released the brake and coasted down the road to where Jonna was probably growing impatient.

Jonna. Damn. He'd promised himself that this time, he wouldn't feel a thing. Not responsibility. Not pity. He wouldn't see her as anything more than a piece of the landscape. He had steeled himself against it, but already the challenging tilt of that chin, the steady, soulful eyes had planted a creeping admiration in his mind and made her seem all too human.

Don't feel *anything*, he added to his list. Don't let feelings get in the way. This final confrontation was going to be difficult enough without caring who or what interfered.

Jonna Sanders was simply a tool, a very small part of the big picture. After the mess he'd made of the last one, he would do well to remember that.

He probably should have corrected her impression that he was sent by her unknown friend, he realized. *But you couldn't take the chance, old buddy.*

After her initial, wary reaction to him, he couldn't chance her choosing someone else to fill the job he'd gone to so much trouble to get. He'd just have to deal with any problems that little white lie brought when they came.

Just as he'd deal with the man Moss—whoever Moss was—was sending Friday. Maybe he could get rid of him the same way he'd gotten rid of his predecessor.

And waylaying anyone coming to see Jonna shouldn't be difficult. From now on, they'd have to come past him.

Slowing, he turned the last curve leading back to the farmhouse. He pulled to a stop beside the steps with a sober sense of satisfaction.

She was waiting on the front porch, her arms wrapped around herself in a warming hug. She shivered in the chill night wind.

He felt the stirring again, the magnetic pull she seemed to exert. He hardened his heart to her. He was susceptible, he realized, but he was also in control. Control. From here on in, he was in control.

With mixed emotions, Jonna watched him return.

She couldn't help but like his honesty. Most people would do or say anything to get what they wanted, her father had always said. She couldn't accuse Sam of that. He'd been recklessly blunt, brutally determined she would hire him. Anyone who wanted, needed, a job that badly...

He gracefully unkinked his long frame and stepped out of his surprisingly sedate, four-door, family-type car. Somehow, she'd expected him to drive a flashy black sporty thing with darkly tinted windows. He's down on his luck, she reminded herself, but had no doubts looking at him, that it was temporary. "I didn't think it would take you so long," she called.

"I stopped to admire the view," he explained.

"It's different, isn't it?"

He nodded and joined her at the front door.

"Where's your luggage?"

He lifted a large barrel-shaped bag.

"That's all?" she asked.

"Most." Again he nodded. "I'll get the rest out of the trunk later."

He grazed her body with his eyes and she turned away. Compared to the sensation she'd felt when they actually touched, his visual touch was almost restful. "Come in." She pulled the screen door open and waved him in ahead of her.

The house was much warmer than the world outside.

"This is where I grew up," she said as he looked around the large foyer. She gestured to one side where the French doors of the dark living room stood open. "I'm afraid most of the furniture is from that time period, too," she added.

He was looking the other way. He eased past her, through the open arch leading into the dining room on the other side. He was careful to avoid brushing against her, but she tingled with his passing.

"Turn out the light," he said from the window, surprising her with the request.

"Why?" She automatically did as he asked.

"The view fascinates me." The heavy drapes her mother had chosen for the room muffled his words.

"Oh, the other side is much better," she said. "From the living room you can see the highway and down the open range. At sunset, the colors are gorgeous."

He left the window. The measured beat of his boots against the hardwood floor emphasized their quiet isolation.

"The view from this side is all uphill. About all you can see is my house," she said softly. Something about the way his broad-shouldered form flowed toward her in the dark made whispering seem appropriate.

He rejoined her in the foyer, noting the broad staircase that ended before the dining room door. He walked on past it, staring down the long hall that echoed its length and width. Then his gaze returned to her, void of the slightest flicker of expression. He absently lifted the receiver from the old black desk phone on the hall table and held it to his ear.

"It works," she offered, "but you'll have to get the account transferred to your name."

He nodded, crossed his arms in front of him and looked at her as if she were a guest who'd overstayed her welcome. "I think this will do just fine."

His polite dismissal irked her. "Well, that's good." She couldn't help the sarcasm. "I'd hate the house to be such a big disappointment that you wouldn't stick around."

"I'll be here."

"Why? Why *do* you want this job, Sam? I mean, you admit it isn't what you normally do. And you said you aren't going to stay."

"I need the peace and quiet. I need time." He lifted his square chin and turned slightly away, as if he didn't much like saying the *n* word and he'd already said it too many times.

"I *need* this to work, too," she said. "I'm leaving town in a week or so and someone has to be ready to take care of things here when I go. I don't expect you to stay forever," she said, suddenly very busy rubbing at a scratch on the heavy wood trim around the dining room arch, "but it would be much easier to believe you'll be here a week from now if I understood."

His dark eyes narrowed, then he sighed. "I don't expect you to understand, but my sister died about two years ago." He looked down at his long fingers, then stuffed them in the pockets of his jeans. "So far, I haven't been able to deal with that. I intend to do that here." The steel in his voice clawed at her.

"I'm sorry." She couldn't put a name to the uneasiness that settled over her. It rested heavily, like a winter storm cloud, waiting for nightfall to let loose its fury.

"So am I." His face was half in shadow.

"There aren't any miracles here," she told him, half-afraid he would believe her and leave. Half-afraid he wouldn't.

He gave her a sad smile, the first really sincere thing he'd shared. "I hope you're wrong."

"I'm not." The man needed something more than the peace and quiet working for her would give him. "Have you thought about getting professional help?" she asked as gently as she could.

He let loose a short, bitter laugh and a shiver ran down her spine. "If the professionals were any help at all, I wouldn't be here." The abrasive pain he worked so hard—but didn't quite manage—to hide, stroked her like sandpaper. This time she turned away.

His touch on her arm was feather light. As soon as he had her attention again, he withdrew his hand. "They're my demons. I'll do my darnedest to keep them away from you." A half smile twisted his mouth to one side. And though tired lines around his chocolate eyes crinkled, the smile didn't reach them.

"I'd appreciate that," she said sincerely, wondering warily what she'd gotten herself into this time.

"And whatever happens, I won't desert you before you get back from your trip."

"I appreciate that, too. Now, let me show you around." She let herself really smile.

He straightened. "Oh, I can check everything out on my own, Ms. Sanders." He sounded almost more distant and formal than before.

"Jonna," she corrected. She thought they had cleared the air.

"Jonna," he repeated in a toneless voice that seeped around her like a cold fog.

"And on that note, I guess I'll leave you alone," she said crisply, heading for the front door. She crossed the porch, wishing she had on her riding boots. They would have expressed her irritation much more definitively than her tennis shoes.

She slammed her pickup door instead and glanced back at the house. The half-painted screen door perfectly framed his mannequin-still form against the backdrop of the brightly lit room. He watched as she reversed.

She had intended to ask him to dinner since there wasn't a thing to eat in the old house, but he was just too... too dangerous, a voice countered in her mind.

She preferred to establish a friendly, neighborly relationship with her hired men and their families. But with Mr. Sam Barton, things would be different. She had a knack for being attracted to men who weren't good for her and she was very attracted to him. His world-weary look intrigued her. He'd made her heart pound and her blood pressure soar. Even her knees had betrayed her, quivering with anticipation as he approached her across the dark dining room.

She supposed she ought to feel grateful that he wanted to keep a safe distance. She suspected that was what he was doing anyway. He'd grown colder every time his eyes had grown warm. He'd recognized the attraction, too.

She could feel him still watching as she waited impatiently for the garage door to lift on its track.

She knew it was her imagination, but only when the door was down again, separating her from the night, did she feel immune to his cautious stare.

She slammed the truck door and reached over the side of the bed to get her painting supplies. Something warm slithered against her bare ankle. With a muffled scream, she jumped and prepared to dive over the edge of the truck. In the dim light, she saw black fur disappearing beneath the vehicle.

"Magic?"

A head appeared and the half-grown kitten brushed between her legs. "Oh, Magic." She squatted to pick the cat up. "You scared me to death, you silly."

Magic curled against her and purred enthusiastically. "What are you doing out here?" Jonna murmured. "You're just warm dinner for any ol' thing wandering these hills."

She repositioned the kitten on one arm. It snuggled closer. She tried to pick up the paint things with the other hand. The timed light in the garage went out and Jonna froze, dropping the bucket. Her tools scattered noisily. She cursed again.

"Forget it," she whispered to Magic. "We don't need to take this stuff in tonight." The paintbrush could dry gunked up. She'd buy a new one rather than linger in the shadowy garage. She was suddenly, inexplicably, very spooked.

Jonna crooned softly to the fur ball in her arms as she hurried to the side door. Making her way across the covered porch to the house, Jonna felt vulnerable, naked to any sinister whim of man or nature. A random gust of breeze tugged at her shirt and crept beneath it. She shuddered as she reached the house.

Slipping inside, she turned the lock behind her, walked quickly through the door that separated the enclosed entry from the main room of the house and flicked on the light. She set Magic on the floor and was about to sag against the inner door when she realized the other outside door, the one facing the drive, wasn't locked. A rush of adrenaline multiplied and divided the disquieting feeling. This was crazy. She almost never locked the house, rarely even thought of it. So why did she suddenly feel terrified knowing it wasn't locked now?

She forced herself to reopen the second door and stepped back into the foyer. Pretending a nonchalance her shaky fingers didn't emulate, she rotated the lock on the doorknob. She reached up and slipped the deadbolt into the home it had seldom known, then repeated the motion on the other side. Finally, with a controlled sigh, she returned to the other room and let its well-lit familiarity embrace her.

Magic sat exactly where Jonna had dropped her, her head tilted as if she thought her mistress was crazy. "You're right, Magic, this *is* ridiculous," Jonna said. "You'd think I'd never had a stranger on the property before."

Never one like Sam Barton.

Lifting the cat back into her arms, Jonna stroked Magic's one white spot between her eyes. "I'll bet you're ready for some milk after being outside all this time."

Jonna opened the refrigerator door. Her hand flailed in midair as she realized with stunning certainty *why* she was so unnerved.

"*I* didn't let you out, did I?" she asked, lifting the surprised pet to eye level. Magic just purred.

Jonna had come back into the house twice before finally leaving after her late lunch. Once to answer the phone that rang the moment she opened the door and stepped outside. The second time, she returned to put Magic, who had escaped when Jonna came in to get the phone call, back inside.

She forced a calm as she filled Magic's saucer, then walked tentatively around the room. Was anything missing? Moved?

Some of her friends had accused her of building a stage where she could perform for the whole world when she'd designed the house and perched it up here on the hill.

The glass wall, slightly tinted to keep out some of the sun's heat, held no shades, blinds or drapes. Now, as she crossed the room, looking for hints or indications of invasion, her movements felt self-consciously jerky, awkward; she felt exposed.

Usually, no one got this far onto her property without her knowledge, so she couldn't believe there had been two interlopers. That meant Sam Barton had let Magic out. That meant he had come in. She could feel his presence as ominously as if he were standing in front of her.

What right did he have just to walk into her house? Though she didn't see anything missing or messed with, it didn't matter. A stranger—that stranger—had come, uninvited, into her home. She felt violated.

She stopped beside the window wall.

She could see everything for miles, but her gaze focused in one direction.

The farmhouse was dark but she could feel him there.

"What were you doing in my house, Sam Barton?" She firmed her mouth. "Tomorrow, you'd best have some answers."

CHAPTER TWO

She could have been walking right toward him. Her hand curved around her waist. Her long legs, paint splattered and bare in the cut-off jeans, moved her erratically across the room. A delicate smattering of freckles peppered her cheeks and arrogant nose. Loose strands of honey-brown hair fanned unceremoniously around her face. She was a beauty, he acknowledged, a find any man would be proud to add to his collection.

Desire hit him like an unexpected punch below his belt. But he refused to be sidetracked by instincts his mind couldn't control. He had very few actual needs—food, occasional rest, shelter. He had room for only one want. Desire for the woman staring sullenly at him didn't fit on either list.

She paused here and there, scowling, looking for something, and finally arrived at the vast expanse of window. She planted her feet determinedly.

Her hazel eyes narrowed and fired at him. Her wide expressive lips moved. The memory of her voice, lyrical, edged with that subtle husk, said his name inside his head.

Then he realized with a jolt, she *was* saying his name, but not kindly. He lifted his hand as if to ward her away and felt extremely foolish when his fingers came into contact with cool glass.

Sam sheepishly lowered his binoculars and frowned. She'd been irritated, a little uneasy when she'd left here. Now she was upset. Why?

He let the musty weight of the old drape fall back in place, separating him from the night and her searching eyes.

She'd talked to Moss? Found out he hadn't sent Sam, maybe? No. The time between when she'd left here and when she stood at her window saying his name was too short for her to have called anyone.

She knew he'd been in her house. The answer came as sure as if she had said it. Maybe she had. Maybe he had more of a talent for reading lips than he thought. But how? How could she know?

It was accidental that he had arrived while she was down here, not paying attention to what he or anyone else might be doing. He'd grabbed at the chance to check out her territory, watching constantly in case she started to return to her house up on the hill.

On his mission inside, he'd been careful not to touch anything, not to so much as curl the corner of one of the bright throw rugs that warmed the monotone, modern interior of her house.

He'd haunted the edges and shadows of the rooms, careful to stay where he wouldn't be seen if she looked up from her work on this house.

He had moved a chair nearer to the table and out of his way to get to the broad open risers that led upstairs. Could the chair have been in a certain position for a reason?

He quickly discarded that idea. She had no reason to suspect anyone would go inside. If she did, her doors would have been locked. He was getting paranoid.

He was fairly certain she hadn't examined the polished oak handrail for fingerprints either. Something else had given him away.

His mind moved to the upper story.

Her office was a loft overlooking the living area. On either side of the work space were bedrooms, each with its own bath.

One had been very impersonal, a guest room, he'd assumed. The other had looked like her.

Sunshine had streamed through the skylight above the bed and warmed the potpourri pots sitting in various places about the room. He had smelled roses and vanilla mixed with a seductive perfume that he'd whiffed later, every time she passed within two feet of him.

Poppies spilled over the comforter covering the water bed and splattered, like blood, over the wallpaper and in the drapes hiding the window wall. He'd left that room quickly, before the patch of sunlight burned her essence on him as indelibly as a brand.

Sam refrained from lifting the corner of the heavy dining room curtain again to spy on her now. She'd never see him—but he had messed up twice. He couldn't afford a third error.

He couldn't even turn on a light. He'd said he was tired, and she'd clearly seen that the house was dark. He didn't dare do anything to elevate her suspicions.

He stumbled through the dark, unfamiliar surroundings, lurching against the heavy furniture. He finally found his way up the stairs. The house creaked, echoing an empty, eerie sound back to him as he made his way to the bedroom he had chosen.

He crept to the side window and opened it an inch. He crouched there, sucking the sharp night air into his lungs. Lights still blazed in her house. He waited impatiently for her to call it a day. When his joints stiffened and pain began to shoot into his extremities, he eased himself over to the bed and extended his full length on the bare, twin mattress.

Bone-weary, he decided to rest until she went to bed. Then he could turn the lights on and move freely as he did the things he needed to do.

Flinging his arm across his eyes, he listened to the quiet. The wind, the aches and groans of the old house and the occasional chirp of a cricket were the only distinguishable sounds. He should identify and memorize them. When the time came, he needed to recognize any noises that didn't fit.

The mattress curved soothingly around him and drew him into the dream.

Denise was there. Waiting. Taunting him. Telling him to go away and leave her alone.

"Quit trying to run my life, Sam," she said insolently, tossing her dark hair. She showed him her back and fixedly ignored him. He felt his anger all over again and warned his heavy feet not to take the steps, not to close the distance between them. His fingers clenched, rebelling against him as he reached for her, intent on regaining her attention. Inside his head, his own harsh voice demanded that he not lose his temper, that he stop. Panic rose. And the woman he turned in his grasp was a lifeless doll—one that had only borrowed Denise's likeness. The eyes were dull, streaked with red. The head lolled aimlessly, un-Denise-like, to the side.

The figure before him mutated. Sun-drenched brown hair hair replaced the dark; clear hazel eyes supplanted the brown ones. Sam jerked himself awake with a muted cry. Even as he took an unsteady breath and sat up, he continued to see a lifeless Jonna in his mind's eye.

Cold sweat dampened his clothes; his body shook. His heart pounded as if it would burst out of his chest cavity. His silent scream continued long after he propelled himself out of the bed. He moaned and dragged himself to the window, wondering how long he'd slept.

The edge of morning had faded the night in the eastern sky. Her house sat peacefully on top of the hill. Nothing had changed except the sounds. He sighed. It was only a nightmare, one that wouldn't become reality. This time.

In the distance, some early bird trilled and Sam slanted his arm to the dim light. His watch showed it was a little before five in the morning.

He'd lost time, but he still had probably an hour or two before Jonna would be up. He needed to lug in the guns. Figure out how and where to rig his equipment. And if he was going to get any more sleep from here on in—which wasn't wise, but probably unavoidable—he had to rearrange things in this house. Then he had phone calls to make.

Sam's stomach growled as he made his way into the tiny upstairs bathroom. He brushed his hand over his jaw. A hot shower, a shave, and then he would get a lot done before he presented himself on her doorstep.

Somehow—without getting close enough to put his plans at risk—he would mollify her, charm her into forgetting whatever it was that had made her angry.

The phone rang twice before Jonna got one eye open wide enough to see the clock. Who would call at six in the morning? She lifted the receiver from its niche in the headboard, cutting dead the third ring.

"Jonna?" The male voice was wispy, excited. "Jonna Sanders?"

"Huh?" Jonna cleared her throat and tried to banish the morning grogginess.

A reedy laugh rippled through the receiver, into her ear and down her back like ghostly fingers.

"I'm so glad I caught you." The unknown caller paused, waiting for a response.

Jonna wasn't good at breathing this time of the day, let alone carrying on a conversation. "It would be hard to miss me this early."

"Oh? This isn't a good time?" He sounded smug, delighted to have disturbed her. "Maybe you could suggest a better one?"

She sat up, frowning.

"Would you like me to call back later with my good news?"

"I'm awake now," she said, growing impatient, trying to decide if she knew the caller's voice.

"Oh, Jonna Sanders," he reprimanded her. "Don't rush me. You're out of step with the rest of the world, you know, still lazing about. Most people have to work for a living and this is the time of day the old rat race starts."

"Who is this? Who's calling, please?"

"Ahhh. You're hurrying me again. I like to take my time," he chided, "savor these little announcements."

The mocking voice filled her with a strange dread. She started to hang up, irritated with herself for having listened this long.

"You've been chosen, Jonna Sanders. Chosen to be inducted into *The Record*."

"What?"

"The Record," he said indignantly, as if she was brash for asking.

She obviously should know what *The Record* was, Jonna thought. She frantically searched her mind.

"Oh, don't worry about it, Jonna Sanders. You've been chosen to be included in a very exclusive book with some other very important award winners. I'll be in touch real soon. We'll finalize the details and I'll explain everything. All will be made clear." There was something eerie in his enunciation. He talked slowly, softly, as if he were awed by his own words. "We'll meet soon, I promise."

"Who did you say—"

"The award." The voice darkened. "Surely you remember the award?"

"Of course, but—"

"That explains everything, doesn't it, Jonna Sanders?" He returned to his singsong delivery. "Your place in *The Record* is reserved. And you don't have to do a thing. No one can take it from you now."

"I'm afraid I don't und—"

"I assure you, when it's important, you will fully understand," the voice promised. "I'll be in touch." And the receiver clicked in her ear.

She was wide awake now. She held the phone away from her, eyeing it questioningly, reluctant to break her end of the connection until the bizarre conversation made sense. Slowly, she replaced the receiver on the hook.

What was that all about? She glanced at the clock again. The revelation that less than five minutes had passed sent her snuggling back beneath the heavy comforter.

Drowsing on Jonna's feet at the end of the bed, Magic reshaped herself around the tent Jonna's toes made as she sprawled and stared at the ceiling.

That damn award. She wished she could get half as excited about it as the rest of the world seemed to be. Her winning design had made the front cover of *Architectural News*. They'd run her picture with the house plans in *Classic American Home*.

Shoot, even the Whitfield weekly had done a front-page story on her. Half a page. But then a trip to New York City could get you front page coverage in a slow news week in a town the size of Whitfield. And the stories were more about the renowned traveler not getting mugged or murdered than about what the local hick did while he was in the big, bad city.

She guessed she ought to be glad the story focused on her award rather than on the fact that she was a woman architect.

Jonna shook her head and yawned. What she wouldn't have done to get the recognition while her father was still alive. He would have been so proud.

She contradicted the thought as quickly as it pierced her brain. "Don't kid yourself."

She punched her pillow, turned over and burrowed deeper into the gentle wave she caused. Her father would have been surprised, but not necessarily proud.

When she had chosen her career, he'd admonished her for taking on a man's job. She found it only mildly amusing that all the people who had come out of the woodwork to side with her father then were rallying around her now as if it had been their idea for her to study architecture in the first place.

Maybe he would have been *impressed* that someone was going to put her in some kind of who's-who book—even if he realized the whole thing was probably a scam to try to sell her an expensively bound copy of it. But proud? No.

Jonna smothered another yawn with the back of her hand and glanced at the clock again. Why would anyone call so early?

Probably one of those Easterners who assumed that if she was capable of winning an award, she had to be in the same time zone as he. Everyone on the East Coast assumed all who lived a hundred miles west had dropped off the face of the earth and rendered themselves ineligible.

Maybe the caller was the kook who had been phoning people all over town and asking questions about her. Kooks might actually get up this early.

Whatever. The caller had definitely been weird. Just thinking about the way he'd said, "Your place is reserved," gave her a chill.

When he contacted her again to "finalize the details," she'd hang up on him, she decided. But something about his voice, the way he'd said the words, niggled at her until she fell back to sleep.

He slammed down the telephone. He should have stopped with the call to Jonna Sanders. He'd felt such control, such power as he talked, he'd wanted to call *her* and gloat. After his success with Jonna Sanders, he'd thought he was masterful enough to handle *her*. Now she had ruined everything.

The stupid bitch. *She* had lost him his last job, bothering him all the time, haranguing him to take her here, take her there. *She* had given him the ultimatum that had landed him here.

It was *her* fault he was so far away. How dare she refuse to accept a collect call from him?

He stalked out of the antiquated phone booth, trying to yank the door off its rusty hinges as he left.

A fat, sloppy slug got out of one of the few cars in the supermarket parking lot and eyed him suspiciously. He realized he was still glowering and threw her an appropriately friendly grin, adding a little leer of admiration for good measure.

He laughed to himself as she lifted her head, tucked in her stomach and smiled back. Women were such fools. And so predictable. She looked fresh out of bed, hadn't even used a comb on her hair yet the woman almost broke her neck as she entered the store, trying to see if he was still watching her. He lifted a hand in a final salute.

His car brought him up short. "Damned, cheap, old woman." All that money and he was driving a car no self-respecting man would drive. She'd probably bought her current drinking partner, that old man she'd let move in, a Mercedes by now. The last beau had "earned" a Corvette.

"What are you whining about?" *she*'d say. "A sturdy, reliable car to get you to work, and you can go anywhere else you want in style. Anyone else would die to be in your shoes."

Yeah. His father had. And *he* had the unlimited flying privileges his dad had earned in the bizarre accident at the airport that had killed him. He couldn't enjoy all those "privileges" when he was tied down to a job. Selfish old lady was rolling in settlement dough while the man's poor son had to have a worthless two-bit job.

What else had she bought her new paramour? he wondered, his thoughts suddenly stone sober. She'd always been good at finding men with what she called "exotic tastes." He'd been quite a draw because—unless they were your own—attractive young boys didn't come cheap. And she'd used him quite shamelessly to seduce the weirdo freaks.

The car rocked as he got in and slammed the door.

But he had Jonna Sanders, he reminded himself. Looking forward to adding her to *The Record* made it easy to stand anything for a little while. Even this lousy job and his two-bit whore of an old lady.

Yeah. Wouldn't be long now. Jonna would go to Los Angeles to get her award soon.

And he would be waiting when she returned.

Jonna had barely closed her eyes again, it seemed, when the doorbell rang.

"Jiminy Christmas!" She glanced at the clock. At a little after seven, it was at least *starting* to be late enough to classify it as morning. She swung her feet out of the bed as the doorbell repeated its chime.

"Just a minute," she muttered, lifting her robe off the hook on the back of the bathroom door and sliding her feet into fuzzy slippers. The bathroom mirror said she needed a brush and she grabbed it and gave her hair a quick smoothing stroke. She still looked like a zombie, but anyone who came to call at this hour surely couldn't expect much.

"Just a minute," she said again as the bell pealed another time.

Magic, always ready for a romp first thing in the morning, hopped one step in front of her the whole way down the stairs, making descending a game. Halfway to the bottom Jonna bent and swept the kitten up in her arms. Between Magic jumping from side to side in front of her and the long flannel robe, she was going to wind up a tangled heap.

At first she didn't know the man at the door. She was about to say something inane, like "Can I help you?," then memory reasserted itself. "Mr. Barton." She nearly gasped with recognition. Of course. The new hired hand.

His face held a charming grin. The dark circles under his eyes had faded to a dull smudge. How in the world could this startlingly handsome man be the same one who'd looked so sullen last night?

"I'm hoping you can spare a cup of coffee," he said.

She hesitated, then yawned and opened the door wider. She studied him, bemused, as he walked in. His dark hair, in need of a trim and curling slightly over the back of his turtleneck collar, was carefully parted and groomed. She had the urge to reach out and muss it. Somehow, the uncontrolled look had been more—

"Frankly, caffeine of any kind will do," he said. His voice was even more controlled today, more even. "I'm not much good first thing in the morning without it."

"Me either," she agreed. "I don't do mornings. But at least you're dressed." And nicely, she added to herself.

Maybe the old saying, "Clothes make the man," wasn't so far off. Yesterday, dressed in dreary black, everything about him had seemed ominous. Today, in jeans and a plain, long-sleeved knit shirt, he looked...carefully prepared, but wonderful. The bright blue of the shirt was reflected in his almost blue-black hair and darkened the deep coffee color of his eyes. The crinkled little scowl that she had supposed was permanently in place over his nose had almost disappeared.

"Did I wake you?" he asked.

"It must be my day for ringing phones and dinging bells. Don't worry about it."

"The morning chores are done. I thought you would want me to get an early start."

Jonna gestured for him to follow her into the kitchen. "It's been more than a year since I've hired a new hand. I tend to forget that whoever I hire doesn't automatically know what to do next. I'll make a deal with you," she said, reaching the counter and turning to gaze up at him. "You make coffee while I take a quick shower. Then maybe I'll be able to carry on an intelligent conversation." She indicated a drip coffeemaker sitting by the sink.

Hanging cabinets divided the kitchen from the rest of the room. She pulled a canister from one of them. "Here's the coffee." She shoved it into his hands and started to go back upstairs.

"Want me to make breakfast, too?" he offered.

She rubbed at one eye and suppressed another yawn. "Sure, if you want."

"Anything in particular?" he called to her retreating back.

"Whatever you can find."

"Great. I'm starving."

Of course you are, she started to say, and suddenly remembered why she hadn't invited him to eat supper with her the evening before. He'd all but asked her to get lost.

And right on the heels of that came the memory that he'd been in her house. She was suddenly wide awake. She felt his eyes on her and froze halfway up the stairs.

A wave of apprehension pricked her neck, spreading through her shoulders as she heard his soft footsteps start toward her.

"Something the matter?" Sam asked.

"Magic." She glanced over her shoulder and gave Sam a wary smile. "I just wondered where my cat has gotten to," she said brightly. "Here, kitty."

Magic leapt from behind the sofa, pouncing toward her playfully.

Sam reached down and scooped up the kitten by the scruff of its neck. "Here you go."

Jonna involuntarily shrank away from the limp and lifeless-looking cat he held over the banister.

Sam's eyebrows raised. "That's the way a mother cat would carry her," he said. Their fingers brushed in the handoff.

"No." The frisson of energy that had passed between them almost crackled around her. Horrified, she curled the kitten to her breast. "Nature doesn't always do things right," she said, avoiding his look.

"Maybe not," he agreed with a shrug. "If a male cat gets a chance, he kills them." His voice sounded hard, well acquainted with nature's realities. He abruptly turned back to the kitchen. "I'll fix us some breakfast."

"Wait, Sam." She hurried back down the few steps. "We need to talk."

She resisted looking at him. She didn't need to, anyway; she could *feel* exactly where he was from anywhere in the room. He stood motionless beside the kitchen counter.

Jonna fixed her attention on Magic, stroking the soft fur in an apology for gripping her too tightly. "You were in my house yesterday." Her voice shook.

"What makes you think so?"

She felt his deadly stillness. "Magic was out. She was inside when I left after lunch."

"Magic?" His face and voice were lifeless.

"The cat."

"Yeah, I know. I just don't understand what it has to do with me." His voice was so low, she heard it vibrate in his chest.

"Unless I'm out riding or some distance from either the house or the barn, I always know when someone comes." It worried her. "I have difficulty believing *two* people could get past me in one day. I would have noticed," she added.

"*I* got past you. If you'd been on the porch painting, I would have seen you when I passed that house on my way up here, even if you didn't see me. Where were you when I came?"

She hesitated. Suddenly she wasn't as sure as she'd been. Daylight seemed to cloud the issue, to make her suspicions seem like wild imaginings.

"I arrived probably around six-thirty, seven," he offered quietly.

"I was in the barn, finishing the evening chores and taking care of the horses," she admitted.

"Were you there long?"

"About forty-five minutes," she said.

"Could someone else have come during that time?"

"All I know is that Magic could not have opened the door herself." Was Magic the only reason she had thought he'd been in her house? She couldn't remember.

But she did remember the hair standing on the back of her neck as she had toured the rooms, looking for any hint of something out of place. And she had felt his *presence* in the room.

"You're sure someone was in the house?" he asked.

Had her imagination convinced her of something that wasn't true? She suddenly didn't know and realized she had conjured something up from the one thing that had failed her time and time again—her nonexistent feminine intuition.

"I did try the door, opened it and called out for you when you didn't answer." He shrugged. "Then I wandered around outside, looking for you. I was getting ready to leave when I saw the porch light come on down there and decided to walk down and check it out." His only movement was the twitch of a muscle in his jaw. His dark eyes were unreadable.

"You didn't let Magic out?"

He frowned. "I may have when I opened the door. I didn't notice if I did."

"Then you weren't in my house?"

"No."

Jonna should have breathed easier, but some creepy-crawly sensation still nudged her. She ventured a glance up at him. His eyes were watchful but his expressive mouth was silent as he waited. She suddenly wanted . . . wanted . . .

She wanted to believe him, she realized. It was a little reminiscent of how she'd felt about Jeffrey early in their relationship. Only not this early. Not after two meetings. And she'd had a lot more reason to trust him than she had this guy. She'd be better off accepting that this just wasn't all that important. "Oh forget it. You're right. It was probably all my imagination."

"I didn't say tha—"

"Never mind. You fix coffee, breakfast, whatever." She swung away, back toward the stairs. "I'll go take a shower and join you in a little while."

Sam nodded and turned abruptly toward the kitchen.

She resisted the urge to look down at him as she reached the top of the stairs. No sense freaking herself out if she found him staring at her in that unsettling way.

She went into the bathroom, punched the lock on the door and held her arm under the shower while she adjusted the water temperature.

She wanted to call Moss. A glance at the watch she'd placed on the back of the sink told her she wouldn't catch him anyway. He was usually at the café having breakfast and exchanging gossip with the early-morning coffee crowd about now. Besides, she'd promised herself she wouldn't rely on him so heavily.

Jim Moss had been her father's life-long friend, and she loved him dearly, perhaps even more than she'd loved her father. She'd been tied to her father by blood and by birth; she was tied to Moss by choice. Who else would have sided with and defended her during the tumultuous years of father-daughter battles, and encouraged her to go after her dreams? Who else would have helped her understand her father's frustration that she wasn't the son he had always wanted?

When her father's will had been read, Moss had been named her guardian. And, though she was too old by then to legally need one, she and Moss fell in with the spirit of her father's wishes. Lord only knew, she was incompetent at this farming business and she trusted Moss more than she trusted anyone—let alone herself.

She'd been much more self-reliant lately, though, she congratulated herself. But Moss was instrumental in that, too. He continually told her she had good instincts and encouraged her to follow them.

She frowned. So where had her good instincts been last night when she was so certain Sam had been in her house?

Same place they were when you were sure Jeffrey was reliable, she thought with a sigh. No, despite what Moss thought, she couldn't trust her misguided intuition any more now than she'd ever been able to. And at some point in time, she would realize that and quit trying.

And much as she loved Moss, trusted him, from now on, when he encouraged her to believe her own instincts, she would replace the word with "common sense." That quality was one of her strengths as long as she didn't let feelings get in the way.

Common sense: Why would Sam have wanted to come into her house anyway? Robbery? Nothing was missing. To find her? No, what he'd said about his efforts in that direction made good sense—pretty much what she would have done. And Magic *could* have escaped without him noticing when he opened the door. Magic had a knack for appearing and disappearing unexpectedly. That was one reason the kitten had earned the name Magic.

And common sense told her she needed Sam to be ready to take care of things when she went to L.A. So why was she looking for problems?

She'd proved time and time again that her instincts were way off. This time, she wasn't going to let them lead her astray. Especially now, when the award was generating a lot of interest in her work. She'd use common sense and Sam to take advantage of the kind of career boost anyone would kill for. And put her female intuition back in the closet where it belonged.

CHAPTER THREE

"Something smells good," Jonna said brightly, coming down the stairs a little later.

Sam sat at the table, cradling a cup of coffee and staring off into space. He stood politely to greet her. "I have a couple of omelets warming in the oven," he said. "But I couldn't find the toaster."

"Probably because I don't have one," she said. "Give me a minute and I'll put us each an English muffin under the broiler."

"This is an interesting house," he said as they sat down at the table a few minutes later. "One of your designs?"

She nodded and shook off another wave of apprehension. One of the things that had bothered her about him last night was his lack of interest in anything about her or the farm. Everyone else she'd ever hired had asked a million questions. Yet he seemed to know a lot. Common sense, she chided herself. Moss had told him. She wondered why she was so determined to find everything Sam did disturbing?

She supposed that was better than blind trust. But she wasn't being very fair to him, either. He was a grieving man who had turned it all inward. He blamed himself for his sister's death, she realized with a flash of insight. She wasn't sure where the flash of insight came from, but knew somehow that it was true.

Oh, good. She was doing it again. She was about to push the theory aside until she realized it wasn't just a feeling, it made good sense. If he was blaming himself for his sister's death it would explain a lot about Sam.

"And is this the house you won your award for designing?"

She nodded again. "Sort of," she said. "I fine-tuned the original plans a bit, and the final version was built by a builder in Kansas City. He's the one who actually entered the design in the competition." She looked around her at the open concept, at the world at her feet twenty feet away outside the huge expanse of window.

"You don't sound very pleased."

"Oh, I am. It's just..." She fluttered her hand helplessly and knew that she was scowling, something she did a lot when she wasn't sure how to explain something. "It's just that suddenly I'm not doing what I wanted to do at all."

"What was it you wanted to do?"

"I wanted to design nice middle-class houses, you know?" she asked sheepishly. "Homes that families could afford and enjoy."

He raised an eyebrow and looked around him again. "Isn't that what this is?"

"Pretty much. This is affordable, energy-efficient, cozy."

"But this isn't what you're designing now?"

"The one I designed for Bob was very energy-efficient, but it's almost three times this size—it's the class of homes my design won in, Energy-Efficient Luxury Class—and now with all the publicity, I'm custom-designing two- and three-million-dollar homes. I can't keep up."

"Sounds like good business to me."

"Especially since I've been struggling just to make ends meet since I left the architectural firm I was with and came back here."

"So why *are* you here?" he asked.

"I love it," she said simply. "I didn't think I wanted to come back and then Dad had his first heart attack. He bribed me with this house—said he would pay for any kind of house I wanted to design if I built it here—and promised he would leave me alone and support me in 'my ivory tower' until I could get my free-lance career off the ground and support myself. He knew that's what I eventually wanted."

"And it didn't work out that way?"

"Of course not. I built my house and then he promptly had another heart attack and I ended up running the farm until he died. With his direction, of course."

A sympathetic smile hovered on his face. "The best laid plans..."

"You speak from experience?"

"I had my own plans until my mother changed them."

Sam quickly took another bite. The closed look was in place again.

He obviously wasn't going to answer any questions along that line. "What were *you* doing before you came here? You never did say last night." He'd told her about his farm-related experiences last evening but they hadn't gone into any details, and she didn't think working around his grandfather's wheat farm while he was growing up had much to do with what he'd been doing lately.

"I was working security," he said.

"Like a security guard?" she asked.

"Close enough."

"At a bank or something?"

"At a college," he said. "And before that, I was in the service."

"So what brought you here? How did you find out about this job?" she said.

"I wanted a change of scenery. The Midwest sounded good. I started calling around, talking to people I knew in the area."

Calling around? "Were you the one calling and asking questions about me a couple of weeks ago?" she asked, certain of the answer before she finished the question.

"How'd you know?" He produced a tautly stretched grin that gave him the sheepish look of a kid caught with his hand in the cookie jar.

"This is a small town, Sam. Believe me, everyone keeps tabs on everyone else. No one has any secrets." She got up to pour herself another cup of coffee. "Why?"

She resumed her place across from him and he picked up both plates, carrying them to the sink. Cleaning up the kitchen seemed automatic. He must live alone, she decided.

"Like I said, I wanted a break from what I'd been doing. A second start. A friend in Emporia gave me a lead in this area and after a lot of dead ends, I heard you might have a opening. It was worth checking out." He closed the dishwasher and at the same time shuttered his face, lowering his eyes. "Do you want me to start this?"

"No, there'll be more later." Her eyes narrowed. "Someone was calling and asking questions about me a good two weeks before Max told me he was leaving."

He shrugged. "You wouldn't be the first employer to be the last to know."

He was probably right. Max's wife hadn't been happy here. Jonna'd known they'd both looked at this as a temporary stop until something better came along. Max had probably had feelers out for a long time, the same as Sam. And Sam's call and questions had led him to Moss.

"Well, you're obviously willing and capable of doing the job and I'm glad you found me." She rose reluctantly. "And we'd better both get busy or I'm not going to be ready to leave next week. With doing the farm stuff for the past week, I'm way behind."

"So what do you want me to do next, boss?" Jonna found the tinge of cockiness in his voice very appealing. "The truck? The fences?"

Jonna let herself enjoy looking at him for a second. "The truck would be a good start. Then the fences."

"A slave driver, huh?"

She laughed and everything suddenly felt right with the world. And with Sam Barton.

"And what are *you* going to do the rest of the day?"

His question took her by surprise.

"I mean, if I have questions, can I come back here? Will you be available?"

"I'm going into town in a little while to run some errands, but I'll be back around noon."

Sam's casual smile stayed firmly fixed, but one of the nearly unnoticeable lines over his brows twitched and deepened. The air around her felt thick, tense again.

"If you aren't sure about something, put it off till this afternoon," she reassured him. "I can't think of a thing that can't wait that long."

He said okay, thanked her for breakfast, then let himself quietly out the back door. Instead of going directly up to her office as she'd intended, Jonna went to the sliding glass doors and opened them. She told herself she was checking out the day, but stepping onto the narrow deck, she watched him go.

Sam's stride was as restrained as the foreboding day. He scanned the horizon as intently as if he would be expected to draw it from memory later.

Clouds rode ominously low in the vast sky, mirroring the suddenly oppressive feeling in her chest, but the day was gauzy bright. It was the kind of day people around here valued—very little wind, cool without being cold, a clean nip in the air that energized as it filled your lungs. The weather held hints of dark winter things to come and subtly issued warnings to take advantage while you could. It wouldn't last long.

As he turned his dark head toward the east, she saw his brows lower over squinting eyes. He looked intense and more than a little intimidating.

Despite the sun spilling over her as it eased out from behind a cloud, she shivered as his slow, even step gradually shortened, then reduced him to nothingness over the rise.

She was certain he knew she was watching him. She felt his awareness in prickles along her skin.

The breeze picked up for a second, shaping the sweats she'd put on when she got out of the shower to her legs. Chilled, she stepped inside and ordered herself upstairs to work.

From her office, she had a much better view of the farmyard, and she stopped a few feet from the darkened windows.

Sam glanced up, directly toward the spot where she was standing. Even though he couldn't possibly see her—the day was bright, the house dark—she withdrew a little farther into the room.

He found her anyway. She felt his eyes focus on exactly the point where she stood as surely as she felt her heart stop.

She managed to sit herself down at her drafting table only when he finally disappeared into the barn. But she didn't manage to concentrate. She couldn't quit thinking about Sam. And not just as a hired hand.

He was the most attractive man she'd seen in a long time, with a lean strength and an easy grace that made her jealous. And those dark eyes, despite the troubled shadows beneath them, seemed to see directly into her soul. With every fiber of her being, Jonna knew the loneliness she'd seen in Sam too closely resembled her own. And even as Sam's intensity unnerved her, it drew her and made her wonder…and think about all sorts of things she'd managed not to think about for a long while.

Maybe all the things she had read were true. Maybe her biological clock was winding down. Could some primitive compulsion to mate be stronger than her sanity? She squirmed uncomfortably. She didn't even want to consider how eagerly she had accepted his slightest suggestion about how Magic had gotten out.

Jonna reached down and stroked the cat's head. "That is how it happened, isn't it?"

Magic stretched lazily as if she was comfortable with Sam's explanation and Jonna went to work.

She was in the process of putting an address label on the preliminary drawings she had to get in the mail when her father's rusty, red-and-white, dual-cab pickup wheezed up the sharply inclined drive a little later. She couldn't have been more surprised if her father himself had been driving it.

She flew down the stairs, still carrying the mailing tube. Sam got out of the vehicle as she flung open the door.

"You got it fixed?"

He paced determinedly toward her. "Temporarily. I've got it jury-rigged for now." He shrugged. "Once I get into town to get a new part, it'll run just fine."

"I can't believe you have it running."

"I don't dare turn it off."

"Do you want me to get whatever it is you need while I'm in town? Write it down so I know wha—"

"You sound like there's no real hurry to get started on the fences," he interrupted. "Can they can wait until tomorrow?"

She frowned. "I guess as long as they're in good shape before winter sets in . . ."

"I was thinking maybe I should go with you. I need the part. I need supplies," he added. "And I'd like to get some gloves before I start work on the fences." He extended one of his hands. They were uncallused and his long fingers looked expressive and strong.

Her arm tingled, remembering the way his fingers had felt touching her.

"And of course food—"

"Coffee, for sure," Jonna suggested, impatient with herself for helping him come up with excuses. He'd come up with plenty of his own. "I don't supply it on a regular basis first thing in the morning." She snapped the cardboard tube against her leg decisively. "You may as well come with me. I have to finish getting this ready to mail. Then I need to do something with my makeup and hair."

A carefully impersonal admiration flickered in his eyes and she checked her watch so he wouldn't think she'd stopped to dig for a compliment. "We'll go in about . . . fifteen, twenty minutes?"

"I'll be ready," he said, climbing back into her father's old truck. "Down by the barn?"

She nodded.

"I see what you mean about the terrain," Sam said as they finally started for town in Jonna's truck. "You don't see these little gullies until you're right on them. Do you ever get used to it?"

She slanted him a curious look, surprised that he was so observant. But then, Sam didn't miss much, she decided. "That's exactly what I meant about getting to know the lay of the land on horseback."

He nodded at another small ravine. "The vast nothingness. Then the surprises. Do you ever feel like you really know your own land?"

"Sure. But I've been over it more times than I can begin to count—on horseback, in hay trucks, on sleds, bikes, foot. Even so, every once in a while I notice some little detail I hadn't before. You remind yourself that whatever the new discovery, it's all been there forever and you just overlooked it. It's kind of timeless." Maybe all this *would* help him get over his sister's death, she realized.

Sam sank back in the passenger seat. She could feel him gradually relax, as if verifying that this peacefulness was exactly what he needed. Maybe the rolling prairie would have the same soothing effect on him it often had on her. The infinity of it, the ever-changing sameness did tend to put things into perspective.

Autumn had transformed the green hills to a murky brown and copper, and the tall grass bent mournfully in the steady breeze, whispering centuries-old secrets as they passed.

His gaze rested on her for a moment, then turned toward the side window. "It's beautiful in a quiet way. Very restful."

"It's not always pleasant," she warned. Clouds still hung oppressively low. "You should see our thunderstorms."

The storms out here were devastating to watch—dark, hypnotic, sneaking up quietly, then exploding with power. He reminded her of them.

"They're violent and wild."

"Hope I get to see one."

"You will," she assured him. "We have quite a few this time of year."

He answered with an "Mmm-hmm" and another half mile went by before Jonna broke the silence again. "What college did you say you worked at?" she asked.

"I'm head of security at North East Texas State," he answered absently.

"That's where I went," she said in amazement.

"What?" he asked, much too vaguely, intently absorbed with the world outside his window again but sitting straight up in the seat.

The truck crested a hill and plunged down into a wisp of a low-lying cloud. It seeped under Jonna's skin and chilled her from the inside out.

"I graduated from NET."

His mouth curved in one of those rare smiles. "What a coincidence," he drawled.

Jonna slowed for the city limits and examined his oh-so-indifferent profile. A car pulled onto the highway at the next corner and driving reclaimed her attention. This information couldn't have come from Moss, she realized. He couldn't keep one college straight from another if his life depended on it, except for his beloved OU. He remembered that only because he was a Sooner football fan.

"I don't think it's a coincidence," she said quietly. "Why do I get the feeling you know a lot more about me than you should, Sam?" She curved the vehicle into one of the marked spaces in front of the feed store and let it bump gently against the curb.

He stared at the storefront. His long lashes shaded his dark eyes and emphasized the faint circles beneath them.

"I was a good Boy Scout. I've *always* liked being prepared. I find out as much as I can about a situation before I put myself into it," he said, not denying he'd more or less investigated her. "The couple of years in the military, the time working in security have exaggerated the habit." The line of his jaw was sharply defined. He was on the defensive.

Jonna gripped the door handle. "It just doesn't seem very reciprocal," she said. "You aren't very anxious to share information with me."

His mouth tightened. "Maybe I'm wrong, but I don't see how my past history—except my work experience—could be of any importance to you. And you know what curiosity did to the cat."

She shivered. It was an old saying. It didn't sound as if he meant it as a threat and yet—

"I came about your opening because, God only knows, I need peace. Solitude." He faltered as her gaze lifted to his, but for once he didn't look away. His eyes were brilliant, sharp slivers of pain.

She curled her hand into a tight ball around the steering wheel. Whatever she wished, a touch couldn't stop his self-inflicted torture.

"I can't tear open my wounds so you can analyze them and spread them out in the sun for quick healing. Some things are best left alone."

She shuddered and opened her door, layering a frosty hard glaze of unconcern over her curiosity. "It won't happen again. And as long as you do the work I hired you to do I guess I don't care about your past—until it affects your work." She clamped her mouth shut.

He opened his door. A second later he stood outside.

"Let's get our stuff done," she said, joining him on the pavement.

The pickup buzzed an insistent reminder. "Get the keys," he ordered.

"This is Whit..." she started to say, then lifted a conciliatory shoulder and reached back in to yank the offending items from the ignition.

They stepped up onto the curb at the same time and their eyes met. His searched hers. She lowered her gaze and shifted the long strap of her purse to the other arm.

"Jonna—"

"Charlie will be out to find out what's going on in a minute." She nodded toward the store. "I really don't look forward to explaining something I don't understand myself."

A joyless smile twisted Sam's lips as he stepped out in front of her toward the building. She avoided public confrontations. That might be very useful information.

But not if he didn't *think*, dammit. He'd relaxed his guard for a few moments and almost blown it all.

In a few short hours, he'd learned a lot about Jonna. For such an intelligent and capable woman, she had a lot of self-doubt. Unfortunately, he hadn't taken full advantage of the knowledge.

When he should have been humming, taking over the kitchen, acting confident and friendly, he'd handed her the cat and let his all-too-human weaknesses take over.

He'd stood, electrified by her touch, hypnotized by the perfectly rounded slope of breasts he'd glimpsed between her loosened lapels. His mind had snagged on wondering what she might or might not be wearing beneath the long robe. He'd fought the urge to drag her over the railing that separated them and use her. When he should have been friendly and working hard to gain her confidence, he'd been longing to annihilate his primitive frustrations with her body.

He resented his body's betrayal. And he resented her for causing the jagged, harsh wanting, for putting his senses on alert and his brains on hold.

He held open the door of Weston's Feed and Seed for her, and she stepped in front of him and into the store. Her faded jeans fit her almost as closely as her skin. How in the hell would he ever concentrate at this rate? He had to put the tightening in his groin out of his mind just to listen to her.

"It's probably good that you came with me today," she was saying. "If you're going to be able to do what you need to without bothering me over every little detail, I need to introduce you to Charlie. Let him know you're authorized to charge on my account."

His brows rose in surprise.

"I guess it doesn't matter whether or not you trust me," she added. "You're worthless to me if I can't trust you."

She pasted on a wide smile and headed to meet the plump man with a rim of white hair around his shiny bald head who was moving down the wide center aisle of the store toward them. "You'll find those gloves you need right here," she said louder, over her shoulder. "Right, Charlie?"

"You betcha," Charlie said, clasping her hand and pulling her in for a one-armed hug. "The best you'll find anywhere in town. How ya' been, Jonna?"

The rest of the morning passed quickly as Sam followed Jonna from store to store, place to place, watching her take care of the business they'd come to do.

He kept his friendly pose plastered on as she introduced him to a variety of people. The postmistress offered him change of address cards to send out. He took them without comment, slipping them into his back pocket for disposal later.

Jonna again introduced him as her hired man to the men at the hardware store and the service station, asking them to please allow him to charge supplies and fuel to her account.

The owner of the service station eyed Sam closely and Jonna watched with noticeably heightened interest. This was someone she trusted, Sam decided, and consciously put on his most practiced, confidence-gathering grin.

The man turned to Jonna approvingly. "Glad to see you found someone so quickly, Girlie."

Jonna rolled her eyes and explained, "My father's nickname for me."

Mr. Phillips made several disparaging remarks about the hired man who had just deserted her, and Jonna said she'd expected it eventually.

The whole experience was an ordeal. Sam didn't want to see her personal relationships, hear her friends and acquaintances offer congratulations on the award. The reminders gnawed at him. But he finally knew *when* she would go to Los Angeles to accept it.

He knew now how long he had to prepare; how long he would have to keep up the smiling farce that made his face ache.

Eight days. Eight days to maintain control.

"Well, Sam," she said as she pulled up outside the Whitfield Mercantile, no longer wearing one of the plastic expressions she'd been wearing for the world, "you're on your own. I'll let you finish whatever shopping you have to do, and I'll go here." She indicated the small café next to the general store.

This was it. Moss. "What about groceries?" His arrogance over how well their morning had gone ebbed away. The tightrope he'd been dancing on with such finesse began to shake and pitch.

"We may as well have lunch before we get groceries and head for home, don't you think?"

He searched for a reason not to separate.

"I'll have a cup of coffee while I'm waiting for you." Before he could blink, she strolled toward the café.

This must be it, he thought fatalistically, then realized that if Moss owned the café, she was already inside, learning that the man didn't know Sam Barton any better than he knew the man in the moon.

"May I help you?"

Sam started. His legs had carried him along with Jonna's suggestion, and he was inside the Mercantile.

Not much later, Sam paused inside the small café's door, searching for Jonna. He honed in almost immediately on the spot she brightened near the rear of the room. Her head was bent toward her older male companion's. Sam held his breath.

Jonna looked comfortable, open, approachable. If that was Moss, Sam was fairly sure Jonna didn't suspect anything out of the ordinary yet.

She lifted her head, arching and displaying the elegant length of her neck. God, but she was seductive. Her low melodious chuckle carried over the clatter and din.

He wasn't that anxious to find out if her friend was the infamous Moss, and this, he realized, was a perfect opportunity to take care of one of the necessary odds and ends—if he didn't waste it, staring and imagining and letting his hormones take charge again.

Quietly, he reversed his movements and went back outside.

CHAPTER FOUR

Jonna shivered as the sun went behind a cloud and turned the café ten degrees cooler.

"You sure are jumpy today," Sol Steward said, placing his bony old hand over hers. His leathery face looked as if it would crack if he smiled any wider.

"Silly, huh, Stew? Seems like everything makes me feel cold. The phone ringing, the sun going behind a cloud..." She waved a hand toward the window and Sol burst out laughing. "Maybe I'm coming down with something."

"And maybe your imagination is working overtime," he said, pointing vaguely toward the outside. "Some man is standing out there. With those shoulders, ain't no way much sun is going to get past him and in here."

Even without looking in the direction he pointed, Jonna knew who was standing there. Sam's broad shoulders filled the storefront window of the small café. She watched as he cupped his hands in front of his face to light a cigarette.

"Shoot," she said, "I'm going to have to go, Sol. That's my new hired hand. I guess he's decided not to come in."

"What'sa matter? He shy?"

She shrugged. "I wish I *knew* what his problem is. I'll get your coffee," she offered, setting a quarter on the table for the waitress.

"Thanks anyway, but Moss already got it," he said.

"Oh? How long ago was Moss in?" The stains in the mug Sol lifted to his lips said he'd been here long enough to know. "I hoped to catch him today."

"Won't have much luck, I don't suppose." Sol retamped the pipe he never lit anymore. "He was headin' for Em-

poria this morning," he added, "to pick up some supplies."

"Well." She grimaced. "Nothing else has gone exactly
like I planned today. I guess I shouldn't be surprised Moss
isn't around."

"He's usually back by two," Sol said helpfully, scouting
around the rapidly filling restaurant for another patron to
join with his mug.

Jonna glanced at the clock over the cash register. "I've
already spent longer in town than I intended. See ya, Sol."

She plunked her fifty cents on the cash register and waved
at Millie.

Sam had moved over in front of the pickup by the time
she got outside. With one foot propped on the bumper, he
studied the small town.

"I didn't know you smoked," Jonna said, joining him.

"Is that a problem?" he asked.

She lifted one shoulder. "I guess not."

"I only smoke occasionally. If you'd prefer I didn't—"

"I said I didn't mind," she snapped.

He raised an eyebrow and flicked the cigarette away.

"Sorry," she said. "I didn't mean to bark at you."

"I hope your bite is worse than your bark," he quipped.

He *did* have a sense of humor. Amazing.

"You'll need these." He extended her keys. "You left
them in the truck again."

She was careful not to touch him as she reached out, a
precaution she need not have taken. He dropped them into
her hand from six inches away. "Thanks." They were warm
from his body heat.

"Do you leave your keys in the vehicle often?"

"This is a small town. We're all probably a little lax."

"And I'm probably too security conscious."

Yeah, so security conscious he couldn't, wouldn't talk
about the work he'd done at her alma mater. Thoughtfully,
she watched him round the truck to get in the other side.

"Leaving your keys in the pickup is not a very safe habit," he added as if he couldn't help himself.

She crawled behind the wheel. His warning was almost funny. He hadn't thought twice about opening the door to her house and he was the most dangerous thing she'd seen in a long time. It smacked of the fox telling the hen to keep the chicken coop latched.

"You leave your house unlocked, too," he admonished, as if reading her mind.

"Not always."

"It was unlocked when I came. It only takes—"

"You shouldn't have tried to open it in the first place," she interrupted irritably.

"Pure habit, from checking campus doors at night," he said. "You really do need to be more careful. You're very isolated. A beautiful woman, all alone in the middle of nowhere...."

Her mind stuck on the "beautiful." Her hand stuttered over the keys in the ignition. She'd seen it in his eyes, but hearing the words...in his most matter-of-fact voice...

"You also said everyone in town knows everyone else's business." He'd warmed to the subject. "And you wander around at the farm alone at all hours of the day and night, I imagine. Don't you think anyone who wanted to hurt you would make it a point to know that sort of thing, too? That makes you a prime target for any burglar or rapist or—"

"You're hired," she said. "You are now the farm's official security guard." She didn't *enjoy* feeling defenseless when she thought about those kinds of things, so she didn't. And most of the time, she felt very safe. "Do you feel better?"

He laughed and the tension that had hung between them all morning eased.

"You decided you didn't want lunch?" she asked, changing the subject.

"You came out of the café. I thought you'd changed your mind," he answered.

"I thought you weren't coming in."

"I just stopped to have a cigarette," he said. "My last for a while," he added quickly.

She smiled. "You hungry?"

"Not really."

She put the vehicle in reverse.

"Where to next?" he drawled a moment later.

"Groceries."

"Could we stop by the phone company when we're through there? I need to get the phone transferred to my name."

"Sorry," she replied. "I should have thought of that myself."

She was pleased with their almost normal conversation.

Sam's phone company business took forever, and by the time he was through inside, the wind had sharpened and he wished he'd worn his jacket. He scrunched his shoulders and hurried to where Jonna was waiting in the truck.

Then he saw her.

Panic clutched his throat. His nonexistent lunch pitched frantically in his stomach. *God! Not again.* It wasn't time yet. What had he done?

His knees were weak but they carried him the twenty or so feet as the pure strength of his rage took hold and moved him down the sidewalk.

He forced himself to her window. A horrified fascination chained his hands as he stared helplessly at the ominous curve of her neck. Last night's nightmare overlaid her face with a swirling and flashing montage of the dead faces of Jonna and Denise, until he couldn't distinguish the two.

She slowly sat up, bright-eyed and blinking, and her image swam, then focused. He realized she'd only been asleep. Surprise that she was alive devastated him almost as thoroughly as thinking she was dead.

"What, Sam?" She opened the door and hopped out. "What happened? What's the matter? You look like you've seen a ghost."

The icy wind bit into him like a sandblaster and he began to shake. Jonna was out, beside him, her hand on his arm. "Are you all right, Sam?"

"I will be." Even his voice shook. He tried to stop it, stop the uncontrollable shivering. He braced himself against the pickup hood and watched the wind pitch the hodgepodge of dead leaves against the curb.

"Come on, Sam," Jonna said gently. Her arm draped his waist. "Let me help you."

"I'll be okay," he said thickly, but didn't resist as she led him to the passenger door.

"There," she said when he was settled. "Are you going to be sick?"

He shook his head.

She went around and climbed in behind the wheel. "Let's get you home." She let the motor idle a minute and reached over to lay a cool palm against his forehead. "You sure you're okay?"

He nodded but it was all he could do not to jerk away. He didn't want her concern.

With a fractured satisfaction, he realized his overreaction might have saved him. He had to fight a smile. She wouldn't take a sick man to visit a friend.

But he'd lost, too. How in the name of all that was holy could he justify caring what happened to her? You did not let yourself care about someone who might be doomed— even for a second. That was when you lost control, became obsessed.

He'd seen what his obsessions with Denise had led to. If they hadn't fought that night—

He yanked his mind from that train of thought and watched Jonna put the truck in reverse. He felt her examine him before she backed onto the street. "Better?" she asked.

He didn't feel so green now. "Must have been something I ate," he murmured and wanted to tell her to keep her concern to herself.

"Or didn't eat," she said. "I get the impression you don't take very good care of yourself." She slowed a bit on the outskirts of town. "Do you think it's the flu? Do you have anything you can take?"

He glanced at her blankly.

"Pepto-Bismol? Alka-Seltzer?"

"I'll be okay."

She turned in at the convenience store edging the city limits. "I'll run in here. Moss'll have something."

He felt himself go pale again and she hesitated.

"Can't we just get back to the farm? I bought ice cream and TV dinners. They aren't going to be edible if I don't get them in the freezer soon."

"Definitely a man thing." She laughed, shaking her head.

He reprimanded himself for taking a brief pleasure in the sound.

"Sick, and you think about food. Oh well, I've probably got something at home in my medicine chest."

Keep your medicine and your concern. He closed his eyes and willed himself to ignore her. It was good practice. Better yet, he decided, he should keep playing the image of her dead over and over in his mind. In just a little more than eight days, the monster might win another one.

Some kind of employee she'd hired, Jonna thought, pounding on his door. On his very first day, she was going to have to do the evening chores herself.

Of course, it wasn't his fault he was sick, she thought guiltily. And her father's repaired pickup was testament that he was going to be valuable to her.

She had brought soup with her—and the key. With his fetish about security, she knew his house would be locked, and if he was sleeping she would leave the soup on the kitchen counter with a note. She was getting ready to use the key when he opened the door.

"Sorry," he apologized, roughly drying his hair with a massive white towel. "I was in the shower."

That was evident. His bare chest gleamed with beads of water. His loose jeans clung damply to his lean hips and long legs. She was sure that was all he had on. The thought left her breathless.

"I was just . . . I wanted to. . . . You must be feeling a little better," she stammered.

"Much," he said, draping the towel across his broad shoulders. The fluffy material contrasted dramatically with the faded golden planes of his too thin, but well muscled chest. His eyes landed on the keys, and his expression hardened.

She sighed and thrust a quart jar of homemade potato soup into his hands. "I was just going to leave this on the counter. I thought you might be hungry." The jar slipped and both of them grabbed for it. One of her hands covered his and she gingerly released her hold.

The effect he had on her, just standing looking at her with those dark, dark eyes, was bad enough. Touching him was disastrous. And she didn't want whatever bug he was fighting.

"Well," she said, backing away self-consciously, "I just wanted to see if you were feeling better. I'd better get going. I still have the evening chores to do."

He followed her slowly out onto the porch. "I'm sorry I've let you down. That was never my intention."

"I know. It's not your fault you're sick," she protested, backing away another step.

"Shall I get dressed and come help?"

"Oh no. I've done this all a million times. You rest up so you'll feel better tomorrow."

She backed up again and he caught her arm to keep her from falling off the porch.

Heat flooded her face and seemed to burn her all over. And the fingers that splayed briefly against his abdomen as she'd tried to stabilize herself felt as scorched as if she'd touched a hot pan. "Sorry," she murmured, trying to side-step him. Her heart picked up an uneven tattoo as he guided her back to the center of the porch and then released her.

"You want to come back after you're done and share this?" He hefted the jar and looked as perplexed as she felt by the invitation.

"Oh, I don't think…" Dammit, she thought. He looked relieved as she started to refuse. If he didn't want her to come, he shouldn't have invited her. "That would be nice," she agreed. "I'll be back as soon as I finish the chores. In about forty-five minutes?"

He nodded and she turned, stalking quickly away so he wouldn't have a chance to renege.

His offer was obviously as big a mystery to him as it was to her. But he *had* wanted her there—the invitation had come as inevitably as his touch. Something in her chest fluttered, pleased yet apprehensive at the same time.

With his dark hair mussed and damp and the reluctant pleasure at seeing her in his eyes, she'd be smarter to stay away. But he'd be dressed when she came back, she told herself, and she'd be neighborly. They would share a brief meal, get to know each other better, then she'd be on her way.

He was still shirtless and shoeless when she came back almost an hour later. At her knock he flung the door wide. "Perfect timing."

"The soup's ready?" Her eyes caught on the faint brushing of dark hair forming a V down his chest. The point disappeared beneath the sagging waist of his jeans.

He nodded and waved for her to follow him.

She draped her jacket over the banister of the stairs leading to the second floor, and joined him in the dining room where he was putting the hot pan at one end of the table.

Her eyes wandered to his taut, nicely rounded buns. At least his jeans weren't hanging on him there.

"Have you been sick a lot?" she asked.

"What do you mean?"

"I just noticed that…" Shoot, she couldn't say she'd been staring at his behind and happened to notice that the only thing keeping his jeans from falling off were his rounded hips and tightly cinched belt. "It looks like you've lost a lot a weight."

He poured her soup, catching the drip from the side of the pan with a paper towel as he moved the pan over his own bowl.

"I guess you could say I haven't bothered much with eating regular meals lately." Sam slid out a chair at the end of the table. "Here, sit down." He returned his attention to the pan.

Though a bit shabbier because of the casual use of a number of employees, the dining room hadn't changed much. Except for the dust, of course. Her father hadn't tolerated dust.

"I meant to have this whole house cleaned before you moved in," she apologized, puzzling over the scattering of wood shavings that littered the opposite end of the big, heavy table. A handprint indicated that someone had tried to brush them away. She glanced at the floor and saw a matching heap of trimmings there.

"I'm afraid that mess is mine. I meant to clean it up before you got back."

She frowned at him questioningly.

"I forgot the crackers," he said and hurried out of the room.

"One of the windows upstairs was stuck. I brought it down here, took it apart. Planed a little off the side," he said as he came back in, purposely meeting her eyes. "Hope you don't mind."

Her dad's pickup, now the old house? "Of course I don't mind," she said.

"Good." He was obviously relieved. "Shall we eat?"

"Some of the electrical wiring could also use some work, I noticed," he added as he took his place. "I'll work on that, too—in my spare time of course."

"Since Dad died, most of the people I've hired have pretty much treated this job—and the house—as temporary. Something that would do until something better came along. It'll be a nice change to have someone around that cares about the condition of this house."

He looked uncomfortable. "Don't nominate me for sainthood," he said bluntly. "I just like to keep busy."

"Even when you're sick?"

"Especially then," he said. "If I'm busy, I at least forget for a while how bad I feel—works every time."

"I wouldn't know. The last time I was sick, I think I slept all the time."

"You must not be sick very often if you can't remember the last time."

"It's that good healthy farm stock I come from," she said wryly. "The last time was probably when I was thirteen and had the chicken pox."

"Must not be too healthy. Your parents both must have died fairly young."

"They were older when they had me. Mom was thirty-four, Dad was in his forties." She was telling him an awful lot for someone who had checked her out. "You didn't find all this out in your 'investigation?' "

"Only that they were deceased," he admitted. "I mostly wanted to know about you—now," he added, one corner of his mouth turning up subtly. He added, as she opened her mouth to ask, "The reports were glowing."

She smiled and shook her head in genuine amazement.

"How old were you when your mother died?"

"Six," she said, ashamed of being so catty when he was trying hard to be congenial. "Natural causes," she added.

"That's definitely the way to go if you've got to," he said, his eyes troubled again.

And not the way his sister died, she surmised.

"How long ago did your father die?" he asked.

She raised an eyebrow and he raised his hands.

"If this is a sensitive subject—"

"Four years," she interrupted. "I don't mind talking about this, but it's strange you ask so many questions when you're so reluctant to answer any." She pressed at the corner of her mouth with the paper towel he'd dropped beside her, and pushed her bowl away.

He shrugged, his jaw squared, the little white scar prominent again. "I promised you I'd keep *my* problems away from you."

"I guess that's up to you." She stood, picking up their empty soup bowls and headed for the kitchen with them. From years of past experience, she flipped the light switch with her elbow. He followed her, filling the doorway as he leaned against it, watching.

"I'd think you would want to perpetuate all that good farm stock. I'm surprised you're not married," he commented.

She half smiled and shook her head again. "And you ought to give lessons in that," she said.

One questioning dark eyebrow disappeared beneath his casually styled hair.

"You could start your own seminars. How to get information without asking questions or without having to reciprocate with any information of your own," she explained. "For the most part, you do it very inoffensively."

"Does that mean I just crossed the line?"

"You're on the edge," she said.

"You aren't going to tell me anything?"

"Not much to tell, except that I was engaged once and it was typical of my luck with men," she confessed. "I've found it easier not to trust any of them."

"Except me, of course."

She laughed. She couldn't help it. "No, Sam. Not you. I think you might be *very* dangerous."

"Oh?" He moved nearer, and she knew it was her imagination but she could feel his body heat surround her. She felt her breathing grow shallow. "In what way?"

"Oh, I don't know." She rinsed her hands, then dried them on the towel by the sink, tossing it onto the counter. It gave her a chance to back another step away. "So far in our short acquaintance, you've been a big bag of contrasts. One minute you're secretive and solemn, the next you're friendly."

The intriguing little lines between his eyebrows deepened, but he didn't say a word. Or reclose the widened gap between them—not physically, anyway. His gaze held steady on her mouth.

"Sometimes, you're very intimidating."

"Intimidating?" he asked. "How?"

She knew she was getting in deeper and deeper, that she should stop, but with him just standing there watching—

"You're very watchful," she said. "I supposed it's an occupational habit."

"I've learned to be very cautious, careful." He smiled slightly. "Especially with women. Like you, my luck with them the past couple of years hasn't been good."

"Except with me, of course." She borrowed his phrase, trying to turn the conversation playful again. It had suddenly become very somber.

"Especially with you, Jonna," he said without a smile in sight. "I don't plan to get caught up in the idea of taking care of you."

He'd done it again. Without her being aware of it, he'd moved closer till he was practically on top of her again. She flattened herself against the hard edge of the kitchen counter. "I can take care of myself," she said, and knew it was time to leave if that were true. The predatory way he was looking at her was beginning to do funny things to her insides.

He boxed her in, his hands gripping the counter on either side of her, his face inches from hers, his lips drawing her gaze.

"And what do you do now, Jonna?" he asked silkily, his low voice caressing her skin.

"I push you away," she said, planting her hands on his chest. He didn't budge but she felt his heartbeat quicken under her fingertips.

"Not so easy, is it, Jonna?"

Though his face remained impassive, a wariness had crept into the coffee-colored eyes. He didn't *want* to be affected by her, she realized, but he was. And with sheer will and wits he was waging this subtle battle with himself as much as with her.

"What next?" he asked again.

He stayed away from women, especially her? Jonna wondered. Maybe she could scare him away. "I try a new tactic," she said. The palms still against him softened and shaped themselves to his rock-solid chest.

She heard his sharp intake of air as she raised her lips and brushed his. For a moment, her strategy worked. He froze; she felt his arms fall away. She felt his sudden withdrawal, and she ignored the message to her brain that said now was the time to escape triumphantly.

But his lips seemed to hold hers like a magnet and his arms came around her like a vise, pulling the length of her tight against him. She parted her lips, inviting him to deepen the kiss.

She could feel his skin through the lightweight material of her sweater. Her hands moved to his back, exploring the planes and hollows, creeping up to discover the texture of his hair as he increased the pressure of his mouth against hers. His fingers formed some peculiar brand on her as he caught her arms, gently tugging her away.

She inhaled deeply, intending to retreat, but his earthy scent lingered in her nostrils and incited some primitive, long-forgotten need.

His lips were sweet, as addictive as chocolate, and his skin was as warm as the sun. It had been so long, so long since she'd felt want this intensely, and she clung to him.

"You're playing with fire, Jonna," he whispered. "Do you want to get burned?" He moved against her, his desire evident, contagious. An aching throb started somewhere low in her belly and rose, opening like a budding flower until her chest felt as if it would burst from the pressure.

His lips brushed hers, then her cheek, then right below her jawbone. They dipped toward the sensitive place behind her ear. Her body weakened even further to his tantalizing assault, and she was suddenly terrified by her reaction to him, by his calculating, analytical discovery of her weaknesses, by the way her attempt to turn the tables on him had backfired. She finally managed to push herself away.

He released her abruptly, then stabilized her and let her go. Where she had been hot, she suddenly felt icy cold. "I'm sorry," she said, avoiding his eyes.

"My pleasure," he said. "And it's nice to know you can take care of yourself. But I'd be very careful who you try that tactic on."

She felt her face flame. "A miscalculation on my part," she whispered. She brushed past him, headed for the front door, anxious to get away from him and the humiliation and raging mess of emotions she couldn't define.

He grabbed the jacket she had flung over the stair railing. "You'll need this," he said, tossing it without coming closer.

She caught it and stepped outside, stopping, startled by the darkness that had engulfed everything outside the half-open screen.

He flipped on the porch light. "You want me to walk you up the hill?"

"Thanks, but no thanks," she flung over her shoulder.

"Be careful, sweet Jonna." His soft tone seemed to stir the air around her. "Life is full of surprises. You never know what might be waiting in the dark."

She shivered, reminding herself he was just doing his intimidating thing again. But the night suddenly seemed deeper.

And all the way to her lonely house up on the hill, she could feel him watching.

CHAPTER FIVE

Nightfall!

Sam loved the night. The most interesting things happened between dusk and dawn: crickets hummed outside open windows on warm summer nights; fires crackled, shedding light and heat in a darkened room on crisp, cold nights. A nice Chablis was nicer, sentimental songs were more stirring, and willing women—Jonna Sanders came to mind—were much more willing, late at night.

He had always known how to make the best of this special time...until the killing started.

Now, night was no longer a predictable, comforting time. Since Denise's death—1:13 a.m.—night had fashioned itself into something to be dreaded. He dreaded it now.

He'd followed Jonna up the hill using the night scope on his binoculars. Then he'd watched her house until her lights had gone out a half hour ago. It ought to be safe now, he decided.

The wind slipped icy fingers under his coat as he crept out the back door. The length of electric wire he'd curled and draped over his shoulder slapped against his side. He uncoiled it as he retraced the path he'd laid out that afternoon.

He hated chancing it but snapped on the flashlight he carried to find the reflectors he'd planted to mark his course.

The light caught the first one and he turned it off.

If he hadn't been concentrating on wiring his device to the electricity inside, he never would have impulsively invited Jonna to share the soup she'd brought him. Or maybe he had a deep-seated need to torture himself.

Sitting with her, watching her seductive body flow from one position to another, smelling that subtle perfume and her own unique Jonna scent, all of it was torture. And he congratulated himself again on his control when she'd tried to seduce him. It still amazed him and brought back memories of every night he'd spent in some woman's warm and willing arms.

Damn, he had to quit thinking of her. It had been too long. He could feel the fever building. And what was worse—every time he thought about her, a bundle of emotions crowded in, cluttering up his well-ordered discipline.

The fourth reflector mocked him, glimmering briefly in the dim light, then hiding in knee-high dry prairie grass.

By the time he found it, his concentration was back where it should be.

He fastened the wire to the ground with one of the small hooked stakes he'd found in the hardware store, then retraced his steps, tightening and making sure the wire lay flat and invisible on the ground. Fluffing the matted grass back in place, he picked up the reflecting markers as he went, hooking them beneath his belt.

It was close to three o'clock by the time he finished wiring the motion detector he'd modified for his purposes. It now buzzed inside the house and out in the barn. And it buzzed over everything. Small animals. Bugs. The wind stirring the branches of the bush he'd hooked it up under.

Weary, uncertain what to do next or how to fix it, he crumpled in the chair in the dining room where Jonna had sat.

Jonna. Thinking of her revived him. Completely. Every inch of his body came alive. Thoughts of what he wanted to do to her crawled over him, like an ache, like an itch. At least those thoughts had nothing to do with caring, the terrifying feeling that paralyzed and made the bearer a victim.

And the damn buzzer went off again, but he didn't care.

He went through the motions, taking the infrared scope into the living room and studying the virtual peace and quiet at the end of the drive. Nothing.

The warning lasted sixty seconds. He waited impatiently for it to go by. He could almost feel the second it would quit now.

He thought of Edgar Allan Poe's "The Tell-Tale Heart" and sympathized with the poor, crazy sap in the story. Listening, anticipating, hoping without hope that *this,* in his case, the outrageous alarm he'd rigged up, wouldn't be the thing that gave him away.

Insanity. So this is how it feels.

He thought about Jonna again, ambivalent about which was worse, wondering whether he had crossed the line into total madness or torturing himself with his desires.

God, he'd enjoyed her this evening. Much too much. Yet not enough. He wished it had gone further, warm skin against warm skin, the weight of her soft breast against his hand. She'd practically issued him an engraved invitation. Would she have pushed him away if he hadn't held back?

However uncomfortable the physical desire, it was ten times safer to think about than some of his other longings. How he longed to absolve himself of any responsibility, to go about life as he wanted to and refuse to feel any of the guilt or pain.

He jumped a mile as the alarm sounded again. Damn! He brushed a weary hand through his mass of heavy hair.

Grabbing his jacket from the back of the chair, he strode out of the house, thankful for the fresh nip in the air that jolted him awake. With a deft movement, he zipped out the night breeze and went back to work.

Finish, he promised himself, and you can have a reward. He could think of only one that suited him. But that one was terrific incentive. He'd test the keys he'd had made . . . and check on Jonna.

He rearranged the detector. Now to check it.

He was in fair shape, an above-average athlete, but that didn't make him an Olympic-class runner. With more than a quarter of a mile between here and the end of the drive, he had to be completely certifiable if he thought he could set it off and be back in the house to hear it in under a minute.

He waited fifteen minutes to see if every little movement the size of a blade of grass would set it off. Nothing.

Then he went back, taking his car. Might as well test the sucker with what he wanted it to spot. Jonna's house was still dark and lifeless but to be on the safe side, he didn't turn on his headlights.

At the end of the drive, he let the car idle while he scurried up the tree to reset the time. Then he drove slowly up the drive. Plenty of time, he assured himself.

The alarm pitched a fit for a full minute and a half after he got back in the house.

One more trip to reset it back to the one-minute spot, and he would claim a well-earned night's reward.

Something disturbed Jonna's restless dreams. She held her breath for a moment, listening.

A car? She frowned. She rarely heard cars going by on the highway, only occasionally in the summer when her windows were open wide, and then only if the car was especially noisy.

A glance at the clock told her it was after three in the morning. Shuffling Magic off her legs, she threw back her heavy comforter and slipped out of the toasty-warm bed.

The hardwood floor was cool against her bare feet as she stepped off the throw rug. She hugged herself and stopped near the window. The cold radiated and permeated her bones.

It was a starless, quiet night—no headlights weaving in and out of the far hills even on well-traveled Highway 50. She'd been dreaming, she decided, and headed to bed again.

Then something caught the corner of her eye. Something at Sam's house. She turned back to the window, searching the deep shadows beneath the trees and around the corners of the old homestead. It was as dark and silent as the rest of the night.

The huge yard light perched between the house and the barn was out, she noted, giving the landscape a haunting quality, like the difference between a dull watercolor of a familiar scene being replaced by a sepia drawing of the same scene.

One more thing to add to the growing list she'd have to tell Sam in the morning—assuming, of course, she could face him. Right now, all she wanted was to get him out of her mind. He wouldn't leave it even while she slept.

What was it her grandmother had always said? Sleep comes easy to a guiltless mind? Well, it sure hadn't come easily to this mind earlier.

She crept back to bed, feeling weak and oh so foolish. Heat invaded her cheeks as she tugged the covers back over her chilled feet.

Why? Why had she acted so irrationally? Because you thought it was rational at the time, her forgiving side answered. She barely knew Sam. If you're going to make sexual overtures to an employee, you'd better know him well enough to know what to expect, her chastising side piped in.

At least when she fell for Jeffrey, she'd known him a good six months. By the time he betrayed her, she had had every reason to trust him. She didn't even know Sam—and if she dwelt again on him, she wouldn't sleep.

"I refuse to think about him," she said aloud, using the same technique she'd used to get the ghosts out of her closet when she was younger.

Like a programmed robot, Magic moved back to one of his two resting places, choosing her stomach instead of her legs this time. Jonna nudged aside the covers, releasing one arm, and stroked the kitten's soft fur, but she didn't try to fool herself about whom, exactly, she was comforting. She knew she derived more from the soothing motion than Magic ever would.

"You don't think I'm an idiot, do you, Magic?" she crooned, realizing immediately she had broken her own rule.

"I refuse to think about him," she repeated quickly, then concentrated on deep breathing. She relaxed her big toe, then her foot. With a little luck, by the time she relaxed her nose, she'd be lost in deep, forgetful sleep.

Every footstep seemed to echo. Sam paused after each one, letting his eyes adjust to the dark room, waiting almost unbearably long before taking another. It seemed like hours passed before he reached the bottom of the stairs.

Should he go up? He'd used a lot of excuses to rationalize this mission and the excuses were gone. He'd discovered the one thing he really needed to know, that the keys would let him in and that she had taken some of what he'd told her seriously. She'd locked her doors. Any move past this point was strictly a fool's errand.

So do I care if no one ever considers me wise?

Admitting that he wouldn't turn back now for anything less than an earthquake, he shifted his weight. He planted his foot close to the side of the bottom riser to avoid squeaks. Jonna was up there—sleeping, he prayed—and going on seemed as inevitable as the fast-approaching dawn.

The second stair creaked noisily when he settled there. By the time he felt secure that she hadn't heard him, his muscles ached from the strain of trying to turn himself into a statue.

Then he heard a soft snore—like a message from God or a welcome from Jonna herself—and the rest of his trip didn't take nearly so long. One more anticipated obstacle evaporated as he approached her room. The door stood wide open.

She was a lump near the edge of the king-size bed in the dim predawn light.

A small shape rose from the rumpled blankets and Sam's heart stopped beating.

The cat. The damn black cat. Two bright eyes pinned him. They stared at each other unblinkingly for what seemed like eternity. Then the animal moved in that sleek, almost motionless cat way, gliding, then leaping from the edge of the bed. Magic stood, sizing him up, several feet away.

Another movement from the bed grabbed Sam's attention and the cat was forgotten.

Jonna turned to her side. Her features blended in shadow as her hand came up to rest beside her face on the pillow. Again, he held his breath as the kitten brushed against him and strolled on out the door.

Sam walked softly toward her, stopping only inches away. Jonna's breasts rose and fell gently. She stirred, tugging the pillow deeper into the curve of her neck.

He heard the lapping of sedate waves as she repositioned herself. "Refuse ta thin...bou'..." she murmured, her voice dissolving into to a weak feminine snore. She talked in her sleep.

He smiled, froze and watched for a long, long time.

The dark red pillowcase rendered her brownish hair a pale flowing mist fanning around her.

God, he wanted to touch her. His fingers felt stiff and swollen with the effort of holding back. He gave himself ten points for his control and inched backward, stopping when she tossed again.

His heart thudded frantically, forcing the air from his lungs. He watched her resettle, her back to him, her face to the growing light in the sky.

He gave her a few moments to get comfortable. He was at the door when she lifted the covers and flipped them away. She deftly swung her feet out and over the side.

His pulse pounded so loudly in his ears, he expected her to turn to find the source of the clatter. It would only take one glimpse to spot him standing there. He cursed himself and tasted blood as he bit his tongue.

She rose. Her long white gown flowed behind her as she wandered to the window.

The moonlight silhouetted her slender form beneath the old-fashioned frilly gown. The air his lungs needed caught between his throat and his chest.

He watched in paralyzed fascination. *Idiot.*

He had a heck of a lot to lose—and not a lot to gain—if he stayed rooted to the spot. He crossed his fingers and took a careful step. He planned to keep right on going until he was outside.

Two steps. Three steps. One more and he would be out of the room, out of sight. He felt rather than saw her freeze. Her hand came to her chest in consternation as if she sensed his presence.

Don't turn around, Jonna Sanders. Don't turn and force something drastic. It's not time. I came to make sure I could get in. And to convince yourself you were still firmly in control, another voice added in his head. What a delusion, the same voice shrieked with maniacal laughter.

The kitten weaved a wide arc around Sam and rushed toward its mistress.

Sam scurried through the door with little caution. Only when he was plastered against the wall beside the door did he breathe again, amazed that she couldn't hear his blood coursing through his veins or his heart thundering in his ears.

Relief filled her voice as she greeted the pet. "Oh, Magic." The words whooshed as she bent, Sam was sure, to pick up the animal. "You're beginning to make a habit of that," she crooned. "I thought you were—" He could picture her shaking her head. "Never mind. It's just leftover images from ridiculous nightmares.

"You wouldn't believe . . . well, maybe you would. Was I thrashing around? Is that why you deserted me?"

A barely discernible rustle of fabric told him she was on the move again. He sucked in a breath and closed his eyes.

Her words were louder as she came nearer the door. "Is there such a thing as daymares?"

He somehow managed to stifle a groan. How was he going to get out of here? He sidestepped to the corner, slipping around it into her work space.

"Magic, dammit, you are freaking me out."

Keep talking, Jonna Sanders, just keep talking.

With every fiber of his being, he listened to hear her soft footsteps. He thought he heard waves in the water bed, thought he heard the covers rustling again. It was probably wishful thinking but he didn't hear anything else for a long, long time. His knees nearly gave way as some of the tension finally eased.

Get out of here, Sam. The words became a rhythmic litany in his head.

He gave himself a second to catch back his breath, then took two giant steps toward escape.

"Meow."

The damn cat startled him so badly he almost lost his balance. It stared at him from a foot away.

"Meow."

Sam suddenly didn't care whether Jonna was asleep again or not. He hurtled for the stairs, treading as softly as possible without giving sound a high priority. The importance right now was getting out. Getting away.

He sped down the stairs. He didn't slow, didn't stop until he was outside, with the door firmly locked behind him.

The crisp dawn air pierced his lungs, exhilarating him. He wanted to laugh.

Damnation! What insanity possessed him? Did he *want* to be discovered?

No, he realized, he wanted her to share the haunting, incapacitating terror that made you question where reality left off and madness began. It was all beginning to feel so heavy, he'd longed to share it, give her a personal stake. Let her wrestle with the demons for a while. He wanted to break his promise.

He leaned against the door, bracing himself in a semi-crouch, his hands on his knees.

When he'd checked into Jonna's life-style and background, and then decided on this scheme, he'd believed he could handle it sanely, methodically. He'd convinced himself he could control the situation. All he'd proved tonight was how well he could delude himself, how close to the edge he really was. And that it wasn't the situation out of control—it was him.

Lifting himself away from the door, he slipped his fingers into the pockets of his loose-hanging jeans and trudged wearily toward the steep decline of the drive.

"And it's Friday." He had to prepare for the hired man Jonna was *really* planning to hire. *You've finally figured out what you have to do to regain your life. Don't blow it by acting insane.*

Jonna showered, ate a light breakfast, drank a pot of coffee and restlessly straightened the house. Then she worked on the house plan she'd been playing around with the past couple of weeks—all before seven-thirty in the morning. It had to be a record for someone who was normally a zombie until at least nine.

Without seeing any of it, Jonna gazed out over the gentle wave of hills and valleys expanding as far as one could see. Movement caught the corner of her eye, jolting her back to her drafting table and the land of the living. Sam walked across the flat, open yard behind the farmhouse, intent on the barn.

She was relieved to see him, to know she wouldn't have to call him to make sure he was over his bug. She felt she should automatically know how he was. She felt as if she'd spent the night with him—he'd been so firmly entrenched in her dreams and her mind.

She threw her pencil into the large cup on the desk behind her—a habit born of picking pens and pencils that rolled off her drafting table's slanted surface—and settled her chin in her palm.

She didn't know why she let him haunt her. Maybe because he had played her like a gifted musician played a violin. Just as Jeffrey had.

Oh, Jeffrey.

She didn't want to think about him but maybe she should. His betrayal didn't hurt any longer, she realized, letting her thoughts probe that used-to-be-tender place in her heart—except maybe for her pride. Maybe it was pride that made her believe, down deep in her heart, that Jeffrey had been basically a good man. He was just weak and she'd been too foolish to see. Maybe if she reminded herself what a fool she'd been, she wouldn't be in such a rush to do it all over again.

But thoughts of Sam wouldn't leave her alone even while she slept. Seductively, he'd entered her dreams, made her want him, then stalked her and finally turned the dreams into nightmares.

She swiveled and flounced out of her chair, irritated with herself. She wasn't making much progress this way.

Monica had called last night to say her tickets were ready and waiting at the travel agency. Jonna had to pick them up sometime; it might as well be now.

A half hour later, she sat in her little pickup at the end of the drive. Darn, but she hated it when her conscience kicked in. She really shouldn't leave Sam to his own devices, and she had to face him sometime.

Reluctantly, she turned around and slowly drove back to his house.

A strange buzzing, like one of the high school bells that used to ring when it was time to change classes, emanated from inside the house as she stepped onto the porch. It stopped almost immediately.

She frowned. Sam's alarm clock? If so, it was awfully loud. Perhaps he still didn't feel well and had gone back to bed after he finished the chores. She pounded the door, the sound of her fist startlingly loud in the sudden silence.

She raised her fist for a second go.

"Hi." Sam came up behind her.

She whirled, grabbing her chest. "You scared me."

"I'm sorry." He was out of breath as if he'd been running. He paused, one foot on the ground, the other on the step, as if wary of coming closer. Could she blame him?

Except for his clothes, Sam had reverted to the character she'd met in this very spot two nights ago. His face was pale; dark shadows minimized the usual brilliance of his eyes.

"You're not feeling better?" she asked, trying to decide where he had appeared from. She would have seen him come around the corner of the house from the direction of the barn.

"Sure. The potato soup must have helped." If he'd smiled, she would have thought he was teasing her. Instead, he was silent, watchful.

"You sure you're up to doing the chores?"

"Just finished."

"I wanted to let you know I'm going into town. So if you have any questions or need anything...?" She let the words trail lamely.

"I'll have to wait," he finished for her.

The smile she offered felt stiff and awkward. "Well, that's all I wanted to tell you." She hesitated. She'd have to pass him on the steps—steps that usually seemed plenty wide and roomy. With him and his broad shoulders occupying them, they seemed very small.

She turned sideways to avoid brushing against him, but one of his hands closed over her shoulder. His look was as potent as his mouth had been.

"Jonna?" He drawled her name softly. "Would you mind if I put off working on the fences one more day? I still feel a little weak," he explained. "I'd like to stay close to the house, if you don't mind."

"I guess it doesn't matter any more than it would have yesterday." She headed for the minitruck.

"Any suggestions about things that need to be done around here?" he asked, following her to her door.

The list was endless. She thought of all the things that had been neglected the past few years. "No one's really looked at the equipment in the tack room since my father died. It all needs to be gone through," she said. "Some of it needs minor repairs. Some of it needs to be thrown out. Do what you know how to, and put aside anything you have questions about."

"Okay." He nodded.

She had one foot inside the pickup before her conscience caught up with her again. "And Sam?" She draped her arm over the top of the door. "If you feel bad, go back to bed. I am really not a slave driver. You look exhausted."

He hid some indefinable emotion behind a long slow blink. "I didn't sleep well last night," he admitted.

"That's only fair," she said. "Me neither."

He grinned as if he couldn't help himself and she felt a sudden, shared warmth. And she wanted to thank him effusively for subtly trying to tell her it hadn't all been her, that the evening's activities had kept him tossing and turning, too.

Be careful, Jonna Sanders. You're letting him under your skin.

And she had. She knew she had. He was there like an itch that couldn't be scratched.

She watched him in the rearview mirror until she rounded the curve in the drive and couldn't see him anymore. He hadn't moved an inch.

A car slowed, its turn signal came on.

Someone wanting directions, probably.

She glanced over her shoulder to see Sam jogging down the drive to meet the visitor. A warning scowl as dark as thunder marred his face. He really took all that you're-alone-and-unprotected nonsense seriously, she realized, and suddenly felt just the opposite. And maybe not such a fool.

CHAPTER SIX

Jonna's watch said a little after nine by the time she reached Whitfield. Usually, she was barely on her second cup of coffee by now. After she picked up the tickets for next Friday's flight, she joined the coffee crowd at Millie's.

"Hi, darlin'," Millie greeted her from behind the cash register. "Two days in a row? How'd we get so lucky?" She glanced behind Jonna toward the door. "And you didn't bring your handsome fella," she added in mock disappointment.

"Someone has to work," Jonna said, giving back Millie's banter. "How else do you think I can come in to town two days in a row? Where is everyone?"

"My! It *has* been awhile since you've been here at coffee time. I moved the early crowd back to the meeting room several months ago. Those old codgers were running off the paying customers, taking over all the tables and spreading out like they owned the place."

Jonna laughed and made her way toward the private dining room that housed most of Whitfield's "state" dinners. Entering reminded her she'd never gotten around to joining the Chamber of Commerce. This was where they met once a month, and Moss had been after her about it for three years.

Moss was at the far end, engrossed in a good-natured but passionate discussion with two of the town's councilmen. He raised a hand in her direction, then dived back in to defend his argument.

Mr. Wedman, the owner of the property next to hers, pulled out a chair, inviting her to join the group.

The circle grew smaller as, one by one, they drifted away, back to jobs and their various responsibilities.

"So-o-o-o, how's my Girlie," Moss finally said, scooting his coffee cup and moving to the chair beside her.

"So-o-o-o, when are you going to quit calling me that?" she asked, buzzing his grizzled old cheek with a kiss as he sank his lean, slightly bent body down next to her.

"Soon," he said, "real soon."

"Yeah, you said that twenty years ago." Jonna grinned.

"I'm working on it," he said. "Now. Are you going to catch me up on all your happenings out there?"

"I was kinda' hoping for the chance."

"Then I'm all ears," he said.

"Well, I'm pretty much ready for the trip to California," she started.

"Did you get something to really razzle-dazzle 'em at the awards ceremony when you went to Kansas City last week?"

"I *hope* so," she said.

"Nerves setting in?"

"Yes," she answered truthfully. "I had a heck of a time choosing something to wear. You should have gone shopping with me. I could have used a second opinion."

Moss chuckled. "And what I know about women's fashions you could fit in this." He doffed his ever present baseball cap, smoothed the few strands of gray hair back down across the top of his head and replaced the cap, wiggling it until it settled just so into the permanent groove that circled his head.

"You could have kept me from buying *two* dresses."

"You can finally afford it," Moss said.

Jonna lifted a shoulder and sighed. "One, I'll *never* wear and the other I'll wear only once. Now how much sense does that make?"

"You work hard. You deserve your rewards."

"But this isn't a reward. It's an extravagance because I couldn't make up my mind."

"And if that's the worst thing you ever do, you're in good shape." Moss covered his cup with his hand as the waitress reappeared with more coffee. "Come on. Millie's going to charge me rent." Moss slowly lifted his lanky frame. "Walk with me down to the post office."

They both said their farewells to the few remaining drinkers as Moss dug in his pocket for his wallet. "I'll get it," he warned Jonna as she started to open her purse. He plunked down the money for both coffees and a tip on the cash register a minute later, and Millie zinged them with a few parting shots as they walked out into the warm, sunny morning.

Moss led Jonna between a couple of parked cars to the street and they crossed to the other side, disregarding Whitfield's one traffic light half a block away. "Wish Becky would have lived a while longer," he said as they stepped onto the opposite curb.

"I remember her vaguely. But I don't remember what having a mother was like," Jonna admitted. "Isn't that horrible? You'd think I would."

"Probably because your daddy was such a strong personality," Moss assured her, stretching out his arm in front of him and rubbing his chest just below his shoulder. He eased back on his long stride and Jonna thankfully slowed the too-fast gait she'd had to use to keep up with him.

"You're a smart and beautiful woman, Jonna." He hooked his thumbs into the tool loops of his loose overalls. "Just like your mother. It's too bad she wasn't around to give you some of her confidence."

"But she wasn't," Jonna said. "And if you're right about me being so wonderful, I'll surely gain some someday, don't you think?"

Moss didn't chuckle. Instead, the corner of his mouth curved up slightly. "You don't have any reason not to," he said seriously. Turning, he started up the incline leading into the post office.

"I'll wait out here," she murmured. "The sunshine feels good." She watched his stooped shape go, a huge lump forming in her throat. God, she loved that man. He kept warning her he wouldn't be around forever, and she couldn't face the thought. She buried her hands in the pockets of her jacket and pulled the loose ends taut down over her jeans, warding off a shiver.

He appeared a moment later with a small bundle of mail. He leafed through it as he walked, then stashed it in one of the huge pockets of his overalls.

"I take it you hired the new man," he said as he wandered back toward Main Street. "Otherwise you wouldn't be in town so early."

"Yeah," she admitted.

"You think he's going to be okay?"

"I'm reserving judgment," she said after a moment.

"Yeah, I guess it's a little early to tell," he agreed.

"He's . . . different than anyone else I've hired," she said after a moment. "What's with him?"

"What do you mean?"

"Well, his background. He said he didn't have a lot of experience—and I don't have a problem with that. You'd already told me—but he's so . . . so . . . private. And his attitude!"

"Bad?"

"Well, not really," she said. "He's willing enough to take initiative. He had the chores done yesterday before I even got out of bed and he's already fixed Dad's old pickup—"

Moss stopped. "He wasn't coming until today."

She shrugged. "I know that's what you said, but he showed up Wednesday evening."

Moss frowned.

"We planned to come by the store when we were in town yesterday, then he got a touch of some kind of stomach bug," she explained. "And Stew had said you were in Emporia anyway." She lifted one shoulder. "Having him here early was really nice. I didn't have to finish cleaning the house."

Moss harrumphed a chuckle. He knew how little she liked that type of work.

"I guess it's working out," she said.

They had arrived back at Jonna's little mini, and she opened her door, took her purse off her shoulder and slung it inside. Moss closed the door and leaned back against it, studying her with a frown as he stuck the toothpick he'd picked up in the café in the corner of his mouth and started chewing. "But?"

"Oh, I don't know," she said with a sigh of frustration. "I don't have anything concrete to be concerned about, but I keep imagining that... that he's watching me. It's weird, and it's probably *my* problem, not his. Or yours. And I should be thrilled. He's even started fixing up odds and ends around the old house. No one has cared much about that kind of thing in a long time."

"Probably for Carla."

She scowled. "Carla?"

Moss eyed her expectantly. "She probably wants the house spiffed up. And she's one who'd nag a husband to death until everything is just her way. She's real picky about things."

A husband? "But he—" Damn. She couldn't say he wasn't married. She didn't *know* if he was or not. She hadn't asked, and he sure hadn't volunteered the information. A sinking, repugnant feeling landed in the pit of her stomach.

Well, if Sam was married, it would explain why he hadn't brought much with him. His wi—she changed the word to Carla. Carla was bringing the majority of it when she came. And he was preparing the house for her arrival.

But damn him, why had he— Besides feeling foolish, she now felt cheap and dirty.

She tossed her hands up in the air and let them fall against her legs. "Oh, who knows, Moss. You know me, I didn't ask any of the right questions and now I'm just being my usual insecure, should-have-done-it-differently, uncertain self.''

"You quit saying stuff like that,'' Moss threatened gruffly, tugging at a strand of her hair as he had when he wanted to get her attention as a child.

"Yes, sir,'' she replied. "And I guess when his wife gets here things—"

"She's not with him?"

"No. He hasn't said a word about her.'' She quickly looked away.

"Well, I guess it's understandable why they didn't stop by then. Carla would have been the one to insist.''

"Then you don't really know him?"

Moss grinned at her. "Ah? You're starting to question my wisdom a little?'' he teased. "That's a good sign. It's just what I keep telling you. I can give you advice, but you sure as heck shouldn't always take it.''

"Hogwash. You've never steered me wrong.''

"Everyone's judgment is a little faulty from time to time.'' A suspicious light dawned in his kindly old eyes. "You didn't hire him just because I suggested him for the job, did you?"

"It isn't like anyone else has expressed the least bit of interest,'' she said dryly. "And with the trip getting so close, what choice do I have?"

Moss grasped her chin between his thumb and forefinger. "Well, if you're having doubts about him, you follow your heart, Jonna. All I know about him is secondhand.''

"What *do* you know about him?'' Jonna couldn't help but ask.

He rubbed at the gray stubble on his chin. "His wife is Marge Franklin's daughter. She worked for me...oh, 'bout five years ago... back when I first opened the store and she was in high school. She was a good worker because she is so picky and Marge says Darrell's a hard worker, a wonderful son-in—"

"Who?"

Moss cocked his head to one side.

"What did you say his name was?" she prompted, an awful feeling creeping into her stomach.

"You mean Darrell?"

"The man I hired is Sam Barton," she said slowly.

"Who the hell is he?" His bewildered voice said it all.

"I hoped you could tell me."

Moss gnawed at his toothpick as one of her cattle might chew its cud. "Well, since I don't know him, I can't help you much," he drawled.

"Well, dammit." Jonna grabbed the door handle and started to open it.

Moss placed his hand over hers. "Hold on, hold on. Don't do anything rash here, girlie. From what you've told me, he sounds like a fairly good guy to have around. He's fixing up the old house?"

"Yes, but I've got to fire—"

"Why? Who says?" Moss interrupted. "You don't have to hire *anyone* just because I referred him. Don't fire this guy just because I suggested Darrell," he said firmly.

"But he said..." No, on second thought he hadn't said anything about Moss. "I guess I jumped to the conclusion that he was the man you had sent," she corrected sheepishly, running a hand over her nape. But Sam hadn't corrected her. He'd let her believe it, and in her mind that was as bad as a lie. She put a damper on her agitation and tried to concentrate on what Moss was saying.

"So who is he?"

She told him the little she knew.

"And he thinks being here might help him get over losing his sister?"

She nodded.

"He may be right. There is something sane and sensible about this kind of work. And there are a lot worse places in the world," Moss agreed.

"But what about Marge's daughter and—"

"Darrell and Carla have been wanting to get back to this part of the country for a long time," Moss interrupted. "I just told Marge this might be a good opportunity—nothing else. I didn't give any of 'em a guarantee you'd give him the job. Besides, I just saw an ad in this week's paper for maintenance help at the school. I noticed because I thought it was a coincidence since that's what he's been doing in Ohio. He'll have other opportunities and you've got to hire who *you* want to, Jonna," he said. "If you thought this Sam Barton would do all right for you, then don't get rid of him just because you think you should hire someone I refer. Trust your instincts."

"But..." No, dammit! She wasn't going to tell Moss what her *instincts* had initially been. She'd put them aside just because of him. Besides, now she had something concrete. She wouldn't tolerate a proved liar.

She looked up into her guardian's caring eyes. "Poor Moss," she said dolefully. "What are you going to do with me?"

"Same as always," he said with a crooked grin. It crinkled one whole side of his wind- and sun-worn face. "Same as always." He opened her door, swatting her bottom as she climbed in. "You just use your own good sense. Everything will work out with the new man. You wouldn't have hired him if you didn't think so."

He slammed her door and she rolled down the window. "Thanks, Moss." She wanted to say she loved him but knew from past experience that it would embarrass him.

"Just let me know how things are going." He touched the brim of his hat. "And bring him by to see me," he added.

She waited until he was back up on the sidewalk before she started the truck. Lifting one hand in response to his goodbye thump on the hood, she reversed the truck and drove somberly toward home.

The strange buzzing Jonna had noticed earlier accompanied the sullen beat of her boots as she clumped across

Sam's porch. The noise stopped abruptly with her last step and her fist hung in the air as she listened to the lifeless silence.

She wasn't surprised when he didn't answer the door. His car wasn't by the side of the house where it had been when she left, either.

Almost without thought, she tried the knob. No surprise there, either. The door was locked.

She wandered to the edge of the porch, leaning out across the rail to look around the large yard. No sign of life there, either.

Determinedly, she paced down the steps and toward the barn.

His car was at the rear of the house, she noted as she passed. He'd moved it to the back door leading into the closed-in porch that doubled as a laundry room. She couldn't decide whether to be relieved he was here after all or sorry. She told herself she was anxious to get the showdown over, before she lost her nerve. But if she was truthful, she would have to admit she'd like to forget what Moss had told her and pretend everything was just hunky-dory.

Jonna stopped inside the barn door. "Sam?" Her eyes adjusted to the gloom as the smell of hay and manure, dust and old leather assaulted her nose. The sweet scents were comfortingly familiar.

She walked slowly to the center of the two story room and looked up, turning slowly to check the hayloft. The dim interior was cool, and she wrapped her arms around her waist to ward off the chill.

He wasn't here, though he'd obviously made progress on the task she'd given him. Worn bridles, an open can of dried and cracked leather cleaner and an assortment of debris lay in a pile by the door as proof.

Candy, her buttermilk mare, snorted a greeting from just beyond the corral door. Jonna jumped, then cursed herself for her nervousness. "Hi, girl." She lifted the latch and picked her way carefully through the pen.

Candy met Jonna halfway and nuzzled her soft nose against Jonna's hand. "Sorry, girl, I don't have anything for you." She patted the horse's silky long neck and Candy followed as Jonna went outside to look around. "Where's Murphy?"

Candy stared at her with those big somber eyes.

"Come on. Let's get you saddled." She led the mare back inside.

"I'll get you an apple later if you'll find Murphy for me now," she promised a few minutes later as she mounted and gave the horse free rein. Candy cantered to the worn track that led to the south pasture.

Ten minutes later, Jonna spotted Murphy and Sam sauntering slowly along the fence up the next rise. Sam dismounted and wiggled a post as Jonna lightly pressed her heels against Candy's haunches. The horse eagerly quickened her pace.

Sam cupped his palm over his brow at the sound of her approach, and the breeze lifted a dark wing of hair.

He needs a hat, she thought as he lifted a welcoming hand. No, he didn't. Sam didn't need protection from the sun or wind here. He'd be gone before either could hurt him.

"I felt much better by the time I finished in the barn," he explained as she drew near. "I decided to go ahead and start on this."

Candy snorted as Jonna yanked the mare to a stop and barreled off the side. Jonna gripped the reins. "I'm sorry you went to the trouble." She gazed back into his questioning eyes. She didn't let herself dwell on the way his lips had felt or on the twinge of regret.

Sam's squint into the sun changed to a questioning scowl. "You changed your mind about me doing this?"

Jonna looked down at the ground. "No. I changed my mind about everything. Game's over, Sam. You have to leave."

His halfway pleasant smile disappeared.

"I know the truth."

"Oh?" An ice-hard glint frosted his welcoming eyes. His mouth flattened into a grim, hard line. "And what truth is that?"

She was almost grateful for the gust of wind that slapped a strand of hair across her face. It seemed like some protection from him. "You lied to me about Moss sending you."

He crossed his arms across his broad chest. His razor-smooth jaw clenched. "I didn't lie," he said, his voice as cold and sharp as a winter wind. "You believed what you wanted to believe," he corrected.

"You let me believe it. That's the same as a lie," she challenged, meeting his stare. "You . . . said you were honest."

"I said some people couldn't handle the truth. You're still not ready for it, Jonna."

"What truth? Tell me." She held up her hands, warding off what he had to say. His voice was so low she had to lean closer to hear.

"You don't really want to know."

"The truth—if you really know there is such a thing—doesn't matter. And I think you also lied about being in my house," she added impulsively. "I can *still* feel you there."

Both his eyebrows rose, and she felt her face burn furiously.

"I had breakfast there," he reminded her blandly.

"I'm tired of your riddles and intimidation. I want you gone."

"What are you going to do for a hired hand while you go to Los Angeles?" he asked.

"The man Moss *really* recommended is coming today," she said, and hated herself for answering. "Not that it is any of your business."

"He's already been." Sam's voice held steel.

"I'll get in touch with him, tell him there's been a mistake."

"Good luck." He crossed his arms and looked bored. His arrogance was infuriating. "It cost me dearly to get rid of your last man," he told her. "I didn't take any chances this guy would come back."

"What do you mean?" His ominous words crawled through her skin and down her body. "What did you do?" she whispered, aware for the first time that she didn't know him well enough to know what he was capable of.

"Does it matter?"

She suddenly remembered the car she'd seen turning into her drive earlier this morning. Ghastly visions filled her head and her knees went watery. "His wife was with him," she whispered.

"Yeah."

"What did you do with them?"

"Like I said, it doesn't matter. I'm not leaving, Jonna."

The tiny hairs on the back of her neck stood on end. What was he capable of? Denise ... His sheer audacity held her transfixed. She couldn't breathe, she couldn't think. Candy sidestepped and Jonna's numb fingers tightened shakily on the reins.

The lips that had kissed her moved, but he changed his mind about saying anything else and stood an arm's length away, his feet planted, looking as permanently grounded on her land as the rocks that lined these hills. And all she could think of was her hungry response to him last night and a thousand images of the past two days overwhelmed her, jumbling all together in chaos.

"You're fired, Sam," she said determinedly. "Get your things. Get off my property." She turned to remount her horse.

Sam's fingers clamped over her hand.

She swallowed a whimper.

His grasp loosened slightly but he maintained enough pressure to steer her around to face him. "I'm not leaving, Jonna," he repeated, his voice cold, his eyes sharp and hard.

She cringed. Her unfeeling, frozen body bumped Candy, who protested softly and danced the length of the reins away. "It isn't open for discussion." She forced the words between senseless lips.

"No, it's not." Sam's humorless chuckle sliced the quiet afternoon, putting a choke hold on her chest. She was sure she would never be able to breathe, her heart would never be able to beat again. It would hurt too much. "It's just a fact, ma'am, just a fact." Some wild spark edged into his eyes. His jaw tightened and the muscle twitched.

"You have an hour," she whispered, glancing over her shoulder. She'd lost track of Candy. The horse waited patiently several yards away.

"If you want the truth," he said, "you'd better stick around to hear it."

"You wouldn't know the truth if it slapped you in the face." She resented the quiver in her voice. "You're only trying to scare me again...." *It's working. God, it's working.* She felt limp from trembling.

She didn't see him move but his hands were suddenly on her upper arms. He hauled her to him, breast to chest, nose to nose. Her toes barely skimmed the ground. "I'm trying like hell to scare you, Jonna Sanders. You need me and I'm not leaving."

He released her abruptly. Her hands flayed the air and the whole world seemed out of kilter. Jonna lunged for Candy, stabbing clumsily at the stirrup with her foot. Her lungs battled to pull in air. She shook in anticipation of his strong hands clamping over her shoulders. Out of the corner of her eye she saw him move and choked back an alarmed sob as he emotionlessly watched her stumble, then clamber onto the horse's back.

Candy stutter-stepped sideways as Jonna finally swung her leg over the wide rump. Jonna tossed an agitated look at Sam, and was relieved to see he wasn't coming after her.

"You're crazy, Sam." She wasn't sure she'd said it aloud until the corner of his mouth twitched.

"So I've been told."

His hands were on his hips, his long fingers spread over the pockets of his jeans.

In her life, she would never meet a man whose entire demeanor captured her imagination as his did. And standing there against the backdrop of gray linen sky, she knew she would never meet anyone else who would haunt her the way he would. But his eyes were as unreadable as they'd always been, and his face retained the hard, impersonal determination.

She pulled back on the reins and Candy pranced backward.

"An hour. If you're not gone in an hour I'll call the police," she warned.

One of Sam's eyelids half closed in a semblance of acknowledgment. "The last woman who told me that is dead now."

The words stunned both Jonna and Candy motionless. He moved first, turning to pace resolutely toward where Murphy stood. Then his meaning sank in.

Jonna's sob finally escaped and she jerked on Candy's bridle. The horse shot forward with an automatic prod from Jonna's tennis shoes.

Candy settled into a graceless gallop and Jonna's heart doubled the beat. The wind twisted her hair, flipping it into her face, then away again. Her terrified tears dried on her lashes.

She didn't waste time when she got back to the house. "Sorry, old girl," she apologized, quickly hitching the horse to the front rail of the porch. "I'll take care of you later."

Candy looked at her sympathetically and Jonna almost burst into tears again. Even the horse knew what an incredible fool she was. The one and only time in her life her intuition had been right, and she hadn't listened.

She hurried to the little pickup that still sat in his drive and drove like a maniac toward town.

CHAPTER SEVEN

He watched her go. His lips thinned into a semblance of a smile. She was terrified. She'd ridden that horse up to that ramshackle old house as if the hounds of hell were after her. What the hell could have scared her that way?

Damn, but she was going to be fun—but almost too easy. At least this one was giving him plenty of opportunity to spice things up a little. He applauded himself for his genius and good fortune.

Denise had been simple—but unplanned, almost an accident. A gift to show him his destiny.

JoAnne Campbell from Connecticut had been a royal pain, but in one way she'd been the best so far. He'd had the chance to play with her a bit. The calls. One nocturnal visit before she'd officially won her award. She'd been arrogant, so sure she was much smarter than anybody else that she'd believed every ounce of it. He still dreamed about the way her eyes had finally widened in comprehension. And the moment before she died, her face had acknowledged his power. His superiority. And she'd given him the idea for *The Record*.

Too bad he hadn't had the opportunity to hone some of those skills on Leah Thurston Darcy. Just catching her alone with all that family running in and out had taken him almost four days. Four days, and then he had little time to savor his task. But he'd won eventually. And he'd certainly enjoyed the winning.

They all thought they were so wonderful and bright. Just like his mother. Damn women, tricking people into giving them awards that should have gone to wiser, better candidates.

He had no doubt how they'd won. Just as his mother would have to win—if anyone was stupid enough to nominate her for an award, he thought—by sleeping with the judges. He could still feel his rage build thinking about how Denise Barton had stolen *his* award.

He shook it off, looked around him, admiring the layout of the farm, trying to decide exactly what he could do in the short amount of time he had left. He smiled. Wasn't Jonna Sanders considerate? Leaving like that just when he needed time alone.

And what a display. A nice preview of things to come. With a confident spring in his step, he strode toward Jonna Sander's house a little way up the hill.

The house, the whole layout, irritated him. How arrogant she was, perching a glass castle up here in the middle of nowhere, as if she were queen of the world. She obviously didn't know his mother. Didn't realize *she* had that title.

Too bad he wouldn't be here to see the look on her face when she returned. "No, maybe not so bad," he mumbled to himself. Just multiply the fright he'd caught on her face by ten times, and he could imagine—yes, he was very good with his imagination—how she would look when she saw his talent for *this*.

Too bad he'd been so slow in realizing how he could use his wonderful gifts to improve his little competition.

"But better late than never." His grin widened and he went to work, hoping Jonna Sanders would at least be intelligent enough to appreciate his handiwork.

Jonna screeched to a halt outside the Shop-N-Go. Her heartbeat had slowed from terrified to frantic, but she was so weak, she practically tumbled from the truck. Her knees shook as her legs carried her into the store. She forced her lips up into a casual smile and felt the corners quiver with the effort.

It was lunchtime, and several workers from the paper products factory at the edge of town stood in line, paying for the deli-type sandwiches Moss's employees made fresh daily. Jonna's eyes searched the place expectantly.

Brian Tyler looked up at her as he gave the last man his change. "Oh, hi, Jonna. How's it going?"

"Hi, Brian." Her voice trembled slightly, but he didn't seem to notice. "Where's Moss?"

One corner of Brian's mouth turned down in an apologetic grimace. "Sorry, you just missed him."

Jonna shifted restlessly. "Did he go home?"

"Nah. You know that friend of his from over by Cedar Point?"

Jonna nodded.

"He went over there to look at some kind of wood crafts the guy's been making with his band saw. His wife paints them and he wants Moss to carry them here... 'for the tourists,'" he quoted, punctuating it with a silly grin.

Tourists through this part of the country were as rare as any endangered species, and she knew she was supposed to share his humor but couldn't manage the chuckle he expected. Her lips felt tight and dry as she dragged them wider in what she hoped looked like a smile.

She wasn't sure what to do next. She felt her shoulders slump. Running to Moss was a habit, a dependency almost as sordid as any addiction. But right now she needed him. This time she really did. What kind of advice would he give her if he were here?

"There anything I can help you with?" Brian asked, glancing toward the door to see who had just come in. She started and looked, too, feeling her pulse slow again when she saw that the new customer was a woman.

"Well, maybe." She frowned and chewed at the corner of her mouth. She could go downtown, turn the whole thing over to Police Chief Hardin. No, she'd promised Sam an hour. But she wouldn't hesitate if he was still there when that time was up.

Besides, Mike Hardin would be too smugly satisfied that she was finally "cracking" under the pressure of filling her father's shoes. Hardin was the worst chauvinist in town—which was probably why his nice little wife was always doped up on Valium.

Jonna propped herself against the counter and waited while Brian took the latest customer's money for gas and snacks.

"Actually, you probably can help me, Brian." The bell over the door clanged as the stranger left and the store was empty again. "I was going to borrow Moss's gun. Do you know where it is?"

"Sure." Brian eyed her skeptically. "He keeps it in the bottom drawer of his desk in the office, but—"

"Do you think he'd mind?" she asked politely, knowing she'd take it whatever Brian said.

Brian's thin blond hair flopped down over his eyes as he squinted with doubt. "Well—" he strung the word out "—I don't think he would but..."

Jonna started for the office and Brian came from behind the counter, practically hopping with curiosity. "Got some sort of varmint messing with your cattle?" he asked.

"You could say that," she said under her breath, not slowing a bit.

"Yeah, I heard about a bobcat some of the cattlemen had been having trouble with, but that was a couple of months ago. I thought someone had probably killed it by now."

"I think this is a different one," Jonna said, opening Moss's bottom drawer and gingerly reaching for the small handgun lying near the back of it. Jonna lifted the weapon carefully.

"Well, that .38 ain't going to be much good for hunting a cat."

The gun was heavier than it looked. "Why?"

"That's pretty much a people gun. You need a rifle to go after a cat," Brian said matter-of-factly. "Don't you have one? I thought big John had a whole collection."

"I hated them," she said regretfully. "I sold all of Dad's guns at the auction last fall. Having them around made me nervous. Is this loaded?"

"Nah." Brian pulled out the middle drawer. "Moss says that'd be like keeping a time bomb on hand. Here's some bullets."

The bell in the main part of the store went off again. "Just a minute," Brian said, plopping the small box in her empty hand. "I'll be right back."

Jonna had watched her father load and clean his guns a million times. She fiddled with the weapon and the cylinder swung out into her hand. She tentatively slid a few shells into the empty slots, then upended it and let them fall back into her hand. By the time Brian returned, she had the bullets back in the box and was tucking the box into the larger of the two pockets of her purse.

"Gonna take it with you?" Brian leaned over the desk and watched as she tugged at various pockets on her clothes, looking for a place to stash the gun.

"I can't wander out of here just carrying this," she murmured.

"Here," he suggested, pulling at the waist on his own jeans. "Stick it in your belt."

"Don't have one. This will work." She slid the barrel beneath her waistband and pulled her knit shirt and the thin Windbreaker she wore into place over them. The gun felt cold and deadly against her skin. She squirmed uncomfortably.

"Tell Moss I borrowed it, okay?" Rearranging her purse strap over her shoulder, she walked determinedly toward the door. She felt weighted on that side, very lopsided.

"Sure," Brian said, following behind and closing the door of the office.

She paused beside the outer door. "You won't feel unprotected without it?"

Brian settled himself behind the cash register inside the U-shaped counter. "Sure." He laughed as if she'd cracked a huge joke. "You taking that gun is the closest thing we've had to a robbery in the three years I've worked here, and Moss has laid down so many rules about when and if we could use it, by the time any of us decided whether the rules applied to a particular situation, the criminal would be in Missouri. I don't think anyone will mind."

She sighed. "Thanks, Brian."

Jonna took the gun out of her pants as soon as she was in the truck. She hefted it again and knew she was being ridiculous but slid it under the edge of her seat. She was certain Sam Barton would be gone when she returned.

I'm not leaving, Jonna. He'd be gone. Her spirit felt heavy. She felt tears welling up again but squelched them. He wasn't worth crying over.

She stuffed the box of bullets into the overflowing glove compartment, then glanced at her watch. She'd given him an hour.

She hadn't counted from the time she'd said the words. She didn't even start the countdown when she left the farm. She had allowed him ten extra minutes to get back to the house and twenty-eight minutes had passed since.

With the little he had with him, an hour should be more than enough time to get his things together and be on his way.

She should have left him money. He surely wouldn't use that as an excuse for waiting for her. She couldn't very well blame him if he did—he had done some work—but she hoped with all her heart he didn't. She was so frightened and confused right now, she wasn't sure what she'd do if they had another confrontation. She reached down, touched the gun under the edge of the seat and wondered what it would take for her to be able to use it. Let him be gone, she prayed, realizing that more emotions were involved now than terror.

Brian came to the door of the store and looked at her strangely. When he put his hand on the handle, she started the pickup and quickly put it into reverse.

What should she do with herself? Still too upset to talk to anyone, she drove slowly through town, in the opposite direction from home. She braked once when she saw the arrow sign pointing the way to the County office building. She didn't have to talk to Hardin, she realized. Crime committed outside the city limits was in Rodney Madden's jurisdiction. Talking to Sheriff Madden sounded infinitely more appealing but she had promised Sam an hour. She owed him that.

She was halfway to the next town, where the hills began to flatten into wheat fields before she decided it was safe to start back. He'd better be gone when she got there.

He was.

Jonna drove completely behind the old house just to be sure his car was gone.

Candy was back in the corral. The fact that he'd taken time to take care of her horse seemed to contradict the hard, cold, warning that had been in his words. All his talk had been a bluff, she decided, detesting her efforts at trying to find something good about him.

She reminded herself of his threats. All bluster. As insubstantial as the breeze.

Jonna's sigh of relief locked in her lungs though. He'd shown himself a terrific candidate for some extensive therapy, but she'd hovered on the brink of falling for him. Wouldn't a therapist have just as good a time with that?

She drove slowly up the hill to her own house, lost in wistful speculation. Would he go back to the college and resume his life there? She wondered what he'd been like before his sister's death had tipped him over the edge. What a tragedy.

She could probably even find him eventually, send him the money he was due. And when or if he recovered from whatever demons possessed him . . .

She was beginning to feel every bit as obsessed as he was and as foolish as she'd been over Jeffrey. But the glimpses of the man she had assumed he was, the one he could be, those glimpses had been very appealing.

She realized she'd been sitting in her garage, her fingers pressed against her cold mouth, for—she wasn't sure how long. She walked wearily toward the house, totally drained by the huge gamut of emotions she'd used up.

The second she opened the door, Magic jumped her, meowing frantically. She'd never felt so grateful to see a warm comforting body. She was going to cry again and Magic always understood. Jonna bent to pick her up, then stopped halfway.

A pile of debris cluttered the door between the foyer and the main part of the house. Jonna rose slowly from her partial squat and pulled the door open wide.

The trash filling the doorway was only the beginning, and the lump in Jonna's throat turned to horror again. She wanted to cry for him. "Oh, God. He's even sicker than I thought."

The kitchen cabinets stood open. At least two hung by one hinge, as if someone had opened them, clawed everything out, then swung on the doors until the top hinges gave way.

Jonna picked her way through the mess at her feet, stepped through the chaos of the kitchen and looked into the living room. Sam was gone, all right, but he'd certainly left his mark.

The living room looked almost as bad. Giant slashes made the upholstered furniture seem to have exploded. He had missed one cushion on the loveseat, making it, not the others, seem mismatched and discordant. Books tumbled everywhere. One of the bookcases stood upside down in the middle of the room.

The small cocktail tables were upended, the lamps destroyed almost beyond recognition.

But there, untouched in the midst of the mess, sat the fragile glass castle her best friend from college had given her the day they graduated.

She slumped to her knees and picked it up, examining it and trying to figure out how it had avoided the destruction. Magic rubbed up against her thigh, purring comfortingly as Jonna's hand absently stroked the pet.

Had the upstairs escaped the attack? One glance toward the loft confirmed that it hadn't. Papers littered everything and her drafting table wasn't there. She could always see it from this vantage point.

"Oh, Magic," she whispered and looked around for the phone.

The peach-colored cord led to a pile of books, and the phone jangled as she unburied it from the bottom of the stack.

A rustling noise sounded behind her and Jonna bolted to her feet.

Sam stood in the doorway, white-faced.

"What are you doing here?" she asked, curling the castle to her chest with one hand, the telephone receiver protectively to her with the other.

Sam's eyes scanned the disaster, then clashed with hers. She stepped warily backward, coming up short as her calf contacted one of the end tables.

"Jonna, I'm sorry. I should have been here. I could have stopped this. Stopped him," he added with an extra layer of venom.

Him? Jonna searched frantically for a way around Sam. If he would keep playing games like this, if he was crazy, he would—

The gun. Damn. She'd left it in the pickup.

"What a con artist," she said, sarcasm disguising her fright. "Do you expect me to believe *you* didn't do this?"

"I didn't, Jonna. I swear on my life." He took a step in her direction, then froze at her yelped scream.

"Jonna, please. Listen to me."

She felt an unwelcome stab of sympathy at his tortured expression, but reminded herself he was one heck of an actor. And dangerous and deranged besides. She had to get that through her head and base every reaction on that fact and that fact alone. Dangerous. Deranged.

"Get out of my house. I told you I'd call the police." She looked at the phone and reached to dial 911.

"Don't you get it?"

"Get what? That you are crazy and . . . and . . . ?"

"That someone wants to kill you," he said, enunciating each word carefully.

"Me?"

"I'm here to stop him."

"Who?"

"I don't know." He bowed his head. His jaw did that tightening thing that made the muscle there flex.

"The man who wants to kill you murdered my sister," he said. "He also killed a woman in Colorado. Probably another. There may have been others—I'm not sure," he said. "But I know you're next."

"Why? Why would anyone want to kill me?" Her heart was beginning to ache from pounding so hard. Why was Sam doing this?

"The award."

Don't you remember the award? The dark, neurotic voice on the telephone? The memory stole the firm, solid ground beneath her feet and she began to shake uncontrollably. "That's ridiculous."

"You know that." Sam lifted one eyebrow. "The police know that, everyone knows that—but someone forgot to tell him. He wants to kill you. Your thinking that it's ridiculous won't keep him from doing it."

He believed it. Somewhere that truth clicked in her head. "Oh, Sam. Let me get you some help."

"I have proof that everything I've told you is true."

"Everything?"

"Everything I told you this morning," he amended, fluidly closing in on her, his movements so graceful that she almost didn't notice. A crushed lamp and a chaotic stack of miscellany were all that separated them. Another step and he would be within grabbing distance.

"Look at these." Sam lifted a sheaf of papers she hadn't noticed in his hand. For a second, they claimed his attention, and Jonna seized the chance she might not have again.

She dropped the phone and dodged right—opposite the direction of the door.

He lunged, just as she'd anticipated, but her flight the other way from what he expected left him off-balance for a second. A whimper of hope escaped her as his fingertips brushed, but didn't get a grip on her Windbreaker. If she could keep him disoriented, she might have a prayer of a chance.

Leaping a pile of clutter, she gave him a wide berth and circled the counter, running back toward the still-open door. Cold wind hit her face as his warm hand brushed her waist.

She shrieked, twisted. Alarm rendered her senseless as she rushed outdoors. She *must* get to the gun.

He caught her halfway to the garage.

Both hands clamped around her midsection. She struggled silently. Squirming, kicking. Her hand formed a claw, ready to swipe at his face, and she tried to turn. He jerked her backward, holding her firmly against him. She whimpered again and realized it was almost a permanent state. She wasn't sure if she'd ever be able to stop. Her brain felt like a quivering mass of matter. She fought mindlessly.

"Jonna." His breath fanned her ear, yet the sound seemed to come from far, far away. "Jonna. Calm down. Listen to me. Please. Jonna."

The words pounded her, like waves relentlessly lapping away at a sandy shore. Gradually, the gentle hold, the soft concern in his voice pricked her consciousness. She started hearing him coherently.

"Jonna," he said urgently as her struggle slowly died, "you've got to listen to me."

His strong arms, his taut body, swaddled her and wrapped her in a tight cocoon. She felt the rise and fall of his chest. His heart thudded heavily in a counterbeat to hers. Both rhythms gradually slowed as if seeking to establish a shared pace.

She guessed she should be grateful her heart was still beating. She was positive it had stopped completely for a few minutes.

"Now, listen to me," he commanded. The words vibrated through her.

She squirmed again, then nodded and his grip loosened, but he didn't let go. "Let's go back inside."

Sam shoved Jonna gently in front of him and negotiated her through the disaster.

Chairs were overturned, and a whirlwind of paper layered the stairs. Sam prodded her forward to the only unmaimed cushion on the sofa and pushed her down there. Standing room only, he thought inanely as he rejected the volcano of fluff on the cushion beside her and crouched down in front.

Safer anyway, he told himself, looking at those wide stunned eyes. She was obviously in shock. Each shard of green, gold and brown in the hazel circle was overly bright. Her pupils were dilated. When she emerged from that state, she might try to run again.

"Jonna?" He spoke as if he were speaking to a child. She looked past him and he felt a reluctant anger.

"Jonna, will you stay put if I get the papers I asked a friend to fax me so I could show them to you?" He waved vaguely toward where he'd dropped them to chase her.

She didn't react, and he didn't take his eyes off her until he couldn't avoid stumbling over the debris any other way.

By the time he got back to her and settled on his haunches again, her trembling had subsided a little, but her breathing was still shallow. He offered her the stack of papers. Anger stabbed him as she drew away, farther back into the cushions. Anger at her for believing him capable of this. Anger at whoever had done it. Oh, God, he hadn't wanted to feel. He couldn't spare the luxury of feeling right now. He hardened his heart.

She was registering some reaction again at least, he thought. That was positive.

And little comfort. He'd screwed this up and the worst was yet to come. He'd cluttered all his plans with delusions last night, and they clouded his perceptions today. The facts. He had to stick with the facts.

"I didn't bring these with me because I thought this would be all over before I had to explain it. But here's verification that what I'm telling you is the truth." He curled her fingers around the first sheet of slick fax paper. "Please, I want you to read these."

Her eyes flicked over the item, then jumped back to him. "Please," he asked.

She looked at the beginning of the article again. He licked his lips nervously as she began to read.

She scowled as she handed the paper back to him. "So?"

For a moment, the image of the woman in Colorado was superimposed on Jonna's. That had been her reaction, too. He glanced down at the next one and a lump thickened his throat. "Now, this."

The grainy picture at the top of the page caught and held her eyes. They grew wider as she read the headline and looked back up at him questioningly. "Your sister?"

He managed a nod, keeping the deep and painful gasp where it belonged, inside. Shifting his weight from one bent leg to the other, he focused on the sky behind her. The expanse of milky gray framed her shoulders and didn't make judgments. If she looked at him with disbelief or accusations or even sympathy right now, he wasn't sure what he would do.

"I'm very sorry," she said at last. "But I don't see what this proves or has to do with me."

Wordlessly, he handed her another paper. She skimmed the page, her face devoid of expression. His restless feet itched to walk away, to leave her to her fate. Today he'd balanced so close to failure once again that he could barely think. Why was he so willing to torture himself this way? Jonna was nothing to him. Nothing.

Standing, jamming his fingertips into the pockets of his tight new jeans, he forced himself to maintain his guarding stance.

She looked up at him and extended the glossy pages toward him. They fell and limply draped her hand. "I still don't see—"

"Read the top of the clippings announcing the awards," he ordered. Two of the articles had the standard logo, *Tiger Watch*, and the date printed at the top of the column. The words were scrawled in a bold stroke across the bottom of the third small alumni news item.

"Yeah, I recognized the NET alumni paper," she said.

"Don't you think it's strange that all three of these graduates died violently within a couple of days of winning some kind of award?"

Jonna eyed him speculatively, obviously wondering whether she dared disagree. "Coincidental, maybe," she said tactfully, "but strange? People die all the time." She lifted her chin slightly. "Some of them are murdered. But these people are probably not the only NET graduates to die in the past two years."

Sam wanted to scream, yell, pull his hair out with the injustice of it. The same old arguments. His muscles tightened with the familiar frustration. She was making him mad. Somehow he had expected more from her. He realized he had begun to *hope* that she would understand.

"Tell me about your sister's murder," she said. "Give me one good reason to believe they're connected."

Sam swept a weary hand through his hair. He felt it stand on end but ignored the impulse to smooth it. Somehow, wild disarray seemed to match the moment. "I've told you the best reasons I know." He told her about being the one to find Denise. About the police investigation. About their concession that it might have something to do with the award. "The police checked into the whereabouts of the other nominees for Denise's award—the most likely suspects if it wasn't a random act of violence," he said. "Except for one, they all had alibis. The one who didn't was clear across the country," he added before she could ask. "He was the only one of the nominees that hadn't been at the ceremony." He told her the police's final decision to categorize the circumstances of her murder as an attempted robbery.

"But how could they all be connected? They all died in far-flung parts of the country."

"The only connection the victims share is the college."

"Someone from the college is doing this?"

"No," he denied. "I don't *know*. I've gone through every bit of information I can find and there isn't a soul—staff or student—at the college who was in all these different places when the murders occurred."

"Then how—"

"I know it doesn't make sense," he conceded. His hands felt especially useless, hanging at his side. *Honesty, Barton, she trusts honesty.* "The killer can't even be a former student who receives his alumni newsletter and then does the deed. In two out of three of these, the murders happened *before* the alumni newsletters announcing the awards were sent out."

"Then how did you—"

"I don't have a thing to go on but pure, gut-level certainty—but I've been right twice."

He felt perversely satisfied when Jonna visibly shuddered, then perversely irritated at himself for caring whether or not she believed. He just wanted someone to, he told himself.

"That doesn't mean the police and the FBI believe me," he added.

"You've talked to them?"

He nodded. "They think I added two and two together and came up with five."

The confusion on Jonna's face deepened.

"But look at the pattern, Jonna," he said. "Look around you."

Renewed horror rioted across her face as she reassessed the chaos around them.

"Think about it. If I did this, why would I come back?" He settled in front of her again, tentatively touching her cold hand.

Her shoulders drooped dejectedly. She closed those incredibly seductive eyes. It was a small, unconscious sign of trust. He was making progress.

"If I wanted to hurt you, why wouldn't I have done so already?"

"How would I know?" she said wearily.

"If I'm not telling the truth, Jonna, who did this? And why?" He waited momentarily for a reaction, then answered his own question. "Someone wants to kill *you*, Jonna. And until someone else believes me, I'm your best— your only defense."

CHAPTER EIGHT

Her best defense? Jonna looked around her. A knot of terror formed around her chest and squeezed. She wasn't sure which was the most terrifying. Him? Or his story?

"I came here to protect you."

"Well, if you're telling me the truth, you aren't any damn good at that." She burst out of her seat, past him. She saw him move from the corner of her eye and turned on him. Her voice broke on the verge of a sob. "Look at this mess."

It was inconceivable. She felt doubly betrayed. He wasn't even similar to the man he'd led her to believe he was. And he was thirty times the con artist Jeffrey had been.

She faltered backward and almost tripped over one of the lamps. The noise made her jump; the chaos around her reflected the cold confusion she was feeling. She wanted to rush forward, to the man she couldn't afford to trust, because his arms had felt so warm. Could they make the shaking go away? "Why would *anyone* want to kill me?"

"The award."

"Why?"

"I don't know. Denise was dead a day after winning hers."

The woman in the picture had been very pretty, a fine-tuned version of Sam. In the picture, Denise's eyes had sparkled merrily; she'd exuded life. Could those hands have strangled his beautiful sister?

He held one more slick fax printout toward her. "The same guy who killed Denise killed Leah Darcy."

Jonna accepted the flimsy paper that emotionlessly reported the bare details of another victim's death.

His head dipped. "You can't imagine how I felt when I read *that* in the newspaper in my hotel room the next morning."

Jonna read of Leah Darcy's death in spurts, glancing from him to the page, from the page to him. "Her children found her?" The article slipped from her fingers.

"Her eleven-year-old daughter," Sam confirmed.

"So you think this...this...nut is some kind of serial killer who runs around the country murdering women who receive awards?" She wouldn't have thought the chill at the roots of her nerves could turn any colder, but it did.

"I only know about the ones who have graduated from NET." His mouth formed a grim line.

"You think there are more?" Comprehension took all her breath away.

"Probably not. I don't know. From the research I've done, this guy would be considered a pattern killer—not a serial killer," Sam corrected. "Females. Award winners. NET alumnae. You fit the pattern, Jonna. And unless, for some reason, he doesn't know about you, you're next."

Jonna closed her eyes, blocking him out. She would have given anything to know what to believe. Her eyes jolted open again and she was relieved he hadn't moved.

God! She *was* too trusting. And it was going to catch up with her soon if she continued to let herself trust everything he said.

"What did you do with Darrell?" she asked suddenly. "The guy Moss *really* sent this morning," she added resentfully at his scowl. "The guy who should have had this job."

"Same thing I did with your last hired man," he said flatly. "I gave him a thousand dollars to get himself settled in Texas and offered him a job in either the Grounds Maintenance or Security departments at the college."

"He took it?"

"The money? Gladly. But not the job. He and his wife want to stay in this area if they can. My only stipulation was that neither of them come back here," he added with a hard edge that plainly told her not to get her hopes up that he would be back.

At this point, she didn't care. Her only worry now was what to think. What to believe. Where was Moss? Where were all the friends she listened to when she couldn't rely strictly on common sense? She had to have time to think.

He seemed to understand her plight and didn't push her. His patience made her vulnerable, though. It made her inclined to simply trust him.

"Shall we call the police now?" he asked, startling her. "Now that he's done something we can pinpoint, actually show them," he explained, sweeping the room with a broad gesture, "maybe they'll listen. And if I'm going to get him this time," he added, "I need all the help I can get."

Rodney Madden, the county sheriff, gingerly picked his way through the debris. "Jonna, this isn't the kind of excuse I like, but it's sure nice to see you again. Has someone taken a strong dislike to you?" He stepped toward her and wrapped an arm around her shoulders as he surveyed the room. "Got any ideas about what happened here?"

Jonna turned to Sam and listened as he told a brief version of his story again.

Sheriff Madden absently rubbed his ear as Sam finished. "We'll have to confirm all that. Now, Jonna." Madden led her toward the kitchen. "We'll let Gary get on with his powdering, see if we can lift a fingerprint or two. Let's get out of his way. How about a cup of coffee?"

"Sounds good." Jonna appreciated the sheriff finding her something to do. Sam and Madden sat down at the table. She listened intently as Sam answered questions.

Rodney Madden was skillful. He managed to sound sympathetic as Sam filled in blanks. She saw Madden perk up when some of the questions brought out Sam's military and security background. She herself was impressed to learn that Sam had pioneered a campus escort service at night, a security measure that was becoming standard at colleges and universities across the nation.

"The police thought Denise caught a burglar in the act when she was killed," Sam explained. "A matter of being in the wrong place at the wrong time. Nothing was stolen, but they believe whoever did it didn't have time to take anything before Denise walked in and interrupted them. I assumed they knew what they were talking about until almost nine months later."

"What happened then," Madden asked.

"One Saturday morning I was hanging out in Barry's office. He's a friend of mine, the director of Alumni Affairs. He was looking up some information for me, and while I waited I read the proofs for the alumni magazine about to go to press. I ran across a couple of items about JoAnne Campbell. The announcement of her award was in the same issue as the announcement of her death."

"And it reminded you of Denise? You thought it was too much of a coincidence?" Madden asked.

"I knew." Sam's voice held an eerie certainty.

A chill crept up Jonna's back and she paused in her search through the debris for mugs.

"You knew...what?"

"I knew the same person who killed Denise had killed JoAnne Campbell."

"Same award?"

"No." Sam said the word reluctantly.

"Different parts of the country."

"Denise was killed in California. JoAnne Campbell lived in Connecticut." Sam's slow response, his defensive tone hinted that he'd been asked the same questions before. And his answers hadn't been believed.

Madden cleared his throat. "And you called the police?"

"The inspector in charge of Denise's case."

"You've kept in touch with him?"

"From time to time." Sam didn't hide his frustration.

"And they hadn't found your sister's killer?"

"No." Sam sighed heavily. "They had checked out Denise's co-workers, they'd talked to friends, to the guy she'd been dating and her boyfriends for the past two or three years. They even checked into the whereabouts of the other nominees for her award. I checked it all again when I started putting things together and came to the same conclusions. Everyone loved Denise. No one had a solid motive."

"Coffee," Jonna announced. "I can't remember, Sheriff, do you take anything in yours?"

"Just straight." Madden took the mug and motioned her into the seat next to him. He turned his attention back to Sam. "So they called the FBI and they, in turn, contacted the local authorities in Connecticut."

"Only because I insisted." Sam sloshed coffee over the top of his cup as he swiveled back to face the table. He didn't seem to notice.

"And the FBI ran the whole scenario through their fancy computers and didn't come up with any similarities?"

"They didn't know JoAnne and Denise had both graduated from the same university. The didn't know they'd both recently received awards."

"And when they did?"

"They believed it was a coincidence." Sam propped his elbows on the table and buried his face in one hand. He rubbed his forehead with his fingertips.

"Did they say why?"

Sam shrugged. "Denise was strangled with someone's bare hands. Her apartment was a mess, about like this. They still think she interrupted a robbery. JoAnne Campbell was strangled, too, but whoever did it used gloves. They can't guess the motive, but she *wasn't* especially well liked. They don't think it was robbery. They believe it was someone she knew and trusted. She'd let him in."

"What kind of award did Denise receive?"

"She was a graphic artist. She'd won an advertising award for some special type of layout."

"And JoAnne Campbell?"

Sam gazed deeply into his mug, as if he'd find answers in the dark pool of liquid he hadn't even sipped. "Hers was some kind of regional award for her work with a local community theater."

Madden's face was unreadable. He gulped at his coffee as his undersheriff came around the corner. "Gary? You findin' anything?"

"Guess we'll see when we get the results back from Wichita," Gary answered.

"So you want to tell me about the third one, Barton?"

The skin around Sam's expressive mouth whitened.

"Barry promised to alert me if he received any more award notifications on female alumnae."

Madden nodded, encouraging Sam to go on.

"It was for journalism. I went to Colorado the day before she was to accept it so that I could warn her." Sam lifted one hand dismissively. "She was dead four days later."

"How?" Jonna asked before Madden could. He patted her hand.

"Strangled?" Madden asked after a moment.

"Yes."

"Was she robbed?"

Sam shook his head.

"Were any of them molested? Disfigured in any way?"

Sam shook his head again. "Not exactly."

"What do you mean?"

Sam lowered his head and muffled his voice with his hand.

"I'm sorry, Barton, but I missed that. What did you say?"

"Denise and JoAnne Campbell were arranged in a . . . he posed them in a suggestive position."

"But not the third one?"

Sam shook his head. "I don't think he had time. He ran out of time."

Madden leaned back in his chair and sighed.

Jonna watched him, anxious to know what he was thinking.

"Well," Madden drawled, "I see why the FBI failed to pick up similarities on their computers."

Sam nodded. "They didn't ask the right questions."

Madden ignored the statement. "Jonna, I need to look around a little more." He rose from his chair and asked Gary if he was finished upstairs.

She started to follow, but he motioned her away. "Let me look, see what I can see without your interpretation," he said. "I'll holler if I need you."

She folded back into her chair and Sam caught her gaze. There was a question in his eyes. *Do you believe me?*

She looked away quickly. What could she tell him? She didn't know what to believe.

"What happens next?" he asked.

"What do you mean?"

"Do you still want me to leave?"

She wanted to cry. For him. For herself. She'd never seen or felt so much pain for no physical reason. "I . . . I really don't know."

"I'm going to get the bastard," he said, hate dripping from the words. "Preferably before he kills you."

She jerked back as if he'd slapped her. Her safety wasn't high on his list of priorities. The doubts flooded back. "He's killing you, too," she said sadly.

"Jonna?"

"Yeah, Sheriff?" She hustled out of her chair, relieved to escape Sam's presence.

Madden was halfway down the stairs and she climbed to meet him. "You working on anything important right now?"

She shrugged. "No more so than usual. I sent out my last project this morning. All I've really done on the next one is a few preliminary sketches." She lifted a shoulder again. "I can't imagine how any of it might be of importance to anyone besides me."

"You're making good money now. Having a lot of success. Maybe someone who's not doing so well wants to steal your current designs." He led the way back up the stairs. "You've been up here?" he asked.

She nodded, then realized he couldn't see her answer. "Yeah," she answered aloud.

"You didn't notice anything missing?"

"Just destroyed."

"Anything irreplaceable?"

"Not that I noticed."

Madden stepped aside and motioned for her to pass him.

"Check around. See if you can find anything missing. We need to cover all the bases. Maybe we're dealing with a professional burglary and all the destruction is to sidetrack us. It's hard to imagine anyone this malicious or vicious for no reason."

Unless whoever did it—Sam?—is simply crazy, Jonna thought. She did as instructed while Madden went in and out of the bedrooms.

"He didn't mess with a thing in your bedroom," he said on his way to the other.

"Thank God." She didn't try to hide her relief. She'd been too freaked out to go in there with him before the police arrived. And she had been wondering if she'd ever be able to sleep peacefully in there again if it looked like this.

"This one either," Madden said from the door of the guest room and watched as she finished picking through the clutter.

"Why did he leave those rooms alone?" she wondered out loud.

"Ran out of time, maybe?" His beefy face scrunched in an I-don't-know. "More likely, he ran out of steam."

She swallowed hard. "Do you think Sam did this?"

"I'd say you're probably the best judge of that," Madden said softly. "What do you think?"

"Absolutely, when I first saw it." The tight ache squeezed her chest again. "But now...I just don't know. Why would he suggest I call you? Why would he stay? Why would he come back at all?''

Madden gently pushed her back in her office chair and half stood, half sat on the tall stool before her overturned drafting table.

"So what did you decide about the damage up here?" he asked, changing the subject.

"Surface," she said. "All my copies of final plans haven't been touched. They're exactly as I left them in that drawer." She waved toward the oversize file cabinets the other side of him. "All my legal papers and files and things are in order. The only thing ruined was stuff I had out, lying on top of the desk and drafting board. In the bookcases."

He nodded. "Well, that about clinches it. No real purpose here besides pure-D-struction."

"How can you tell?" she asked.

"In my experience, vandals are basically lazy," he said. "They don't want to work very hard at destroying whatever it is they destroy."

"He sure did a job on my kitchen," she contradicted him.

"He probably started there first, while his energy level was high. Since vandals go for effect and you don't keep much on your counters, the fastest, easiest way he could get it was by opening the doors and pulling things out. You notice, he didn't bother with the bottom cabinets."

"He didn't?"

"Nope. Too much effort and by the time he was through the top ones, he'd achieved his desired effect." Madden rose slowly from his perch. "Come on. Let's go downstairs and see if Gary's ready to go."

Jonna clutched at Rod's hand. "Do you think Sam's telling the truth?"

"About someone trying to kill you?" he asked.

She nodded. She knew her eyes were far too wide, full of far too much despair as they clung to his face. "About all of it."

"I think *he* believes it."

"But do you?"

"Jonna, darlin', the one thing that *does* add up is that someone has something in for you. In these parts, we don't run into this type of behavior often. Then, it's usually revenge. You already told me you can't think of a single soul that motive might apply to. Sam doesn't have a reason to want revenge, does he?"

Only that she'd fired him. Oh, God. She couldn't think anymore.

She quickly told him about the incident that had sent her flying to town this afternoon.

Madden frowned through the whole story. "Well, he's consistent, at least. Consistent enough to go to a lot of trouble to stay here. It doesn't make much sense to do something like this if his whole intent is staying. Seems to me this kind of thing would have the opposite effect."

She shook her head back and forth.

"And," he drawled, "if he's right about all of this, he may come in handy. And with his background, I like the idea of having him around."

"And you'll be around, too?"

"I'll have the whole department keeping a steady eye on things out here, Jonna. And in the meantime—"

"You'll have someone here?"

Madden grimaced. "Your daddy would do me some serious damage—even from the grave—if I let anything happen to his Girlie. But it's a big county and you know how small my force is. We don't have enough crime here to justify more." He tweaked her cheek as he had when she was a little girl. "But I promise, you just pick up that phone and say your name, I'll have everyone in ten counties out here before you can add a 'boo.'"

Jonna lowered her head.

"And in the meantime," Madden continued, "I'll be doing some checking on my own."

"And if he's lying?"

"Then he's obsessive about those awards. So you don't have to worry about anything until you get back from getting yours. And by then, I guaran-damn-tee you, I'll have a few more answers. In the meantime, I'd rather have him where we can watch him than have no idea where he is."

"Then I *should* keep him here," Jonna said.

"I can think of worse things than knowing what he's up to. You just keep your doors locked, your ears and eyes open and one hand on the phone."

"Sam's been telling me the same thing in a way."

"And *that* sounds like a good sign."

"The house wasn't locked when ... I didn't think about it this afternoon before I went to town."

"You'll think about it now?"

She promised. It was one promise she didn't think he needed to worry about her keeping.

And at least some of the pieces of the puzzle fit. Sam's declaration that he was staying hadn't been so much a threat as a vow. And with no one believing him, she had to admit he had a good reason to lie in the first place. The thought warmed her ... until she reminded herself he could be lying now.

She felt a sudden bitterness toward Jeffrey. Before her engagement to him, she'd only doubted her ability to make wise decisions. Jeffrey had managed to destroy her basic trust in her judgment of people. When she was with Sam, she wanted desperately to believe him. Out of sight, she could only concentrate on the doubts.

"Well, come on." Madden took her hand and led her back to the stairs. "Let's go finish this up so I can get back to the office. I need to make some calls."

Gary and Madden packed up their small supply of paraphernalia as Jonna watched.

As Gary carried the first small load of stuff to the car, the sheriff paused at the door. "Oh, by the way, Barton?"

"Yes?"

"Where were you when the woman in Connecticut was murdered—what'd you say her name was?"

Madden had written it down. Jonna, standing a little to the side and behind Sam, looked at Madden in surprise. She knew he saw the look but pointedly avoided her eyes.

"JoAnne Campbell? I was on vacation."

"Where?"

"The upper Midwest, mostly Minnesota." Sam answered. "I was in Wisconsin the week before that at a seminar."

Madden's reaction was casual, too casual.

"Well. Thanks, Barton." His look at Sam was stern. "I'll be in touch," Madden assured Jonna and touched his hat. "Take care."

The minute the sheriff's car started down the drive, Sam silently tore into straightening things up.

"Why didn't you tell me all of this when you came?" Jonna asked him as he began setting the furniture upright.

"I made that mistake once. I told Leah Darcy." He shoved things back in the bookcase. "She didn't believe me."

"What did you tell her?" she whispered.

"I showed her the same stuff I showed you, minus the articles about her, of course," he added grimly. He paused, sitting back on his heels with a couple of hefty books in one hand. "I told her some nut killed my sister and another woman. That he wanted to kill her and I intended to stop him."

Jonna knelt beside him and picking up one of the tattered throw pillows from the couch. "Did you tell her all the stuff about the FBI—"

"She didn't give me a chance. So I left, but she saw me watching her house."

He looked away and stretched to put the books he held in the bookcase. "I saw her lift the drapes every five minutes. She kept her kids inside."

Jonna hugged the half empty pillow to her chest.

"Finally, she came out to my car and threatened to call the police if I hung around anymore." His voice caught, then hardened. "So I left. I didn't know what else to do. I'd also begun to hope that I was wrong. He killed Denise and the one in Connecticut within twenty-four hours of them receiving their awards. It had been several days since she'd received hers. If I *hadn't* told her, I would have caught the bastard." And *that,* she realized, was one of the things that bothered her. In all his hints and threats and truths, he'd only talked about "catching" the murderer. His intent didn't seem to be *saving* her or anyone else. Maybe with his sister, Denise, it would have been different. His grief for her was almost palpable.

Jonna impulsively covered his arm with her hand. The muscle in his forearm flexed and she carefully took her hand away.

"How long since this all started, Sam?" she asked.

"Two years, four and a half months since Denise died."

She would almost have bet he had it down to the weeks, days and hours.

"It's not really your problem anymore," she said hesitantly, studying her intertwined fingers. "Why not let the police handle it?"

"They couldn't."

She started to protest.

"I don't mean they wouldn't have the capability," he explained, "but our laws prohibit the various authorities from acting on gut feelings. They have to have some kind of concrete proof. They're good laws, but that doesn't mean I could live with myself if didn't try to stop this monster since I *know* what's going on."

"But that's just it," she argued. "You don't have proof either. Just speculation. Doesn't that bother you?"

His eyes burned into her. "I *know,* Jonna."

And therein lies his madness.

"I promised my mother before she died, that I'd take care of Denise. Poor kid was only fourteen at the time."

His eyes took on a glazed look and Jonna thought he was revisiting some distant time and place. But when she leaned closer to hear his hushed words, she realized the glaze was a cloud of unshed tears.

"I failed."

For a second, she caught a glimpse of the soul that used to live in this fine, fine man. He used to care about someone besides his obsession—whatever or whoever it was; he used to be concerned and loving; he used to be someone who was oh so gentle, she suspected. She felt a bittersweet longing to have known him then. Before he'd buried those feelings somewhere deep beneath...what? Guilt? Pain? Insanity?

"Oh, no, Sam. You took care of her while she was growing up, you put her through high school and college. Denise was what? Twenty-three years old? Isn't that what the article said? You can't possibly take—"

"I didn't keep my promise," he interrupted in a rough voice charred by pent-up emotion, "and I can't go back. But I can stop him." He looked at her squarely. "He *will* pay."

Then, as he went back to work, Jonna stared at his long, capable fingers, at the broad shoulders that seemed intent on carrying a far too heavy load. His lean, lithe body moved with such restrained power and grace. She felt a gnawing hunger to have his dangerous energy directed at her, as if somehow that would ease his burden and make her whole, too.

Her mind played with the tantalizing contrast between the two of them. Male. Female. He possessed a controlled strength. She was weak. She couldn't seem to make a simple decision without input from at least half the people she knew. But it must be far, far worse to take on responsibility for the entire world. If Sam was right about any of this—if he wasn't just a madman with an extra personality that could deftly mask another—*he* was going to pay a very high price. And she'd never felt more helpless.

"Do you have a camera?" he asked, startling her out of her reverie.

"What?"

"It might be a good idea to get pictures of all this before we clean up. For your insurance," he added at her blank look.

"We need pictures?" she asked.

"Probably not since you made the police report, but it can't hurt."

Jonna brought the camera and finished the partially used film inside, impulsively snapping the last frame of him as he began picking up with a vengeance.

For the most part, Jonna followed him around with trash bags, telling him which things to throw out and which she thought were salvageable.

Jonna wasn't sure she would have gotten through the task without his help, but by the time they were done, she was anxious for him to go. The strain of being an oblivious entity was getting to her.

Especially when she couldn't keep her eyes off him.

She *hated* her own paranoia and growing obsession. She hated having to match his self-sufficiency with a bravado of her own. She hated her need to impress him with her poise and her disappointment when he didn't seem to notice.

She kept remembering how his arms had imprisoned her when she'd run from him earlier, and how she'd felt they were as much a haven as a trap. And she hated the desire and longing for him that had been steadily growing as they worked.

She managed to stammer an awkward thanks as he finally took his leave.

"You'll be okay?" He paused by the door.

"You're the authority on this. Maybe I should ask you."

A nerve near her mouth twitched with the effort of holding

her scattered emotions at bay. She hoped it was one of those things you felt but no one could see.

He absently rested his thumb against the jumpy nerve, destroying one more overly optimistic hope. She knew her eyes were wide, pleading for reassurance as she looked up at him.

"I could stay with you." His voice was as thick as a gray winter day.

She flinched.

"You're right. Lousy idea. You're right not to trust me."

She blinked, thankful that he'd misread her reaction. Wasn't it better for him to think she didn't trust him than to realize she didn't trust herself with him? In the past hour, she'd let down every defense. Despite not knowing if he wanted to harm her, the part of her that was currently in control longed for him to stay.

"I loaned thirteen thousand dollars to the last man I trusted. I haven't seen him since," she reminded herself as well as him. And Sam was offering company, not the forgetfulness she knew she could find by closing her eyes and lifting her lips to his.

As if reading her mind, he slid his thumb a fraction of an inch to the left and softly traced the corner of her mouth. "Then he was a fool," Sam said.

She told herself to move away from his soothing touch.

"Jonna?"

"What?" she asked, mesmerized by the gentle stroke. She thought she might even have swayed closer.

"I won't let this monster win."

Her heavy eyelids jolted up. A hard and terrible expression flickered across his face and she finally had the strength to draw away.

"You'll be right down there?" Her head jerked in the direction of the farmhouse and she managed a tremulous but bright smile. "Ready for anything?"

He nodded, then swung on one heel and went to the car he'd driven up so many hours ago. He had gotten his coat from the foyer where he'd thrown it when he came in. It was the long, dark coat he'd arrived in, and she realized the ominous aura she'd felt the day he came was one he intentionally created. It was part of his defensive wall and it fit his Clint Eastwood, save-the-world self-image.

She wondered if he'd packed the rest of his things in his car, ready to leave if she didn't believe his story. Would he have left if she insisted? As he said he'd left Leah Darcy?

She'd never know. She shook her head and watched until his car disappeared behind the windbreak of trees. Even then, she could see his headlights slowly bounce and fall with the ruts in the road. They outlined random trees as he turned the car toward the old house.

Jonna switched on the lights she rarely used between the breezeway and the garage. Her first steps were calm and measured. But by the time she reached the side door of the garage, she was running.

She stopped inside. Her gaze flicked around, spastically searching the dark corners of the cool and hollow building. Each move became more jerky and self-conscious as she withdrew the gun from beneath the pickup seat. Her back felt exposed as she awkwardly leaned across the cab and took the box of bullets from the glove compartment.

She didn't breathe naturally again until she was back in the house, locking the night outside.

But as she looked around, she knew she'd also locked the horror in. Sam had rehung the cabinet doors. They'd put everything redeemable back in its place. Together, they'd patched the furniture cushions with silvery electrical tape. But the scars were there.

She lurched self-consciously through the open rooms, leaving the lights on in her wake as she sought the sanctuary of her untouched bedroom.

She popped a couple of aspirins, took her time in the shower and through all the rituals that usually calmed and soothed her. She read. She watched . . . nothing at the old farmhouse.

She branded and counted cattle and drew house plans in her head. It was a long, long while before she slept.

CHAPTER NINE

Jonna's hand hit the snooze alarm four times before she realized the awful noise was the phone. She yawned and moaned a "hi" into the receiver all at one time.

"Jonna Sanders," a voice singsonged in a ghastly whisper.

Her body lunged upright and she was suddenly very wide awake.

"Where did *you* go in such a hurry yesterday?" His words were muffled and Jonna strained to hear.

"Who is this?" She squeezed the words past vocal cords so tight they hurt.

"I'm sorry I missed you or I would have introduced myself." A high-pitched and sinister giggle set her nerves on edge. "Hope you enjoyed my little surprise when you returned."

She wanted to scream. She wanted to reduce the man at the other end of the line to cinders with some devastating remark but her paralyzed brain wouldn't produce one coherent thought. "You can't—"

"Oh, I agree. It's a terrible shame but I really can't include you in *The Record* yet. Until you have your award, it's just not possible."

His raspy laugh bordered on unholy. "But you'll get it soon, then I'll be in touch," he promised and the phone clicked.

All Jonna heard now was her heart pounding in her ears.

The call had been short. The water bed waves she'd created bolting upright hadn't subsided yet. Jonna glanced toward the window to get a time reference. She'd drawn the curtains and she reluctantly turned toward the clock. A little after four.

Sam. She had to tell him.

It comforted her, knowing that hideous voice hadn't belonged to him. Her instincts had always known.

Without consciously moving, she was at the window, standing between parted drapes. Deathly cold oozed through the gap and her nipples hardened painfully.

Except for a light coating of frost that glistened and defined select blades of grass in the waning light of the moon, the prairie below her was a tarnished bronze.

The white farmhouse accented the harsh landscape like a warm refuge, an inviting sanctuary against a storm. It had embraced her throughout her safe and secure childhood, and even dark and sleeping, it beckoned like an old friend.

Her house—her award-winning, wonderful house—suddenly felt hostile and lonely. And nothing in this world said she had to stay here, she realized. She stepped back and let the curtains separate her from the night.

Yanking her gown over her head, she pulled on jeans and a saggy sweatshirt as she slipped her feet into shoes. Her numb fingers zipped and smoothed as she ran through the brightly lit rooms.

She grabbed her jacket and a sleepy Magic, slung her purse over her shoulder and sought the keys in the front pocket of the bag as she hurried to the garage.

Blanking all thought from her mind, she locked her doors and backed the little vehicle out. She forced a calm she didn't feel as she drove too swiftly down the hill.

Sam's house still looked peaceful. Jonna considered honking, trying to raise him. She dreaded getting out, walking across the shadowy yard. Magic had snuggled close to her hip and looked as reluctant as Jonna felt to go anywhere. She picked up the cat and curled her to her chest. No one could have phoned and then made it here to attack her in the five minutes or so since she'd hung up the phone, she assured herself and opened the truck door.

"Come on, kitty. I know this is crazy, but I just can't stand the thought of going back up there."

She concentrated on taking long and confident steps toward the porch because that kept her from watching over her shoulder. "It was only a stupid telephone call," she whispered.

She finally managed a deep breath when she was at Sam's front door.

Her knock sounded loud and hollow in the silent predawn. She shivered and pounded again. This time, as the racket died, she gave in to her screeching nerves and swiveled pressing her back against the side of the house. She scanned the area for a legitimate threat, sure that if she didn't see anything, she'd relax.

Nothing moved, not even the grass in the breeze. Her land, which should be friendly and quietly familiar, seemed gloomy and ominous. And instead of easing her mind, her certainty that the shadows held terrifying things lying in wait, increased.

Without turning back to the door, she hammered on the frame of the screen again. Before the echoes died, she accepted that Sam wasn't going to answer.

Her body launched into automatic pilot. Three fast strides took her to the steps and she lunged above and beyond them, hitting the ground running. She was gasping by the time she reached the pickup, but not from exertion. And locking the door, almost before she closed it completely, seemed like habit now.

She cleared her throat and gulped air. Her heart rate gradually slowed to its usual pace—until another thought struck her.

The tiny hairs on the back of her neck slowly rose, tingling like some freaky sensor as she lifted her eyes to the rearview mirror. She fully expected a strange pair of eyes to look back from beyond the window behind her.

Of course, no one was there. Only trees filled the small mirror, imitating attentive soldiers.

Magic rubbed against her hand and Jonna jumped, whacking her wrist on the steering wheel.

"Damn, you're a fool," she scolded herself, then wished she hadn't spoken aloud. Every whisper of noise startled her and seemed foreboding.

That final bit of paranoia convinced her she was totally losing it. It was time to get a grip, go home and back to bed. She turned the ignition and the motor purred reassuringly to life.

She released the clutch, intending to reverse and go back up the hill. She looked again at the house, convinced that now, since she was leaving, a light would come on inside. Again, nothing.

"Some kind of protector you are, Sam Barton," she muttered. "God, an army could have come in and you would have slept right—"

—*unless you're not here*. He usually parked in back. She'd automatically assumed his car was there.

Jonna put the truck in drive and let the vehicle creep around the side of the house. By the time she reached the rear, she had accepted that Sam's sedate little car might not be there.

Missing in action!

Her fears confirmed, the wheres and whys occupied her mind and weighed heavily on her heart while she drove back to the house that no longer felt like home.

When her headlights lit the garage, she put her questions aside so they wouldn't distract her as she searched each nook and cranny of the suddenly sinister building. Finally finding the nerve to get out of the pickup, she rushed headlong back into the house.

She took her suspicions back out for examination as she heated water in the microwave for a cup of hopefully soothing herbal tea. Sitting down at the table a minute later, she dunked the bag and tried to understand how this new piece fit into the whole puzzle.

He'd said he was here to stop someone from killing her.

Then where would he be at four in the morning? How concerned could he be about her safety if he wasn't even there? The caller could have just as easily come to "visit."

Of course, she didn't have the award yet. The caller had pretty much verified Madden's and Sam's assumption that she didn't have to worry until she had actual possession. That might explain *why*, but it certainly didn't explain where.

When Moss's convenience store, the business with the longest hours of operation, closed at midnight, Whitfield officially rolled up the streets. Even Emporia, forty minutes away and the only town around that was larger than Whitfield, pretty much folded when the bars closed at 2 a.m.

She propped her elbows on the table, burying her forehead in one of her palms. In a few short days, her life had turned upside down. She didn't feel secure anywhere. And suddenly, she was so weary.

And Sam had been here such a short time. How could one man change everything? How could she know what to think?

Logic. She had to think logically. *Why* would he have gone anywhere?

Jonna realized she was slowly lifting the tea bag up and down, up and down. The liquid inside the mug looked thick, undrinkable and cold. She poured it down the sink.

After double-checking and triple-checking the locks and dead bolts on the doors, she again left all the lights on and took her thoughts upstairs to her bedroom.

There she slowly put her gown back on and went to gaze at the house below. She'd been standing there perhaps two minutes when headlights pierced the drive, flickering eerily through the trees as a car came slowly up the lane.

The car pulled behind the farmhouse and Jonna watched Sam's long shape get out, then disappear inside the back door.

She actually got as far as picking up the phone before she realized she had no idea of what she would say if she called him.

What *could* she say?

I got another call? She suddenly realized she hadn't told him—or anyone—about the first one. So many things had happened, she hadn't thought about it. She'd associated it with some who's-who book. It had never occurred to her that there might be a connection.

I came to you for protection. From what?

Where the hell have you been?

No lights came on in the house below. Jonna had seen very few lights there since he'd moved in, she realized. She'd assumed he was just one of those nuts who believed in "early to bed" and all that garbage. He *did* seem to be an early riser.

She wondered now if he'd been home the night of the other call?

Dammit! Where had he been?

Maybe he couldn't sleep and had gone for a drive. Could he know someone in the area and have gone for a visit? Would it be so amazing if he had a girlfriend?

No, she thought uncomfortably. In her entire life, she'd never met a man who was so compelling. Or attractive. Shoot. He probably had dozens of girlfriends. He might even have a wife.

She knew darn little about him, and what she knew she could tick off without using all five fingers on one hand. His sister had been murdered—he said. He had worked at NET—he said. He'd been in the service—he said. And he was obsessed with catching a killer—he said.

Each of those things could be lies. But for some ungodly reason that had nothing to do with common sense, she wanted to believe him.

Her thoughts were disturbing. She looked once more at the dark and quiet house below. The sky was starting to lighten in the east. She forced herself back to bed and her thoughts back to the original question.

Where the hell have you been, Sam Barton?

Maybe he'd gone to town to mail something. To pick something up? To make a phone call?

But he had a phone.

What if he didn't want any record of a call? The shivering started again.

But calling me wouldn't be long distance. There would be no record.

Who knows what the phone company—or the police—can tell with current technology? a small voice countered in her head.

She tried desperately to remember every detail: the low breathy voice, the hushed whispery tone. She would have recognized it if it was Sam's. Wouldn't she? Right now she wasn't sure.

And no matter the technology, no one could prove a specific call had been made by a specific person if that person used a public phone—unless he or she were caught in the act.

The tiny bit of trust Sam had earned earlier evaporated as if it had never been.

The quivering that had never really stopped returned in earnest, and Jonna clenched her teeth to keep them from chattering.

She wished she had paid attention to where he'd been the night she received the first call—the morning after she hired him. Sam could have easily made that call, too.

Jonna gave up her restless attempts at sleeping about ten the next morning.

The phone rang as she was coming out of the shower and she recoiled from the instrument. Wrapping herself in a towel, she let the answering machine pick it up, listening until she heard Sheriff Madden's voice.

"How you doing?" he asked after her hello.

"I've been better," Jonna replied honestly.

"I'm not surprised," he agreed, then hesitantly added, "I've got several reports from last night's patrols. They indicate you probably didn't get much sleep."

"Oh?" She felt a shimmer of hope. She'd forgotten they promised to be watching.

"Yeah. One says Sam didn't leave your place till after midnight. I suspect that means you didn't finish cleaning up until then. Then you wandered around until nearly three—they saw movement in the house anyway; nothing at all the next two trips by, then about four-thirty, they recorded activity at both your place and the old house every time they drove by for the next two hours."

"They saw Sam leave then?"

The other end of the line was quiet for a moment. "Did he leave?"

"Yes." Her teeth gnawed at the corner of her lip. "I got another one of those calls about four."

"What calls?" Madden broke in.

Jonna explained the strange phone calls in detail, finishing, "I'm sorry, I should have mentioned the first one last night when you were here, but..."

"It isn't like you didn't have plenty on your mind," he soothed.

"And I'd forgotten the first one. It didn't occur to me that the two had anything to do with each other and...do you think it might have been Sam?" she asked.

"It could have been anyone with access to a phone, Jonna. We'll put on a tracer."

"Whoever is doing this isn't stupid enough to stay on the line that long," she said wearily. "They've both, especially the one last night, been very brief."

"That's a fallacy, hon. The person *receiving* the call controls it now. We use a device that ties up the line so the person initiating the call can't disconnect until *you* hang up. All you have to do is leave the phone off the hook."

"Then do it." Technology really was amazing. "But that's not why you called, is it, Madden?"

"No, 'fraid it's not."

She heard him sigh and mentally braced herself.

"I wanted to let you know what I found out about Barton's tale. There have been three murders in different parts of the country. As far as the facts go, what he told us was true."

"What do you mean, as far as the facts go?"

"Barton's interpretation of the evidence is questionable, at best," Madden said. "The experts usually focus on the details of the crime itself. According to the agent I talked to, until Sam came to them, nothing in the FBI computer tied the three killings together."

"And with the information he gave them?"

"Well, once they added in that info—where the victims went to college, that they'd recently won awards, etc.—the computer tagged them and noted one other thing."

"What?"

"All the states where the murders have taken place begin with the letter *C*."

Jonna laughed.

"That's what I did," Madden said. "But that's why they don't usually put in the kind of information Sam gave them."

"Why?"

"Because then the computer comes up with all sorts of weird connections. Ones that have nothing to do with anything."

"Well, that lets me off the hook anyway," Jonna said lightheartedly, and realized that one laugh had relaxed her and brightened her day considerably.

"Oh, what makes you think so?" Madden asked.

"Kansas starts with a K."

"Unless you're spelling phonetically," Madden supplied wryly. "*C*alifornia, *C*onnecticut, *C*olorado, *K*ansas. There ain't nothing in this world, Girlie, that guarantees someone who gets away with murder has to be educated or intelligent.''

Jonna sighed and still appreciated the chuckle.

"And even then," Madden went on, "these crimes have as many similarities to other crimes as they have to each other."

"So they think Sam's lying?"

"I'd say it's more likely they *hope* he's a nutso."

"They hope?" Why would the FBI hope for more insanity in an already insane world?

Madden cleared his throat. "Well, you gotta look at it the way they do: If he's a nut who's imagining things because he desperately needs someone to blame for his sister's murder, he's probably harmless."

"But." Jonna heard the reservation in there somewhere.

"But if there is any truth to his suspicions, he's the only one they can identify who had access to the information he says the murders are based on *and* the opportunity to commit every one of 'em."

"So he might be dangerous?"

"Not 'might be,' darlin'," Madden said gently. "*Is* dangerous. *If* he's right, *if* there really is one person responsible for the deaths of those women—as Sam thinks there is—Sam Barton's the *only* suspect."

Sam was saddling up Murphy when the extra phone ringer he'd rigged in the barn went off.

When he got inside, Barry had left a message and Sam dialed the college number immediately.

He interrupted Barry's hello. "What's happening?"

"Got another one, Sam." A heavy concern permeated the words. "I certainly was tempted not to tell you," he added.

"Barry, if you give up on me, too, I'm . . . I'm . . ."

"I know." There was a long pause. "That's why I decided to tell you about it. Besides, this one's a little different than the others. The differences bothered me enough that I went back and did some comparisons to the others."

Barry gave him the details of an alumnus in Louisiana who had won an award. "But," he emphasized, "she won it—and received it—almost four months ago."

"And she's still alive?"

"Yes. I called. She's definitely still walking around, working, talking. Boy, could that woman talk."

"And you told her about all of this?"

"Of course not," Barry said in his wryest voice. "I told her the alumni office always calls to congratulate award winners. You think I want people believing I'm as nuts as you?"

"So why—"

"That's what I wondered," Barry broke in. "If you're right, why hasn't this wacko killed her? I pulled the other files and I think I might have an answer."

Sam waited impatiently while Barry, as usual, took full advantage of his chance at heightening the drama.

"This woman sent her own announcement. You know, the handwritten, guess-what's-been-happening-with-me-since-graduation type note with the mention of the award casually tacked on at the end so we wouldn't think she was bragging."

"Yes. And what were the others?"

"News releases."

A clue. Finally a clue.

"One's from a PR firm representing an international organization," Barry continued. "The others, the one on Denise and the woman in Colorado, were from the associations who presented the awards."

"So the killer is probably someone in publicity or PR," Sam said, as much to himself as to Barry.

"Not necessarily." Barry stopped him. "We print those items. The whole idea of sending out a release is to get as many people to print them as possible. Whoever the madman is—if there is a madman—could have received the release, just like I did, or read the news just about anywhere else."

"So I need to get a list of the people those announcements were sent to."

"It might be a start, but Sam, give it to someone else."

Sam started. Barry rarely used such an intense tone.

"Give it to the FBI, the cop on Denise's case, someone," Barry urged.

"I've had such success with them," Sam pointed out dryly.

"Please, Sam. Think about it? Dr. Simpson in the psychology department—"

"The one in hot water for letting his TAs do all his classroom work?"

"That's the one. His teaching assistants do all his teaching because he's too busy publishing his own personal studies on deviant behavior, remember?"

"What about him?" Sam asked.

"He's starting to get quite a reputation, and a lot of people consider him one of the foremost experts in the nati—"

"And what does that have to do with me?"

"This latest thing. You knew everyone would talk when you took a leave and went off like that? Well, you know Dog-Eat-Dog Simpson. He doesn't mind bringing up some multiple-personality disorder or some such nonsense every time your name enters a conversation. He hasn't actually said your name in the same sentence but the implication is there."

"But no one—"

"He's planted the seed, Sam. You know how this profession is, publish or perish. If you happen to turn out to be a mass murderer, you'll be his ticket to the talk show circuit and a *major* university. Ivy League even. He hasn't been shy about telling everyone that's where he plans to go."

Sam let that bit of information sink in.

"And you can't deny, you've acted a little over the edge the past few months. Unfortunately, Sam," Barry added slowly, "that's not the only news I have."

Sam wasn't sure he wanted to hear more. "Okay. Give it to me, Barry."

"Donna called bright and early this morning. Guess who had just shown up on her doorstep? Asking questions? About you?" He answered his own question. "An FBI agent."

"Why Donna? We quit seeing each other right after Denise..."

"Died, Sam," Barry filled in for Sam when his hesitation dragged on too long. "Right after Denise *died*. It isn't so tough to say. And it's *past* time to deal with it and put it behind you. Son of a gun, Sam, I wish your mother hadn't laid all that baggage on you, but Denise's murder was not your fault. Your obsession with this is starting to make me nervous. Why don't you just come back?"

"I can't, Barry, you know that. You want to publish another story in the alumni news about Jonna?" Even saying it was like tempting fate. He felt a cold sweat layer his entire body.

"But now the FBI is interested. Isn't that what you wanted? Come back. Let them take care of it. You don't have to be involved."

And that word took his breath away. Dammit. He'd broken all his own rules. He *was* involved. The knowledge was like a body blow.

When he didn't comment, Barry went right on. "Get the hell out before something happens, Sam. If you're right about this Jonna Sanders, that's the last place you should be. Especially with them asking questions about you—"

"And *she* would be here, totally on her own, while they're in Texas investigating me."

"Oh-h-h-h." Barry groaned and Sam could picture him wiping his big hand across that plump face in frustration. "Sam, what am I going to tell them when they show up here? You know they will. I've been expecting them since Donna called. Do I tell them you know who is doing this? You don't. Do I tell them you couldn't be responsible for any of it? I, myself, gave you every bit of information you would need to have killed the last one—*and* this one. Try living with that for a day or two. I keep telling myself you and I are both sane, but everyone else thinks I'm aiding and abetting a madman."

"I'm sorry, Barry. You know I never intended you to—"

"How do I convince them you're *not* crazy?" he went on without acknowledging Sam's apology. "You've acted crazy as a loon the past several months. Someone else they interview will surely mention that."

There was a lengthy silence and Sam felt the heavy weight of Barry's concern.

"Barry," he said finally, "just tell them the truth."

"But—"

"Maybe they'll come *here* to keep an eye on me. That would be perfect. You know the problem. We've talked about it before. They don't investigate something that hasn't happened yet. But if they come to watch me, they might just be around when that bastard shows up again."

"Again?"

"Oh, I didn't tell you." Sam briefly described yesterday's "visit." Barry asked if Sam was positive his murderer was responsible for the destruction of Jonna's house.

"She wouldn't have an enemy in the world," he answered, a little passionately he realized when Barry was silent for far too long. "No one else would have done something like this," he added quickly before Barry could comment with something that Sam knew he would have to defend.

"Why didn't you get him then?"

"The faxes. It happened while I was in Emporia picking up the faxes I asked you to send."

"Then she believed you when you showed her the articles?"

"I'm still here," Sam said.

But several minutes later, after they'd said their goodbyes, after Barry had promised to keep him up to date on what was going on in Texas, Sam returned to the work Jonna had hired him to do and admitted to himself that Barry was right.

He really shouldn't be here. Day after day, he was getting in deeper and deeper. After the incident yesterday, he wasn't so confident anymore.

Somehow, at some time during the long lonely night, he had realized his focus had shifted. But he couldn't care about Jonna.

He couldn't risk becoming more preoccupied with *her* than he was with the bastard who had destroyed Denise. That's when he'd slip up and if he failed this time...

Everyone thought he was crazy now. If he let Jonna die, they'd all be right.

CHAPTER TEN

A knife turned inside every time Jonna thought of her conversation with Madden. *Sam Barton's the only suspect!*

For some reason, that seemed to be the one and only thing she could think about.

He's the only suspect!

Madden had promised to keep an even closer eye but cautioned her again about keeping Sam there. "The FBI agrees that you're safe until you get back from getting that award. If he leaves, we may lose him," he'd said.

It still bothered her that she was almost relieved to take his advice. And all the logic in the world wouldn't let her confuse Madden's excuse—keeping track of Sam—with her own. She didn't want Sam to leave. She wanted him to have the chance to grow out of that grim, dark-stranger self-image. And she had to be nuts, for this time, trusting the wrong person could get her killed.

Jonna gave up trying to work and placed the call she couldn't talk herself out of making to Moss. She took a deep breath, preparing to ask if she could stay with him for the next few days until she left for Los Angeles. Instead, he handed her a surprise.

"I was just getting ready to call you," he said, clearing his throat. "I'm checking into the hospital in Emporia this afternoon," he told her quickly. "Doc Benson is a little worried about some pains I've been having. He insists I go in for some kind of balloon test. They'll knock me out and do it in the morning."

Everything she'd always considered stable and secure was eroding out from under her. As they talked about his symptoms, his heart and the possibility of surgery, she buried all hope of running to Moss for refuge deeper and deeper. The most she revealed of her own problems was when Moss asked about the gun she'd borrowed from Brian.

"I haven't seen the bobcat again," she stammered. "I guess the neighbors got it after all."

They ended the conversation with her promise to see him at the hospital tomorrow.

"You can't waste all that time and trouble right now," Moss protested.

"You're the only family I have, Moss." She practically choked on the truth of it. "Of course you're not going through this alone, any more than you'd let me."

That he didn't argue further was evidence that Moss was scared beyond what he would admit and more than a little grateful to know Jonna would be there.

She hung up and fought off a panic attack. What now? Whom could she turn to now? The house closed in around her, tighter and tighter. And though she couldn't *trust* Sam—and she didn't think she had to worry about forgetting that fact—she'd settle for any human company.

She'd seen him leave the barn on Murphy an hour or so earlier. Jonna saddled Candy and rode directly to where she had found him yesterday, then followed along the fence. She didn't have to go far. Raw hammer marks in the dry wooden fence posts indicated she was on the right track.

She spotted them from the rise in the farthest corner of the section. For a moment Candy stopped, and Jonna sat quietly, watching Sam's slow but steady progress.

He sat tall and easily in the saddle, obviously at home on the horse. With little noticeable movement, Murphy stopped, walked and—a rarity for free-spirited Murphy— seemed totally subject to the rider's control.

Nudging Candy with her knees, Jonna urged the mare forward, continuing the insistent pressure until Candy cantered.

Jonna knew the second Sam heard the horse's hooves. Suddenly his broad shoulders were a little more square, his back perceptibly straighter. She wondered if he was remembering her indignant attack on him yesterday.

It seemed like a televised rerun as she anticipated his next reaction. And just like yesterday, with no obvious direction from Sam, Murphy swiveled and the two motionlessly awaited their arrival.

Only Jonna's inner turmoil was different this time. For some crazy reason, the terror had been painted over with a numb acceptance and a morbid, fatalistic sort of anticipation. She'd told herself before she left the house that maybe if she was with him, he'd say something, give himself away. Or do something that would end her doubts once and for all. As she rode to meet him, she realized she *wanted* to be with him.

Sam dismounted when Jonna was within twenty feet. Murphy followed him docilely as he walked to meet her with those purposeful strides. Then the horses were face-to-face and Sam reached for Candy's reins.

Jonna let him take charge of her horse and quickly joined him on the ground. He scowled at her, then scanned the broad prairie behind her.

"What now?"

The first day he'd been here, she had interpreted that tone as insolent and overly aggressive. Now she knew his reaction was dread. He expanded his firmly sculpted chest with a huge intake of air.

"Nothing," she said.

He released the breath slowly. Again she read him differently. The flicker of relief in his eyes, the loss of his intense attention wasn't a dismissal of her. He simply let himself off the sharp edge of horrific expectation.

She offered him a half grin. "I'm not getting anything at all done. I can't concentrate." One hand plucked nervously at the bottom of her sweater.

"So you came out to check on me."

"Actually I thought I'd ride along with you, maybe help you?"

He handed her reins back. "It's your land." He turned toward Murphy.

"Sam?"

"Yes?" He paused, his hand on the saddle horn, his leg bent to lift his foot into the stirrup, his muscled thigh tightening the denim fabric around it.

"We aren't fooling anyone about you being my hired hand. You don't have to do this, you know."

His dark brows drew together and hooded his eyes.

"I really need you to keep up with the chores until I get back from L.A. but..." She lifted a shoulder to finish the statement. "That's enough, given the situation."

His forehead relaxed. A hint of a smile warmed his usually somber face. "Are you firing me again?"

My, even when it was barely there, he had a nice smile. It tilted one side of his face and slightly crinkled into creases around his eyes. "Sure. I'm going to fire the guy who *says* he's going to save my life?"

He stiffened. "You still don't believe me."

She stepped a foot closer, started to touch him, then let her hand uselessly flay the air. "I don't know what to believe anymore, Sam."

His jaw loosened, but not enough to make the tic in his sharply defined cheek go away.

"You asked me yesterday why you would come back if you'd done any of that. Well, why would I let you stay if I didn't buy into at least part of it?"

"Probably so the sheriff can keep an eye on me."

She drew back, the doubts and suspicions raging again. Had he tapped her phone? Eavesdropped on her conversation with Madden? She knew the idea was ludicrous the minute she thought it. Besides, she'd seen him riding out about the time Madden had called.

He smiled grimly. "It's a logical deduction," he explained, reading her mind. "You fired me when you decided I'd lied about Moss. It doesn't take a genius to figure out that you would fire me in a heartbeat over all this." His dark eyes searched hers. "You just can't decide if I'm the bad guy—or the good."

She studied the rough ground between them. What about the phone calls from whoever was doing all this? It was on the end of her tongue to ask, to demand to know where he'd been last night. But she needed to hold at least one bit of information for her very own. How else would she ever decide what was true or false? She didn't know she had bitten her tongue until she tasted warm blood. The world had suddenly become a very dangerous place. She had to quit giving her complete trust to . . . to just anyone.

Sam's long fingers grazed her chin and he urged her face up with a nearly imperceptible pressure.

"You can't decide if I'm the devil or the deep blue sea," he said. "It makes an awful lot of sense to keep thinking that way, Jonna Sanders."

They were sandwiched together by the two horses, and even though the vast empty space around them should have made her feel vulnerable, she felt exactly the opposite. She felt closed off—and for the moment—safe from the rest of the world.

His eyes held her for an eternity. "I won't hold it against you," he promised softly.

"Madden called," she said in a breathless rush. "He checked with the FBI. They verified your story."

"And?" he asked.

"They don't necessarily believe your interpretation of it."

"What else is new?" His index finger explored the line of her jaw; his eyes followed. His thumb traced her cheekbone beneath the hollows of her eyes and down the side of her nose. It came to rest at the corner of her mouth and Jonna vaguely wondered how Sam had managed to make the nerve endings in her face connect with a million others all over her body.

The tip of her tongue dipped nervously out and dampened her dry lips. It drew Sam's gaze, and one of his long seductive fingers slipped an eighth of an inch in that direction.

Her heart pounded haphazardly as his lips parted. She was dancing with danger, skirting lunacy, but couldn't seem to help herself. She felt a mind-spinning rush. He excited and exhilarated some unknown adventurous side of her.

Her head lolled back weakly, forcing her lips up toward his in what he could only perceive as an invitation. And although positive she didn't *intend* the action as a provocation—she was just too weak to do anything else—she held her breath to see whether he accepted it.

The hunger in his eyes satisfied some perverse desire and she licked her lips again, taunting him as if she were afraid she would lose his attention.

"We'd better get busy," he said, but didn't take his hand from her face.

She nodded, hypnotized.

"And you didn't come just to keep an eye on me, Jonna?" he asked.

"I need to keep busy. I needed fresh air and... and..."

He raised one brow, encouraging her to go on.

"And company," she finished. She needed his reassurance.

He closed his eyes and sighed deeply.

She needed him to voluntarily share where he'd been last night. She wanted to ask him about the phone calls, wanted to tell him what Madden had said. The sheriff's voice rang in her ears. *Sam Barton's the only suspect!* She twisted away. She'd already given him more of herself and her knowledge than was safe.

The autumn day turned suddenly cold. She quelled a shiver. Walking around Candy's head, Jonna mounted and waited for him to do the same.

"Come on, Sam," she coaxed. "If you're sure you want to continue working. Let's get busy."

"I'm sure. This waiting is a killer. Maybe it will go quickly if we get something done." He swung himself into the saddle. Sam turned Murphy back toward the fence and she followed.

With the pretense gone, Sam and Jonna shared a quiet camaraderie for the rest of the day. Even without the reassurance she sought, it soothed Jonna's soul and she hoped—thought—it did the same for his.

She spent Tuesday at the hospital with Moss. She was relieved when his tests showed that he would need to change his life-style a bit—no more daily bacon, biscuit and gravy breakfasts at Millie's, more exercise, less stress—but that surgery wouldn't be necessary for the time being. She kept her own counsel about her problems.

Sam called her early the next morning, said briefly that he had coffee on if she wanted to join him. She did, and took along cold cereal and milk. It settled the pattern for the next few days.

After breakfast they would do chores, then saddle the horses. The sun shone warmly as they spent the daylight riding the perimeters of her land.

The second morning, Sam gave her a package. "The mailman said it wouldn't fit into the box," he said, then explained before she could ask, why the man hadn't brought it up to her house as usual. "No one will get past me—and to you—without my knowing."

The seed of trust he'd nurtured so patiently grew. She opened her mouth to ask him about the phone calls.

As if he read the impulsive trust on her face, his chocolate brown eyes looked arrogantly pleased, and she hesitated, giving the doubts time to crowd back in.

"You have a knack for all this espionage-type stuff," she said instead as they stopped and unpacked the sandwiches and cold drinks she had brought. "Is that why you went into the line of work you do?"

"My career choices have had a lot more to do with necessity than choosing." He made the admission equitably. "When my mother died, my friend at the college told me about the opening in the Security Department. He knew that's the sort of thing I'd been doing in the service and that I had a sister to raise."

"But you've stayed."

"I'm satisfied. I think I would have eventually ended up in one kind of law enforcement work or another anyway. Or maybe farming," he added with a wry grin.

She punched him playfully. "Don't make fun."

"I'm not," he said seriously. "I like your farm."

You could stay. She cleared her throat and managed not to say it.

And as the sun started its descent in the sky each day, they fixed dinner together, taking turns at his house, then hers.

They moved about whichever kitchen, carefully avoiding touching. And if they did make that terrible mistake, his hand lingered and she would feel hot spikes of sensation radiating from the point of contact long after the mishap was over. Or if their eyes met, she couldn't catch her breath without looking away.

His wide, sensuous lips seemed to capture her attention when he spoke. She felt his every glance on her body, even when her back was turned.

Then, each evening, as dusk overtook the brash land, they went their separate ways. The nights swarmed with tense and dark imaginings, and the demons returned.

She kept them at bay by packing and cleaning and wandering from room to room in her brightly lit house. Then she'd stop at the windows and wonder what Sam was doing—and wish he were here to quench the fire he'd spent the day igniting inside her.

She longed to ask him a million questions and promised herself that tomorrow would be the day. And once all the questions were answered, she would not spend another night alone and in need.

But with the sunrise, the questions that had obsessed her during the long night didn't seem nearly as important as the peaceful unspoken truce between them.

It was small comfort that the ghosts haunted Sam, too. Each morning, the dark circles were back beneath his eyes and several hours passed before he quit looking over his shoulder.

Then, the night before she was to leave, at a little after four in the morning, the phone rang. Jonna was wide awake, for once, when she picked it up. She didn't even have to question who it was. She knew.

"Hello?" She cursed herself for sounding tentative. She had promised herself that the next time he called, she would challenge him, not just stupidly ask who it was.

Nothing.

"Hello?" she said again, and looked at the receiver in her hand when no one responded.

Wrong number, she sensibly decided. Whoever it was had hung up when they realized they'd dialed the wrong number.

She listened again.

No. He was there. He wasn't breathing heavily like the the classic silent caller, but he was there.

"Sam?"

The line wasn't empty. It literally *oozed* a deadly silence. His ominous presence seeped through the receiver and Jonna found herself holding it farther and farther away. The air around her thickened with virulent gloom. And she felt him *smile*.

She dropped the handset back in its cradle as if it had bitten her, jerking her hand away as if, like a rattlesnake, it might strike again.

"Sam!" Her heart leapt at the thought of him. Scrambling from the bed, she yanked jogging shorts from her dresser and donned them over the camisole and panties she'd worn to bed without a thought for what she was putting on.

And then she remembered. He hadn't been there before. A cold vise squeezed her soul. Still only half-dressed in jogging shorts and a bra, she parted the curtains and gazed down at the peaceful home below.

It looked just as inviting and safe as it had Sunday night.

She realized she was leaning, almost bent in two in the middle, trying to see around the back of his house, to see if his car was there. She felt incredibly silly and stepped away. The drapes fell back in place.

I'm losing it, she thought in despair. She dropped into the chaise longue beside the window and pulled the afghan folded across its back around her shoulders. She was cold. So cold.

She wanted to run to Sam and insist he comfort her and keep her warm. But it could be him. Maybe part of the game was winning her trust first and then—

She couldn't face the doubts and suspicions again.

Why hadn't the caller said anything?

"It was a wrong number," she murmured, jumping at the sound of her own voice.

It wasn't. You know it wasn't.

"No, someone was there." This time her voice was consoling.

But why didn't he speak? He didn't hesitate before.

God, she wished the tracer had been put on. Madden was waiting for some court order he had to get, and never having had this particular request before, the judge was checking the legality of using the equipment. "Maybe he thought the line was tapped."

Why would he care? The calls had all been brief, probably to prevent a trace, but why would he worry about someone listening or recording the call?

Because he thinks his voice might be recognized!

The answer came with such clarity that it jammed into Jonna's breastbone and left her dazed.

"Sam!" This time his name held anguish.

Without conscious thought, Jonna found herself at the window again. She didn't see a damn thing more than she'd seen before. Was he asleep? Was he there?

Rather than leaning, she decided it might make more sense to go to another window. She might be able to see the back of his house from the far bedroom.

Going through the side door into the loft, again she felt vulnerable to the world. As much as she'd loved her open house, as soon as this was over, she was going to invest in some blinds or shades. And she wasn't sure when she would be able to sleep again with the lights off.

Jonna's feet iced up as she stepped into the spare room. She kept it closed, the doors, the registers. She couldn't see heating a room she didn't use. Her toes curled against the hardwood floor. She dragged a deep breath and stepped between and behind the lightweight curtains in here.

Again she could see nothing. The area where Sam had been parking his car was still blocked from her view by the house.

She should go there, she supposed, but remembered the last trip with revulsion. She'd just wait, she decided. She'd make coffee, settle into her easy chair downstairs and watch until she saw some kind of movement at his house.

If he wasn't there, he'd come home again soon, or he'd get up in the morning. Whichever, by morning, she was going to *know* what he'd been doing when she received the call this time.

Sam Barton's the only suspect they've got. A crack formed somewhere in her heart as she realized that every quietly companionable moment that they'd shared the past couple of days, every craving he created just by looking at her, made her want—long—to believe, to trust him.

And somewhere in the midst of all this she *had* grown to trust him, to need him. She realized with an even greater terror that her concern for him wasn't about her safety anymore. This was very personal.

He's the only suspect they've got.

She was halfway down the stairs when she remembered her father's binoculars. She hadn't sold them at the auction when she'd sold his guns and other things. No, she'd put them on the pile to get rid of, then took them off, stood at the window inspecting the land he had loved for almost an hour. Then she had stashed them in the guest-room closet with some other things she'd saved.

It took a few minutes to find them and anticipation denied her the cool plans she made during her search. She didn't put the box they'd come out of back in the closet. She didn't go downstairs where she always left the lights burning now. She flicked off the closet light and went directly to the window.

Her fingers shook as she adjusted the fit to her eyes, then took a moment to focus the field glasses to the outside. It surprised her that the binoculars didn't banish the night. Where shadows hid things before, they still did, only now, they seemed closer, more threatening.

His front porch was a well of blackness, and she couldn't imagine how she'd stood in that dark pool. She felt again her anxious hope and silent terror as she had waited for Sam to let her into the warmth of his house and the security of his protection.

One by one, she scanned the midnight-black windows of the bedrooms upstairs. One by one, they tantalized and teased with glints of moonlight, then kept their secrets.

She lowered her search to the first floor, calling herself all sorts of names as she foolishly hoped for some thread of evidence that would prove Sam trustworthy.

She almost swung on past the dining room windows, then a shred of movement brought her back.

There—bare-chested and staring back at her with his jaw slack with surprise at being caught—was Sam—with a pair of binoculars of his own. And her worst fears were confirmed.

He'd made the calls. Why else would he be there at this hour, wide awake and watching in the dark to see her reactions?

"Who the hell is Sam?"

Quentin Kincaid dropped the telephone into its cradle and screwed up his face with irritation. He didn't waste much time worrying over the question, though. Just a few more days and it wouldn't matter. He would be there to take credit for his own work. And this was going to be an incomparable piece of it. "Mama will be proud."

Damn, he was good. With the others—well, except for that award-stealing bitch Denise Barton—he'd only made one call each. One preliminary call to "invite" them to star in his masterpiece. One little-bitty conversation so they would remember—"Oh, yes, *you're* the one who called about the who's-who book?" they'd all said—and doors had opened wide before they even finished the sentence.

Goddamn right! He was the one. And stupid Jonna Sanders was going to credit his genius to some idiot named Sam. He wondered vaguely if it was the guy who had been riding around her farm the day he'd made his visit.

He sped to his grungy one-room apartment, anxious to look at her one more time. His fingers caught the flap of the small envelope of pictures beside it as he lifted *The Record* from the table and photos scattered across the horrible green shag rug.

He ought to get another book. He grinned, studying them one by one as he picked them up. He could call it, *A Visit to the Farm*. The living room after he finished with it. That was where he would put her. Right there in front of those windows, for all the world to see. Her office. He frowned as he looked again at her stairs, littered in the picture with debris. That would be a good place for her, too. One leg out like that, one leg over here, showing for all the world to see, exactly how she'd ripped off some other guy's award.

How would he decide? He just might have to experiment until he found exactly the right one. And in that desolate place, he would have all the time in the world.

Well, maybe, he cautioned himself. He'd been surprised to see the man and the other house there. It *looked* deserted. He looked at that photo again. Until he'd checked it out and made certain, he shouldn't get so goddamn cocky. *Pride goes before a fall.*

The old lady'd been quoting that one for years. And her fall was coming. As sure as he had only four more spaces to fill before it was *her* turn to enter into *The Record.*

He didn't let himself linger too long over each page. He only had half an hour before he had to head for work. For once, he was almost anxious to get there. Another few days, Jonna Sanders would be permanently enshrined here and he hadn't yet chosen another candidate. The thought made him itchy.

Of course if he wasn't so picky...

But dammit, being picky paid off. He reached for the pictures of Jonna he'd taken. He was almost awestruck by how good he really was. Jonna in the distance, her body curved into the pale horse, her hair fanned out and up behind her like some bizarre flower's bloom.

At first, he'd nearly swooned with distress. She was going to see him. What would he do then? But he'd changed the lens on the camera, saw her close up and figured he'd know the appropriate thing to do when the time arrived. Getting these pictures had been worth taking a bit of a risk.

These were gems. Jonna frowning into the wind. Jonna and the horse, in silhouette against the sky.

But this one was the prize. Alone after tying the horse to the porch, she'd been striding toward that little truck she drove, and she'd looked back over her shoulder. He'd snapped the shot as her eyes had swept past him. But in the picture, it looked as if she was staring right at him. Her hair, the color of honey in the sun, was windswept and wild, and her cheeks were flushed with exertion. But it was her sparkling hazel eyes, wide-eyed and terrified, that drew the viewer in.

Wait till his mother saw this one. How could she possibly say he didn't have an eye for art? Denise Barton had stolen his award and ended his graphic arts career, but here was real proof of his barely scratched artistic potential. In photography. He would probably be famous.

Jonna Sanders should consider herself very lucky to be his first official model.

She freaked! Sam saw her drop the binoculars and scream.

The curtains swayed with her frantic movements, then closed, blocking his view.

Damn! How was he supposed to know she had binoculars of her own? He'd watched her night after night, wandering waiflike through that open and always lit-up-like-a-Christmas-tree house.

He didn't think about his decision, he just moved, taking the stairs two and three at a time. He grabbed the top shirt from the folded stack in the corner of the room he occupied. Jerking it over his head and automatically tucking the tail in, he stopped beside the window and glanced up at the house on the hill as he refastened his jeans.

He debated only a second about whether to take his car. She'd see his lights, know he was coming. That would probably send her right over the edge.

The wind was cold, and he ran back inside to get his coat—and his keys. He relocked the back door behind him.

Her house was quiet when he reached it, and he hadn't seen her moving about. That meant she was still either in one of the bedrooms where she could close out the night, or in the kitchen. There, behind the stairs that separated the dining area from the rest of the room, she could hide from the world.

He took a deep breath and knocked.

She shrieked, but that immediately mutated to a terrified whimper.

My God, I've scared her to death.

He knocked again. "Jonna."

She was maybe fifteen paces away, beyond the door. He could hear her there, practically dancing with fright. A frantic guilt smothered him. He'd never intended—

"Jonna, let me in." He waited. "We've got to talk." He tried the door but the knob didn't turn. "Jonna? Please."

No answer.

"Please let me in. Let me—"

"Go away." The second word was muffled beneath a hysterical sob. "I'm . . . calling . . . the police."

He heard her move, heard a chair or something overturn, heard her muted curse. He could picture her desperate scramble toward the phone.

Damn! He had no choice. He knew he was hammering another nail of suspicion into his coffin, but he took the keys from the pocket of his jeans and let himself in. The inner door banged against the wall as he crossed through the kitchen.

Her heard her yelped mixture of fright and frustration as she realized he was coming. The phone crashed to the floor.

"Jonna, please, listen to me. Think about—"

The words caught in his throat as he rounded the base of the stairs, and the sight of her clawed at his soul. Jonna stood shivering, half-dressed and petrified, beside the mutilated couch. Tears coursed down her pale face. She held the receiver protectively curled against her breast while the phone itself lay at her feet.

And two yards away, the stark, shaking barrel of a gun was aimed directly at his heart.

CHAPTER ELEVEN

"D-d-don't...m-move," she whispered. "I'll sh-sh-oo-t."

How could she shoot him? She couldn't even *see* him. She had to stop this ridiculous crying.

She used the back of the hand holding the phone to wipe at her eyes, and the telephone resisted at the end of the stretched cord, then skidded several inches across the floor. She couldn't dial and maintain her concentration on him, so she opened her hand and ignored the clatter as the receiver bounced at her feet.

She covered the hand gripping the gun with the hand she had just freed, and her violent shaking subsided a little.

Sam sighed and wearily rearranged his features with his palms, raking his fingers on through his hair. He clasped his hands behind his head. The plain white T-shirt he wore hugged his broad chest. The veins in his arms laced his long, tensed muscles as he froze in the classic I-give-up pose she'd seen on a million cop shows on TV. She relaxed a smidgen.

"Will you listen to me, Jonna?"

"How did you get in here?" she demanded, but her voice quivered weakly.

"I took your keys, had copies made that first morning when we went to town," he explained. "I warned you not to leave them in the truck," he interrupted when she would have replied. "I was preparing for when *he* came but I'm glad now I did it. We obviously have—"

"Stop!"

He'd moved a foot nearer and she almost hadn't noticed. She tentatively backed a couple of steps away.

"I can't miss you from this close, Sam. Don't try me."

"Will you please just listen, Jonna?" he pleaded. "I can see why you might be scared—"

"Why were you up in the middle of the night spying on me?" She swayed and widened her stance to brace her trembling knees.

"Think about it," he said slowly. "How am I going to keep someone from killing you—"

"You're the one who wants to kill me."

He ignored her accusation and went on in his measured voice, "If I don't watch you?"

"You said I didn't have to worry about that until I have the award."

"But *I* worry. I don't sleep much. And I get up several times a night—every night—just to check on you, just to make sure everything's okay."

"And you just *happened* to 'check on me,' right after that phone call?" Her sarcasm couldn't stop the hurt or the horror, and her tears began to flow freely again. "Curious about how your sick phone calls affect me? And I suppose you just *happened* to be gone when I got the last one?" She sniffed.

"What phone calls?" He took another step.

"And you just *happened* to not say anything this time because you were afraid I might recognize— I said 'Stop.' I mean it, Sam, if you come one step closer I'm going to shoot you."

He obeyed. Her hands wavered precariously. The gun felt as if it weighed a ton.

"What phone calls, Jonna? I don't know what you're talking about."

"Don't do this to me," she cried. "Don't pretend you don't know and didn't make—"

His hands closed over hers on the gun and she screamed. She didn't have the strength to resist as he lifted their arms, aiming the gun over his shoulder toward the kitchen.

"Give it to me, Jonna. Give me the gun. You know you can't shoot me."

Her hands were stiff as he unwound her fingers and gingerly took the weapon. She gasped as he turned it toward her, but he kept it lowered while he removed the bullets and she crumpled, sobbing, to the floor at his feet.

He knelt and she jumped at the heavy thud when he placed the gun on the rug beside them. She scrambled on all fours, trying to get away, out of his reach.

"Jonna, please, Jonna. Come on, sweetheart, don't cry."

The endearment battered, confused her.

He followed, hand-walking, grappling with her, crooning comforting sounds. He succeeded in capturing her and pulling her to him when they were stretched nearly full-length across the floor.

"Please, Jonna, don't cry."

His thumb flicked away one tear, but they wouldn't seem to quit coming.

She felt like ice. Sam rubbed her arms slowly up and down, up and down, warming her. Gradually, probably for the first time since she'd seen him peering back at her, her shivering stopped—until his thumb brushed the thin material of her camisole.

A shudder of a totally different kind swept through her.

His breath caught. His hands stopped.

Another tear escaped, and this time he caught it with his lips.

She opened her eyes and searched his face.

Suddenly *he* looked as vulnerable and helpless as she felt. And she wanted his strong arms around her more than she'd ever wanted anything in her life.

Shaken outside and in, as in control and coherent as a bowl full of Jell-O, she ordered herself to move away. But telling and doing were two different things. Especially with his hand curved around her bare midriff. His fingers shaped themselves to her, caressed her.

He cradled her back and gently eased her over, hovering above her. "I wouldn't hurt you, Jonna. Don't you know I wouldn't hurt you for all the world?"

Her skin tingled and the intense sensation traveled from her head to her feet. She groaned. "Oh, Sam, I wish I could believe you." Resisting the urge to curl herself against him sapped all her strength.

He took the choice from her, pulling her close, into the hard planes of his shoulder. His hand stroked her hair, the length of her back, fanning flames of some primitive desire.

"Do you have any idea what you do to me?" he asked. "Do you honestly believe I could hurt you when it takes every bit of my energy every day just trying to resist you, trying not to care?"

He leaned away from her, framing her face in his hands, forcing her to look at him. "I'm going to kiss you," he warned in a raw whisper, giving her a chance to refuse.

Whatever her mind said, she knew her eyes were saying yes.

The blood in her veins boiled as he drew her weight in to him. His hips moved suggestively against her. The concrete strength of his arousal left her dizzy.

He lowered his lips to hers tentatively. They were sweet, so sweet. They seemed to draw the very life force out of her with their gentle, undemanding caress. He deepened it gradually, seeming to sip from her every ounce of strength before he generously gave it back. He stopped to kiss her closed eyelids, her tearstained cheeks. Then he returned his attention to her lips.

At some point in the very near future, she knew she'd have to think lucidly again. But her body itched with emptiness and deprivation. And *never* before had she experienced this intense, throbbing, hurting need.

"Sam," she whispered, "Sam, please make love to me."

He moaned and tried to pull away. "Don't do this to me, Jonna."

"Please, Sam." She had to do something about this aching void. Sam was the only one who could fill it.

"What makes you think I'll be able to turn it off, stop, when you start thinking again and decide you don't want to?" He moved far enough away that their bodies were no longer touching, though the fingertips of one hand lingered on her arm, as if he needed to keep that one connection.

"I won't want you to stop." Just the introduction of air between them made the hurt return. And this would surely destroy her dangerous, mindless fascination with him. She had to indulge the craving that had been growing and devouring her by bits and pieces each day. Once and for all, she had to do whatever it took to think logically when she thought about him.

"What scared you, Jonna?"

"Don't you know?"

"No."

She lifted his hand to her breasts. "Then, please Sam, make love to me now. For a little while, I want to believe."

He complied.

His hands flowed over her silken skin. Her tear-washed eyes trusted him, warming him like the sun warmed a rainy afternoon, banishing the hollow cold that had gripped him since Denise's death.

With little fuss, little preamble, her clothes were gone, his lay where they fell and he was in her.

She was moist, ready, receptive, and for long minutes, neither moved. He savored the feel of her involuntary responses to his invasion.

She sighed and he began to move.

He slid his arms beneath her, satisfied momentarily with sheltering her from the coarsely woven carpet. The action offered up her breasts to his lips and he accepted the offering.

A low guttural cry rolled from deep in her throat and she arched against him. He groaned and thrust deeper. He savored the smell of the soft perfume he would recognize anywhere as hers. And for once, he let himself fill his vision to his heart's content with the picture of the warm vibrant Jonna lying beneath him.

Cradling her, he rocked her, then rocked her again.

She closed her eyes. Her hands, which had been complacently flat against his chest, began to roam, stroking, touching and kneading him with impatience.

He renewed his assault on the inviting peaks of her breasts, taking ownership, and grew frustrated that his mouth and hands couldn't touch all of her at once.

Then what their hands were doing grew unimportant. No longer capable of thought, he drove into her very core. She gasped, every muscle of her tightening and clasping him to her as if she never intended to let him go.

He dragged himself away, retreating only so she could seduce and invite him back with the compelling lift of her hips. He stabbed, she parried, and they settled into a rhythm as ageless and unrelenting as the wind that had shaped, then reshaped the rolling plains.

When she cried out, perched at the precipice of fulfillment, he hammered against her once more, then let himself pitch with her, over the edge and into cataclysmic, mind-numbing satiation.

And when he could breathe again, think sanely, he felt her body mold itself around the still throbbing part of him inside her.

And it felt like home.

Morning infused the artificially lit room with warm natural light. Jonna finally moved. Tentatively removing herself from the quiet embrace Sam had held her in for the past half hour, she picked up her shreds of clothing and almost stepped on the gun lying at their feet.

It was a bitter reminder of everything that had happened since Sam had come into her life, and she cringed under the weight of what they had just done.

She should still be terrified, but she wasn't. She still didn't understand everything or his part in it, but she didn't care.

She knew as certainly as she knew she'd misplaced her trust a million times before that she shouldn't trust him an inch. But she trusted him with her life.

She stepped around the ugly weapon and started for the stairs.

"Where are you going?" Sam asked hoarsely, watching her with hooded, haunted eyes. "We've got to talk."

"I know." She attempted to protect her body from his eyes with the brief shorts that had been rendered useless as a cover by a long tear up one side.

She'd acted like an animal. But even as she thought about it, her skin tingled and a throbbing ache grew again.

"Let me get dressed. I'll be right back down."

He nodded his agreement and his gaze skittered away. She had the impression that if she wasn't too embarrassed to look, she'd find powerful, hard proof that he shared her mindless, irresponsible, irrepressible desire.

In her room, she grabbed sweats, then in the act of putting them on, changed her mind and stripped back down. Answers could wait another ten minutes while she took a shower.

The water soothed and teased her overly sensitive skin. She could think of nothing but Sam's magical effect on her. She finally flipped the knob to cold.

Sam borrowed her shower when she was done, and she was setting the table when he came back down. He'd draped a towel loosely about his hips and it didn't do a thing to hide that his cold shower hadn't been very effective.

She was relieved when he took his scattered clothes into the bathroom and dressed.

"I've fixed some omelets," she said for something to say. "I'll bet you're ready for a cup of coffee?"

"Desperate would be a little more accurate."

He leaned back against the counter behind her and she turned to give him a mug. He took it, then caught her hand.

Setting the coffee behind him, he lifted her chin with the fingers of the other hand. "You're avoiding my eyes," he said.

"I'm embarrassed," she said blithely.

"And still scared?"

"Sort of."

"Sort of?" He nudged the underside of her chin, subtly hinting that she should meet his eyes.

She tentatively dampened her lips and gulped some courage. "You making I— Our having sex," she began again determinedly, "doesn't really change a thing. I mean, we still..."

"We still have to talk," he said for her.

"Yeah."

"So talk," he invited.

"Over breakfast." She slipped out of the circle of his arms.

Within minutes they were sitting down with the omelets.

But her omelet grew cold and unpalatable as Sam talked about growing up in Oklahoma, about playing baseball and earning a college scholarship. He was rueful, but not especially bitter about the appendicitis and surgery that had kept him on the bench just when the major league teams were scouting, wining and dining some of his peers.

"That's where you got the scar—"

"Yep." He caught her hand. "And if you want to finish this conversation, don't remind me of the way you touched it."

"I don't remember any spec—"

"Give me your hand and I'll give you a demonstration and we can forget everything else again for a while." His dark eyes were as icy hot as black diamonds. Oh, yes! This was the way Sam Barton was supposed to be.

"How disappointing. Appendicitis?" she teased. "I imagined some great heroic military adventure and you off saving the world from—"

"What was supposed to be my lifetime career in the military lasted exactly two years and seven months." He was somber again.

"Why?"

"A discharge." He'd finished his meal and pushed his plate away.

Jonna got up and grabbed the coffeepot. The change in his mood made her hesitant to hear what was next. "What happened?" she managed.

She refilled their mugs as he continued. "Mom had breast cancer. She'd ignored it too long. I asked for compassionate leave." He shrugged. "I requested the discharge when she died."

"But I don't see—"

"Denise."

And Jonna knew they were back to the heart of the matter. The house seemed to sigh around them. "So tell me about Denise."

"She was only fourteen when Mom died," he said, and he was definitely light-years away from her kitchen. "I was all she had. She was nine years younger than me, an afterthought or an accident. I never asked Mom which. She was unplanned but greatly loved. Denise couldn't remember our dad—he died when she was four."

"That would have made you only . . . what?"

"Thirteen. But the situation was totally different. I had Mom. And my grandparents—Dad's folks—lived with us. It was a tough time, because my dad was a wonderful man who kept us all stable, but we had each other. After Mom's death, Denise had no one."

She had you! she wanted to protest. Instead, she gave in to the impulse to reach for his hand and wondered exactly what he'd meant when he said "My dad kept us all stable." She had a suspicion it meant Sam had accepted the position as family stabilizer at age thirteen.

"So then the job at the college?"

He nodded.

"With Denise I needed something flexible, and Barry—we went to school together—helped me get hired. Denise and I moved to Texas. The position guaranteed her a tuition-free college education." He rose and took both their plates to the sink. "And I was promoted to Head of Security when my supervisor retired two years later. You know the rest."

Hardly.

He prowled about the room like a caged tiger. He stopped at the counter, propped his hands against it and leaned, staring across the room and out over the rolling prairie.

Jonna, one arm resting across the back of the chair, cradled her chin in her hand and studied him. He was easy to watch. There was something very seductive and sensual about the way his dark hair curved over his forehead and around his ears. There was something haunting about the way his piercing eyes could absently look right through you one time, and seem to see your soul the next. And those long elegant but capable-looking hands. She shivered, remembering the way they had trailed along her skin.

"What would you be doing if your mother hadn't died?" she asked.

"I have no idea," he admitted. "I felt at home in the service. I could see myself staying there a lifetime. In fact, just before Mom got sick, I'd been selected to attend training for special services."

"You mean like the Green Berets?"

"Something like that," he said, finally looking her way with a self-deprecating grin. "It's funny you should mention it. I used to imagine *myself* as the hero off saving the world from the bad guys in some great adventure."

"And now instead you save coeds." For a second, she pictured a man optimistic enough to believe he could make a difference. She tried to imagine him without the shadows and with a youthful innocence filling his eyes instead. But the tiny lines around them were hard from too much reality, and as she watched, a cold glint edged out the idealism.

"In the end, I couldn't even save my sister," he said.

"Sam?" Somehow, she was by his side. Her hand caressed his arm.

"I promised I would take care of her," he went on lifelessly. "And I couldn't save her."

A million unshed tears filled his raspy voice. She'd never met a man who needed to cry more than Sam did. Had he let himself when his mother's death put an end to his own dreams? Had he even shed a tear when Denise died?

"And even when I *knew* what was going on, I couldn't convince anyone else." His tortured voice held condemnation directed only at himself. Jonna wondered if this was the first time he'd said aloud some of the things he'd been damning himself for over and over again since his sister's death. "I couldn't stop the third murder from happening."

Suddenly, his intensity, his torment was turned on her. He gripped her arms so hard she bit her lip to keep from crying out. "The bastard won't get you, I promise."

"Sam. Oh, Sam." She didn't realize she was crying until his hands abruptly loosened and with one gentle thumb, he wiped away a tear.

"I've hurt you," he whispered.

"No," she denied, even as she felt the fiery tingle of bruises forming under the skin where his fingers had been. But that didn't account for even one of the tears. They were his. The ones he wouldn't let himself shed.

"Sam." She pushed his name past the massive lump in her throat, letting her fingers dip into the hair falling softly over his brow.

And then he was kissing her and she wasn't sure which one of them initiated it. All she knew was that, as she opened her mouth beneath his, he gasped her breath away. And as his tongue dipped inside, outlining her lips, she felt it in her soul.

"Oh, Jonna. This is crazy, but I want to make love to you again."

"Please." Her plea lingered against his mouth.

He pushed her a little bit away. Jonna's neck hurt from straining to keep her lips feathering his.

"I can't seem to get enough of you."

Her thoughts exactly.

"But this time, it's going to be right," he whispered.

She felt herself nodding an agreement, even as her mind searched for anything wrong in the way he'd made love to her before.

"Come," she said, her fingers lacing in his. She led him up the stairs and to her room.

They were barely inside when he grasped the tail of her sweatshirt and tugged it up and over her head. She helped, raising her arms. As soon as she was free, she reached behind to release her confined breasts from her bra. His hands caught hers.

"Let me." He directed her hands to his waist, then slid them beneath his shirt.

He trapped them beneath the soft cloth and then flattened them against the taut nipples on his chest. His mouth began a gentle onslaught of her face.

He swept kisses along the tip of her nose, across each eye, each cheekbone, then started down the curve of her jaw. He paused, running off course to press his mouth against the pulse point behind her ear.

Her heart thrummed and hummed there as if it would jump right out of her skin. Then his tongue flicked her earlobe and a string of feelings connected to something deep inside. The power surge surfaced in a fine tremor that started where his lips rested and vibrated her clear to her toes.

Her hands smoothed his chest, mapping and memorizing the hard planes, caressing his heated moist skin. Her fingers curved up and over his shoulders and clung so her weak knees couldn't betray her and let her fall.

His lips turned back to her mouth as his long sensual fingers traced the shape of her bra above the curve of her breasts and followed the fabric as it led beneath her arm and on around to the clasp.

The relief and release as he peeled it away from her breasts was short-lived. They swelled and tightened until her skin felt more constricting than any piece of material could have been. Cool air filled the gap he created between them. But he warmly cupped one needy breast in his palm while he appraised and approved the other with his eyes. All thought of anything cold went away.

"You're beautiful." His head dipped and Jonna had to twine the fingers of one hand through his lush dark hair to stay on her feet as his lips and tongue teased the dark nipple. She gasped again and he slipped his forearm behind her knees and swung her up into his arms, taunting the other nipple in the same teasing, barely touching way.

He laid her on the bed, examining her body slowly as he lifted his shirt, disappeared briefly behind it, then pulled it over his head. He discarded it uncaringly behind him.

She'd never realized that a perfect man could be such a visual pleasure. He was classically shaped, each muscle across his broad chest spectacularly defined. Her fingers tingled with anticipation at the thought of tracing them. A fine covering of dark, coarse hair provided contrast and shading to his smooth golden skin. The dark hair led her artist's eye to his jeans. She almost groaned with jealousy over the way they snugly hugged him. He read her mind and ridded himself of the vile things.

The silky hair brushed against her as he lowered himself over her.

Then he began exactly where he'd left off.

His lips tormented her and his hands didn't let either breast go unnoticed as he deftly divided his attention between them. But her nipples, he pointedly ignored.

He kissed and nibbled and tantalized until the buds felt so painfully tender from his cruel neglect that she held her breath to keep from begging. She wasn't as successful with her body and it arched entreatingly, volunteering for his mouth's exquisite ministrations. Her hands fisted and tangled in his hair as he hesitated above her, his moist breath fanning one hard and deprived peak.

"Oh, Sam, don't do this to me."

He sneaked one hand beneath the waistband of her sweats and lifted, letting the cool dry air linger where his fingers had so briefly brushed her skin.

Sliding his hand around the curve of her hip, he inched the sweatpants down. Then the fabric was at her knees and she curled into a shy ball as he peeled the last of her clothes away and flung them across the room. But his fingers deftly found the shadowy cleft between her thighs. His mouth returned to her aching breast.

He stroked and hovered, teasing her emptiness as his lips tortured her breasts. Then his mouth closed around one desperate nipple and his tongue flicked gently across it. And his finger finally slipped inside her.

Sam was whispering her name. His voice made her long to turn him into the senseless mass of aching flesh that he'd reduced her to. She pushed him aside, but his fingers continued to remind her of the emptiness only he could fill. She kissed and teased and taunted him as he'd been teasing her. She savored the feel of his muscles tensing beneath the fingers of her searching hands and her wandering lips and knew she could die completely satisfied just from knowing the power she had over this strong and sensitive man.

Her body arched with an incredible array of feelings that threatened to launch her alone into ecstasy.

"Please, Sam," she pleaded, "I need you. I don't want to be alone."

He rearranged her in the circle of his arms and she opened herself to him, inviting him in.

He gazed passionately into her eyes. "I don't want you to be alone." He braced himself above her, his hot, hard self poised against her threshold. She lifted her hips beseechingly and he pulled away.

"If you don't finish this soon, I will die."

His eyes darkened seriously. "I won't let you."

"I know, Sam," she said and lifted a finger to brush a damp strand of hair away from his moist brow. He pulsed against her and seduced an answering response from her.

This time he thrust and she pushed back, tugging, embracing, drawing him completely in.

He stroked. He stroked again. Masterfully. Slowly. She felt the pressure build. She concentrated on the way he felt deep inside her, then set her mind on holding him there.

He sighed. "That feels incredible."

She could feel every inch of him, like velvet against silk; it felt lush, soothing, yet abrasive in a very, very addictive and inflammatory way. Her fingers crept up his chest. "Yes." It took an extreme amount of effort just to say one word when her body was screaming in anticipation of his next thrust. He was doing such wonderful things.

He thrust hard and his palms cupped her buttocks and held her there. Slowly, deliberately, he rocked and reached and caressed every glorious nerve ending inside her, as if trying to fully compensate for every past hurt.

But while he was offering solace for ancient sins, and sheltering her from the bad guys, who was going to protect her heart from him?

It grazed her mind that any protective measure might be too late.

Then the wicked and heavenly sensations he was creating swept away all thought and she willingly sacrificed everything she was to him.

CHAPTER TWELVE

"I'd better go do the chores," he said as they dressed later.

"I'll help," she said and they left her house together.

They worked companionably. Candy was obviously disgruntled at having been made to wait an extra four hours for breakfast. She forgave all when Jonna offered the mare the apple she'd brought. "See. Just like I promised."

The promise seemed so far away.

Everything—and nothing—had changed between her and Sam. Their conversation was more intimate, but still impersonal. He still looked haunted, the dark circles beneath his eyes were even more pronounced. And she watched him warily for signs of...what? She didn't know.

And he could touch her with his gaze from fifty yards away and make her want him.

They had made...had sex—her mind amended. But the word she avoided lingered and carried so many mysteries and implications that her brain backed away from the subject from sheer overload.

"What next?" Sam asked as he rechecked the latch on the corral and reached to brush something from her cheek. "Dust," he explained.

Dust. It was an excuse. He'd touched her because he *needed* to—and Jiminy Christmas—her imagination was really out of control now. She suppressed a sigh.

"The cattle in the north pasture need new salt blocks," she said, damping down her fantasy with the mundane.

"I can do that," he offered. "Don't you have things you need to do?"

"Lots," she admitted, impatient with him for not wanting her company and with herself for jumping to that conclusion. "But I won't be able to do any of it before I leave."

"Tomorrow."

"Yes." Her heart quickened, thinking of her early-morning flight. She didn't want to leave him almost as much as she hated wondering which Sam would be here waiting when she returned? The lover—the gentle, considerate, heart-stopping man? Or a madman?

Trust your instincts. She heard Moss's voice as clearly in her head as if he were standing right next to her.

"You don't need to pack or get ready?" Sam asked.

"You trying to get rid of me?" She tilted her head, tried to ask it flippantly. But she hadn't fooled him any more than she had herself.

He jammed his hands in his pockets, and this time she was absolutely positive it wasn't her imagination that convinced her the action was taken to keep him from reaching out for her. "You thought you'd hired someone so you wouldn't have to do all this. I don't want to let you down more than I already have. So if you need to do something else... I didn't come here to make your life more difficult."

"Except for things like my toothbrush, I'm packed. Have been almost a month," she confessed. She shrugged at his raised eyebrow. "I'm overanxious. What can I say? And right now, I just need to keep busy."

She swung away. "You load the salt blocks and I'll go down and get the mail."

He caught up with her halfway down the lane. She gazed up at him, surprised.

"I'm nervous when you get too far away," he admitted, and her heart flipped with some trusting, hopeful emotion.

They filled what was left of the morning with odd jobs, then Sam fixed canned spaghetti for a late lunch. The binoculars and rifle by the dining room window chased icy shivers up her spine.

"It's ready, Jonna." He brought the hot meal, but the chill had settled like a cloud blocking out the sun. It stayed with her as they used up the afternoon riding more of the fences, even though neither of them pretended after the first hour or so that they were actually doing anything.

"Tell me about the man who hurt you," Sam invited casually as they rode back toward the barn.

She cast a sideways glance up at him. She hoped he didn't think she was making an indictment against him, just letting him know she'd been around long enough that her expectations weren't overly inflated. "I seem to have no knack whatsoever for judging people in general and men especially." If her dad were around, *this* man would top his list of dangerous, untrustworthy men. And Jonna would be forced to agree. If he betrayed her like Jeffrey had—

"You cared about him?" Sam asked.

"We were engaged." The ultimate betrayal. The ultimate proof that she couldn't tell the difference between good or bad intentions, couldn't tell character and integrity from greed.

They reached the barn. Sam helped her off the horse. "What happened?"

"I loaned him thirteen thousand dollars. I haven't seen him since."

"Then he's a fool."

"Most of the time I think so," she said blandly. "But I suppose it depends on your point of view. I imagine more than a few people would say I was the fool."

"Why would you give him thirteen thousand dollars?" He loosened the saddle strap around Candy's abdomen.

"I had it—Dad's estate. He needed it to pay off the rest of his loan on his car."

"Must have been a pretty flashy car."

Jonna winced and occupied herself with removing the horses' bridles. "He was fresh out of law school, trying to establish a practice in town. But people tend to be slow accepting you, especially as some kind of professional like an attorney, unless you've lived here all your life. It's a vicious circle. You have to prove yourself before anyone trusts you and you can't prove yourself until someone does. He thought a Saab would create that stable and trustworthy image."

"And did it?"

"No." She laughed. "If anything, it made people even more suspicious. And since he wasn't well established, he had trouble making the payments. I thought I would give him time to *get* established by helping him."

"Then he left town."

He took her hand. His concern felt warm and caring. But then she wasn't exactly a good judge of character, she reminded herself with a self-deprecating smile.

"Quit reprimanding yourself," Sam ordered. "There are some things more important than being able to predict exactly what someone will do."

"Sure." She would have turned away, but he brought her up short, chest to chest with him.

"There's an extreme scarcity of people who will give *anyone* half a chance."

"They're the wise ones," Jonna said.

"No, *we're* the fools, Jonna. We're the ones without courage. This all could have been much different if I'd had the courage to tell you the truth from the beginning."

I don't know that you're telling me the truth now. You might be far worse than Jeffrey ever thought about being and I find myself trusting you more and more every minute.

"If Leah Darcy hadn't automatically suspected the worst from me, she might be alive now," Sam pointed out.

"I don't know that I would have believed you, either." Jonna pulled away. "And did you ever consider that it might not have made any difference at all?"

"That's fatalistic. Like saying we have no choice—"

"No, it's just that sometimes, despite our best efforts, things don't always go the way we want them to," she argued.

A chill seeped into his tightly controlled voice. "Things *will* be different this time."

And there was nothing left for Jonna to say. They walked out of the barn into a deep and starless night.

Autumn was making an impact on the Indian summer weather, and Jonna's teeth chattered in response to the nippy air.

"You'll stop by for coffee before you leave in the morning?"

He was obviously not interested in sharing dinner or the evening or even her bed. She crushed out the images rushing in. "Maybe I shouldn't go. Shouldn't accept it," she said.

"That solution occurred to me before I went to Colorado," he said quietly. "I thought about telling Leah Darcy not to accept her award, but realized *he* probably wouldn't know, so that wouldn't stop him from coming. You may as well go, enjoy getting it and accept it with pride. I'll be waiting and watching here."

"I have to leave for the airport by about five-thirty," she finally said.

"I'll have the coffee on by a quarter to five then," he promised.

She bit her lip, wanting to ask him to please share her night, devastated that he didn't mention it himself. But wasn't that why she'd all but told him she didn't expect anything from men? So he wouldn't know how much it hurt when her expectations came true? She cursed herself for hoping this time was different as she went her separate way.

He was a fool. He'd seen the invitation in her eyes. He'd seen her hurt and left it there to gnaw away at her.

He just couldn't risk what he was risking. It was time to step back, take a deep breath and concentrate on reality.

Beside, if he stayed with her, who would monitor the alarms? And she shouldn't see the dream that shattered each and every night. That would terrify her. And in the dream, he thought it was his hands that were doing the killing.

And this night, time after time, Jonna—not Denise—had the starring role. The nightmare didn't stop until he saw her and reassured himself that she was really alive. He was glad he'd suggested she stop for coffee before she left for L.A.

He heard her hushed and uncertain sigh as he opened her car door. "Take care," he said.

"Sure." She stared straight ahead and twisted the key in the ignition.

The muscles in his arms contracted, refusing to let him close her door. She glanced up at him hopefully, her lips parted.

The nightmare was too fresh. He couldn't kiss her. It was too much like a promise of life, one he was no longer certain he could keep. And he especially couldn't kiss her goodbye. That would seem permanent, as if he would never see her alive again. It seemed like making a concession to a killer.

A look of betrayal clouded her overbright eyes and tore at him so he looked away.

He leaned against the door, and the hollow sound echoed in the early-morning gloom even after she drove away.

He had her number at the Century Plaza, where the awards ceremony was to take place, but he didn't call.

Instead, he did the chores and started the countdown, preparing for her return, checking and rechecking the alarms, the guns, the infrared scope he'd attached to the rifle.

He slept in snatches, taking twenty-minute naps, concentrating wholly on the monster her homecoming would bring.

He didn't realize how tense he'd become until Jonna called early Sunday morning.

"I'm not coming back tomorrow," she said at his hello.

A reprieve. The knots in his shoulders loosened even as his groin tightened at just hearing her lyrical voice.

"You mean today."

"Okay, today," she verified, a flatness seeping into her tone. She surely didn't expect him to ask her to hurry back to be with him. He was in hell. "It's three-thirty here. I just got in and haven't been to sleep so it still seems like Saturday night. I forget it's close to morning there."

He felt like someone rammed his solar plexus. She was just getting in? "How was the ceremony?" he choked out so he wouldn't ask where she'd been, who had been with her.

"It was wonderful." For a second the excitement was back and he could hear her glow. "The award is beautiful. Much better than it looked in the pictures and drawings."

"Having your name on it wouldn't have anything to do with that, would it?" The words reverberated through his mind. He'd said the same canned phrase when Denise had won her award.

Denise had hugged the crystal-clear engraved plaque to her chest and practically danced into her apartment. "Oh, Sam, you can't imagine."

"Good," he'd said. His finger had traced Denise's name as she extended the plaque for him to inspect for the thirtieth time. His arm had wrapped around her shoulders. "Now you can come home."

Her face had jerked up to his, disbelief widening her warm brown eyes. "Sam, you promised you wouldn't start that again."

"I'm sorry." He'd spread his arms beseechingly. "I also promised Mom I'd take care of you," he pressed. "How can I do that with you in San Francisco, half a continent away?"

"You've kept your promise to Mom." Denise clenched her teeth warningly. "And I love you for everything you've done. Weren't you listening tonight?" Her hand groped at the side of her sleek-fitting silk dress. She extracted a nearly mutilated paper from the pocket, curling the plaque close to her heart with the other hand. "Didn't you hear the very last of my speech? 'I would never have had this chance without the help of my big brother, Sam. This is for you, Sam. It's really yours.'"

The front of her bright red dress had heaved with her great gulping breaths. She'd flung the piece of paper before him on the coffee table, then placed the award firmly on top of it. Her nails, newly manicured and matching her dress, lingered like drops of blood on the etched symbols. She drew them reluctantly away and his name, stark black on the typewritten page beneath, overpowered the frosty engraved *Denise* above.

She walked away from him, flouncing down in the chair across the room. The harsh apartment light caught in her curls, turning the rich espresso color a satiny brown as she tossed her hair over her shoulder.

"You said you had to work in a major market to get a toehold," he persisted. "You wanted to eventually start your own ad agency." He tapped at the plaque. "Doesn't this do all that?"

"It's a toehold. Nothing more, Sam. And when I start my own agency, I sure as hell won't start it in some backwater place in north Texas." She directed her steady gaze toward him and her eyes glittered defiantly. "I told you not to come if you were going to start this again, Sam."

Anger warred with frustration and he clamped down on both. She had changed so much since leaving college and coming to California. His little sister had acquired an edge he would never understand. It was time he left. Let her settle down. He didn't want to fight. "I'll come by in the morning," he said. "We'll go somewhere and have a champagne brunch to celebrate—"

"Don't bother," Denise had interrupted. "I have plans. Just take your damn award with you."

Even as he told himself he wouldn't let her get to him, he had crossed the room. He told himself he should excuse her irritating insolence because she was soaring around on nervous adrenaline, but his hand had closed over her shoulder to demand her attention. She had twisted away. "Denise, I'm sorry."

"I'm not fourteen anymore, Sam. Get your own life. You can't have mine," she said.

So he'd left. And when he returned the next morning her bright excitable eyes had been glazed in death. If he hadn't left when he did . . .

He'd never had the chance—

"Sam?" He heard panic in Jonna's voice. "Sam, are you there?"

He cleared his throat. "I'm sorry, Jonna. What did you say?"

He forced himself to listen, and a vision of her hazel eyes superimposed itself on the image of Denise he carried in his head.

"The ceremony was very nice. Very dignified," she said. "But the reception *Classic American Home* magazine held afterward was really impressive." She described the ice-sculpture house decorating the table and the molded chocolate blueprint with different exotic fruits overflowing from every room. "Then there were chocolate truffles waiting on my pillow when I got back to my room." She took a hasty breath. "I'll save you one, okay?" she added.

Her voice suddenly sounded desolate. Sometime in the course of the conversation a sleepy, lonely quality had crept into her tone. He could see her wheat-colored hair in a sunburst against a white hotel pillowcase. Even from a thousand miles away, she stirred him.

"I'm glad you're staying an extra day," he said quietly. His body protested, aching to sink into her warmth and lose himself in her again.

"Till Monday," she confirmed. "You think he'll come while I'm gone?" She sounded childlike, seeking reassurance about a bad dream.

"I can hope," he said. "I'd love to have this all over by the time you get home."

"But you'll be there?"

"You'd have to blast me out of here before I take care of that demon."

"I mean *if* you've already caught him," she said tonelessly.

"I'll be here," he said. "I'll be here come hell or high water."

She changed the subject, launching into a preview of her luncheon date tomorrow with the editor of the magazine. "He wants to talk about some special project they're planning. And if I agree, my new designs are going to be the focal point," she finished.

He listened as she told him that no one had seemed the least surprised that she was a woman, just that she was young. And when she said all the other architects who had won awards were men, he asked, "Older men?" and laughed at her delighted giggle.

"At least as old as you—but not nearly so sexy," she added breathlessly, and he wondered how much champagne they'd served at that reception.

"Well, I guess I'll see you between three and four Monday," she said reluctantly and added, "goodbye."

He let her end their connection without telling her what he needed to say about how he felt—because he didn't know. All he could hope was that he'd get another chance and that by then he would have figured it out.

Twenty-four hours later, Sam was tired enough he imagined he would catch his twenty-minute nap without the nightmare.

He thought he'd barely stretched his length on the saggy mattress when the warning alarm went off. But the clock showed two hours had passed.

Damn! He shouldn't have undressed. Shouldn't have relaxed. He'd slept right through the timer he had set.

He darted to the window and scoured the thick nig
along the drive for any movement or motion. He didn't s
a thing.

Hurrying to the other window, he picked up the binoculars. Her house was as vacant looking as it had been for the
past three days. He was about to rush back to check the
drive again when he heard the muted sound of…a car door
closing?

He frowned and searched the area at the top of the hill.

A shadow crossed the rim above him.

Damn and double damn! How in the hell had the bastard gotten *past* him? The savage was at Jonna's house? Sam
had installed a second alarm at her house after she had left.
That alarm had caught the son of a bitch going *back* to his
car.

A sheen of perspiration coated Sam's bare skin and a
cold, engulfing nausea clawed at the pit of his stomach.

He'd flattered himself that he was infallible this time, but
the monster had slipped by and Sam had slept through all
of his bells and buzzers and bangs.

Sam's jeans stuttered over his sweat-drenched body as he
yanked them on. A bead of moisture stung his eye as he
grabbed desperately for shoes. He rocketed down the stairs,
missing most of them as he pulled his knit shirt over his
head. He cursed himself for not picking up the rifle, then
pounded out, seeking the piercing glare of the intruder's
headlights.

They passed a scant twenty yards away. The glimpse he
caught of the man driving froze him. He knew him. At least
he thought he knew him. He'd seen him before, of that he
was certain. Hair and teeth. A bright cap of tight, longish
blond curls, almost an Afro style. A smooth, sadistic smile
as broad as the backside of one of Jonna's cows, all teeth.
Who could forget seeing him?

If Jonna had been here, she'd be dead. For a moment,
reality clutched him and a retching dry heave compressed his
stomach, then jammed it into his tight throat.

...ook over and he thundered through the dry ...neath the thick shelter of trees.

...reached the final curve in the drive as a red, late-model ...ntiac swept past, in touching distance. His fingers twitched and he closed his eyes, imprinting the image of the driver in his brain. Gangly and thin, probably tall, maybe twenty-eight or thirty—about the age Denise would be if she had lived. Sam memorized the man's smooth face, his pale, loose skin. His eyes were—Sam hadn't caught a color—just a wild, excited brightness. Sam knew he would find that face in Denise's yearbooks. He was a NET alum.

The car slowed as it neared the main road. Brake lights came on. Sam took one step in that direction, then realized he couldn't catch the bastard now. Not without his car.

And if he did? No gun? No socks? What would he do? Grab on and hook a bumpy ride?

Hysterical laughter rose at his ridiculous thoughts, but he swallowed it, afraid it would turn uncontrollable and debilitating. He memorized the Kansas license plate, then cursed the fates as he noted a rental company name on the tag holder surrounding it. The license number wouldn't do him much good, but knowing the rental company was a start.

The night wind glued his shirt to his damp, heaving chest as Sam ran for the .44 Magnum and his jacket. He'd filled his tank with gas at Moss's convenience store the night before, and he'd taken to Jonna's habit of leaving his keys in the ignition. The man was only four, maybe five minutes ahead of him by now.

As if to confirm his guesstimate, lights hovered near the top of a hill a couple miles away as Sam screeched around the corner at the end of the drive. Then they disappeared over the other side, leaving only a momentary ghostly glow in the sky.

Sam floored the pedal of his ancient car. He'd bought it from the college fleet for Denise. And since he'd been posing as a farm hand, he'd used it instead of his baby, a turbocharged T-bird. If only he had that power now.

But who would have known he'd be chasing a monster through this eerie, desolate land? The car wheezed over the next hill and he eased back on the gas.

The distant car taunted him with glimpses of lights weaving in and out, up and down over the Flint Hills. At least he isn't driving any faster than me, Sam decided, keeping his speedometer at about eighty. His car neither gained nor lost on the cretin turning onto Highway 50 up ahead. And Sam figured the simple fact that the man didn't know he was being followed gave Sam the upper hand.

The miles fell away and he wavered between hoping a policeman who would stop the man, and praying that he himself wouldn't be picked up for speeding.

Traffic was heavier near Newton, then dwindled to nothing as the midsize town grew small in the rearview mirror. The land flattened as they left the Flint Hills behind and the four-lane interstate stretched wide open for miles.

The back of Sam's eyes felt grainy, his head felt as if it would float right off his shoulders. Thoughts of Jonna squeezed his soul like a vise. Thank God, she hadn't come home when she had originally planned. Knowing she would be home later today brought such a chaos of emotions he quickly decided not to think about it.

Dawn crept up as they neared Wichita, throwing streaks of copper and orange and mauve across a nearly cloudless sky behind him. Sam pushed even harder the car he'd thought would seem in keeping with the farmhand masquerade, ignoring the shimmies and shakes as the speedometer needle edged toward ninety.

Traffic, people getting an early start on their Monday morning, began to distort Sam's awareness of which exact vehicle he was following, and he fought off a desperate rage.

He needed coffee. He needed to catch the damn red Pontiac. He needed to know Jonna could come home to a safe, bright day.

And what are you going to do with him if you apprehend him? Sam's hand rested on and caressed the comforting grip of the gun on the seat beside him.

He slowed slightly as the speed limit changed from sixty-five to fifty-five. The bastard had to slow down, too, didn't he? Or Sam would surely find him alongside the road, his rented car keeping company with a cop's flashing red lights.

His heart lurched. Finally! The cherry-red Pontiac was a block and a half ahead. Sam slowed when he was practically riding its bumper.

Sam changed lanes and pulled up beside the other car.

He couldn't have felt a blow more painfully if it had been physical. The driver of the other car had straight, nondescript brown hair. She glanced his way, her freshly made-up features warily appraising him. She seemed mildly shocked as she quickly looked away.

Sam glanced up at himself in the mirror. Bleary, wild eyes looked back. Strands of hair stood on end. No, he didn't exactly look like a run-of-the-mill good guy on his merry way to work.

Motels, restaurants, the road ahead. Damn, he couldn't examine them all at once. They became a blur and none of the cars straight ahead were even remotely similar to the one he wanted so badly to see.

Sam pressed his brakes lightly, changed lanes and coasted his tired car into the first gas station he came to. Staying far out of the main pattern of traffic, he parked to the side of the lot and disgustedly turned off his ignition.

"For nothing," he murmured dispiritedly. "All for nothing." He rested his aching head in numb hands.

"Sam?"

Jonna's heart missed a beat as she tentatively opened the screen door.

"Sam?" The door inside stood wide open. That was not like Sam at all.

Grisly visions and waking nightmares filled her mind. What if Sam had been on the receiving end of an insane killer's attack? They hadn't even thought of that possibility. At least *she* hadn't.

"Sam? I caught an earlier flight." *I couldn't stand it anymore. I came home to be with you.*

Her footsteps clicked hollowly against the hard wood floor. The old house creaked and seemed to have a life of its own. A nervous tremor feathered down her spine. "Get your act together, Jonna," she said aloud. "Your imagination is working overtime."

She smoothed the wrinkles in her fitted skirt and forced herself to walk like a sane, intelligent person when she wanted to run. She kept expecting someone—or something—to reach for her from one of the dark corners.

The back door was also open wide and Sam's car was gone. She hurried upstairs.

A damp towel lay on the bathroom floor. The bed in Sam's room was a rumpled mess. Pretty normal, she suspected. Nothing to be alarmed by. So why was she alarmed?

His fancy rifle lay on the floor by one window, the binoculars were beneath the other, the one facing her house. She shook off a premonition. Now, she was *really* being silly. She had no 'woman's intuition.' How could she *know* to her very soul that something was wrong. Maybe Sam had caught *him* and was in town with Sheriff Madden, taking fingerprints or giving statements or something.

She hurried out of the chill interior of the house and to the barn.

Both horses were inside. They greeted her with demanding, accusing noise. "Okay, guys, what's going on?" Candy approached her and Jonna patted the soft nose, but Murphy headed straight for the feed trough. "Haven't you been fed?"

Obviously not. She crossed the uneven dirt floor awkwardly in the unfamiliar short heels and performed the bare necessities, promising the horses she'd be back soon to do the rest.

The predicted autumn storm was moving across the sky from the south as Jonna went back outside. One huge cloud blocked the thin sunlight, and it suddenly seemed more like dusk than noon. A gust of wind lifted the lapel of her tailored jacket as Jonna got in her little pickup. She shivered all the way to the top of the hill.

A confused mixture of irritation and nerves possessed her as she opened the garage door and drove in. She decided she'd better save both emotions—and her questions— change clothes and do the chores Sam apparently hadn't done. Her stomach flip-flopped queasily as she lifted her heavy purse.

Where *was* he? Had her faith in him been totally misplaced after all? Had he done the chores at *all* since she'd been gone or had he missed just this morning's?

Or had he prepared God-only-knew what kind of surprise for her return?

And for the 757th time, she wondered if Sam was his own obsession. After all, he was hers.

She sighed, lifted her heavy garment bag from the floor of the small cab and started the garage door rumbling down on its tracks.

She let herself out the side door and onto the covered porch leading toward the security and warmth of her home.

Reality sank in slowly as she screeched to a full stop. Seconds seemed like hours as her horrified eyes focused, denied what she saw, then focused again.

The curly mass of reddish-brown and white fur lying a couple of yards from her feet was crumpled and still. A dark wet blob soaked the ground around the form. A brighter red stained some of the soft fur. Blood. Jonna took an automatic step backward, toward the garage. A glassy dark glaze caught her eye, drew her gaze to the seemingly haphazard splotches across the concrete floor. It was also blood. Almost dry. It took her almost a full minute to understand the splotches really weren't haphazard. They were words, painted bloody words.

She dropped the heavy suitcase and tried to scream but it seemed too deeply rooted in her heart and no sound came. She tried to block the gruesome scene from her vision with her hands. But she could see it with her eyes closed.

The calf, the blood, the words.

I've killed the fatted calf to celebrate your return.

CHAPTER THIRTEEN

Sam rested his eyes for a few minutes, then gassed up his car and bought the monster-size cup of strong, hot coffee. With his change, he approached the pay phone near the front of the lot. He was pleasantly surprised to find the yellow pages intact.

He hit the jackpot on his first call to the rental company that owned the car he had followed. The employee wouldn't give out any information until Sam came up with a story about accidentally leaving a package in the car. The man hesitated, then said hurriedly, quietly, "Your friend is supposed to return that car to our airport location." He wished Sam good luck in catching him.

I'll need it, Sam thought.

"I'm sorry, sir," said the pretty young attendant at the airport lot when he described the man and the car. "It's against policy to give out information about our customers."

"I don't need information, just a package I left in his car," Sam lied again with a hopeful, pleading smile. "Surely you can check to see if the package is still there?"

She checked, then apologized again. "Your friend must have taken it with him," she said consolingly.

"It's very important," he said.

It must be, he could almost see her think as she looked at him. Though he'd combed his hair and splashed water on his face at the convenience store where he'd bought gas, her expression showed him that he still looked pretty bad.

"You wouldn't happen to know which airline he went to? Maybe I could catch him before his flight."

"I guess it can't hurt to tell you he took our shuttle to the American Airlines gate," she said.

He rushed out, yelling his thanks over his shoulder.

The Wichita airport was small and quiet. Sam haunted the American Airlines loading gates until he was sure his quarry wasn't there. Then he wandered through the rest of the airport, examining each person he saw. No one even resembled the blond-haired man who had left Jonna's farm several hours ago.

It was nearly noon by the time he gave up.

He noted the destinations of the four American flights that had departed since six this morning—the earliest Denise's killer could have arrived.

He checked Jonna's airline. There were no flights due from L.A. but he realized she'd probably been routed through another city. The next flight in came from Dallas at 1:51. He'd bet that was hers.

He got his car out of short-term parking and headed back to Jonna's farm. She'd be home between three and four. On the off chance the monster *hadn't* left town, Sam couldn't risk not being there.

The thought of seeing her was fast becoming an aching, horrifying need. He had to reassure himself she was all right. But being home with her award would put her in danger. After this morning's fiasco, he could no longer delude himself that he couldn't make a mistake.

From here on in, he wouldn't leave Jonna's side.

Sheriff Madden came, then the Whitfield police chief, even two highway patrol cars were parked in her drive. It was like a huge, red-letter policeman's circus, Jonna decided, huddling in the entry of her house. She held Magic in her arms and her tears inside.

She answered their questions when they remembered she was there, listened to their technical directives mixed with speculation and pure gossip. As the sky grew darker with the approaching storm, the wind colder as it gusted up over the hill, she brought coffee and tried not to see the macabre mess they refused to let her clean up.

She couldn't look at the calf. Somewhere, out there on the range, a mama cow was wandering aimlessly, bellowing a frightened call. She'd seen it before when a calf died or was lost. The hollow ache the scene always left in her seemed to wear Sam's name this time.

Madden took her aside. "Where's the hired hand?"

"Sam?" she asked indignantly. He had a name. "I don't know." She'd changed into jeans and a T-shirt, adding a sweater, then a jacket over the top of that. Her teeth began to chatter again and she considered getting out her winter coat. She wondered if she would ever be warm again.

Madden studied her, as if weighing each word before he spoke. "We're going to have to arrest him, you know?"

"Sam?"

He nodded and touched the tip of his tongue with his finger to remove a wood sliver from the perennial tooth-pick he chewed. "Yep," he added for good measure. "There's an FBI agent on the way. They called yesterday. They've compared Sam's prints, the ones we took from here, to ones they have on file for the other murders he's been talking about. Sam's matched up on two of them."

"And he's the only suspect they've got," she whispered tonelessly.

"Yep."

"He didn't do this, Rod." The earnestness of her declaration surprised her. And she used his first name. No one had called him anything but Madden for years. "He didn't," she added. Her heart knew with absolute certainty that it was true.

He hefted his thick shoulders. "We'll have plenty of time to prove it, one way or another. The FBI will work with the jurisdictions involved, coordinating full scale investigations, gathering evidence."

Madden ushered her into the house, closing the outer door behind them. "You're freezing. Why don't you stay in here and relax?"

She turned on him. "What will happen next?"

"It's a long process," Madden said, pouring two mugs of coffee. He put them on the table and herded her to a chair. "I imagine first, several states will file extradition papers." He eased into one of the chairs across from her. "Depending on how hard he fights it and how good a lawyer he hires, that alone could take months, even years. Then, he'll be shipped off somewhere to stand trial. What we have on him here is pretty minor."

"What?" Her numb lips refused to move.

"I haven't seriously considered it yet, Jonna. Willful destruction of property, breaking and entering, maybe a cruelty to animals charge or two. Mercy, did you see what he did to your calf?"

Her mind wouldn't put Sam and the mutilated animal in the same thought. "Then you won't really be able to hold him for long," she said. "He could arrange for bail—"

"I don't think so, Jonna. I guarantee you, we'll throw every little thing we can find at him. And there will be warrants all over the place before the day is done."

"Please no, Rod," she begged.

His face stretched with disbelief. "This demented sucker told you you're next."

"But Sam...didn't...do it," she protested again, drawing out every word. "And what is going to happen to me? This nut is going to come back. You'll have Sam in jail somewhere where he can't stop him. And you've already said you can't spare the men to watch—"

"What makes you think it *isn't* Sam?" He turned the tables on her.

"Sheriff?"

They both swiveled. Gary and a brown-suited man stood in the doorway. "Sheriff, this is Agent Connors, FBI." Gary's eyes were wide, his voice full of awe.

Mike Hardin stepped up behind them and called in his best official voice. "Sheriff, you'd better come."

A crack of thunder boomed, emphasizing Hardin's dramatic pause. The sky flashed bright light behind him.

"We've got him," Hardin said when the noise died away. "They stopped him down at the end of the drive."

Sam couldn't believe what they were doing. It took five long minutes and the cold metal handcuffs—they stopped him every time he started to move—to convince himself he was really under arrest.

The small road quickly filled with uniforms and cars and flashing blue and red lights. Shock set in as he realized they were all coming, not from the highway or town, but from the top—from Jonna's house.

"Would someone tell me what's going on?" he begged the cop standing closest as another boom of thunder and lightning ripped the sky.

"Sheriff Madden will explain," the officer replied.

Lack of sleep, dismay, relief that whatever had happened, Jonna wasn't here, left Sam weak. He assured himself that he had an hour, maybe two, of fast talking to get himself out of this mess before she arrived.

Sam had a face now. He could offer suggestions on where to start looking.

But what had the bastard done here? he wondered as the hovering deputies parted. Madden ambled through the gap. Sam hoped he was bringing answers. Sam had been impressed with the down-to-earth, teddy-bear of a man, and he started framing the questions in his mind. "Madden," he greeted him.

The sheriff stepped aside and Jonna, white-faced, wide-eyed and terrified, rushed past him.

Sam felt the color drain from his face and was sure his pallor matched hers. Jonna threw herself against him and he reached to catch her, wrenching his wrists.

She looked down at the handcuffs, then back at him. Salty paths of tears marred her satiny skin, and tears welled in her multihued eyes again. He felt an incongruous urge to kiss them away before they could do further damage.

"What are you doing here?" he managed to mumble gruffly.

"I caught an early flight. Where have *you* been?"

"Good question, Barton." Madden drew their attention.

Sam wanted to brace Jonna against him before he broke the news. "He was here."

"We know, Barton. Why do you think *we're* here?" Madden asked grimly. "You left quite a mess," the sheriff added with disgust. He pulled Jonna close, sheltering her protectively under his arm—exactly the way Sam had wanted to do—away from him.

Jonna's bottom lip quivered, confirming Madden's statement.

"What did he do?" Sam asked, afraid to hear. He gulped in the sight of her, reminded himself she was live and in person. Whatever the bastard had done, he hadn't—

Voices bombarded Sam with a hodgepodge of facts and details. Blobs of rain punctuated the vivid descriptions. And Jonna stared and nodded soulfully, agreeing with everything that was said.

"This is Agent Connors with the FBI," Madden finally said, indicating a small nondescript man. "He's got a few questions of his own." As Connors returned a mute, hard gaze, the ray of hope Sam had felt dimmed inside him.

The giant drops of rain grew smaller, more frequent. Shoulders hunched, and Jonna's soft hair curled and waved and drooped to match her troubled expression.

"Let's get out of here," Madden said. "We can do this in town, out of the rain." The group began to disperse.

"But I—"

"You'll have your chance to talk when we get to my office," Madden interrupted him curtly.

"I saw him. I followed him to Wichita. I can identify him now," Sam protested. "He has white-blond frizzy hair."

Connors, out of place amid the sea of uniforms and jeans, mumbled gibberish about personalizing an alter ego.

"Take him in," Madden said to the officer who had restrained Sam and hadn't left his side since.

"What am I being held for?" he asked desperately.

"Anything and everything we can think of." Madden frowned at Sam's guard.

"I arrested him for breaking and entering," the man told the sheriff.

Madden nodded approvingly. "We'll add the rest when we get to town."

"You Mirandized him?" the agent asked.

The officer nodded.

"What about Jonna? Who's going to take care—"

"That's why we're taking you in," Madden said grimly and gave his undersheriff a few terse orders about what was left to be done here.

The officer holding Sam's arm tugged him toward the blue squad car at the end of the drive with its doors open. Sam planted his feet, lurching as the officer lost his grip. "Jonna?"

Her dazed eyes swept his face. She came closer and laid her fingertips over his arm.

"Are you all right?" he asked.

"For now," she said dully. "You?"

"I will be."

Her jaw set in fierce determination. "What do you want me to do, Sam?"

"Get the hell out of here. Go stay with Moss."

"I mean about you, for you. Shall I call an attor—"

"Bring me the yearbooks," he broke in. He lifted both hands and cupped her face, framing her chin with links of chain. He felt a swift, sweet gratitude that they hadn't cuffed his hands behind his back. His long fingers smoothed the rain away from one cheek. It was immediately wet again.

"I know what he looks like now. It shouldn't take me too long to identify him, convince them. Especially if I can find him in one of Denise's NET yearbooks. I've seen him before. I suspect he was at the college when Denise was."

His keeper dragged at him. Sam talked quickly. "I've got them from the five years she was there. If I can't find him in those, you can call Barry—in the alumni office at the college," he inserted. "He'll help you. He can send you more."

Sam stumbled sideways as the policeman's grip tightened painfully. "Look, man, we're getting soaked."

Jonna followed. "Where?"

Sam scowled.

"Where are the yearbooks?"

"In that big thing in the dining room."

"What?" Jonna's hair was plastered to her scalp. She brushed it from her eyes and blinked against the blurring moisture that dripped off the ends. "Oh, the buffet?"

He nodded and turned to accompany the officer, glancing back over his shoulder to confirm, once more, that she was real, alive.

She looked a little less stunned. And obviously, she was on his side. A burst of warmth bloomed from the inside out.

Dammit. How could he leave her where she stood, surrounded, drifting and lost in the middle of the chaos? The officer covered the top of Sam's head and propelled him down into the back seat.

I'll be back before sundown, Sam thought. I'll hold her and protect her and refuse to leave her until that bastard is dead and in his grave.

"Sam?" Jonna called his name as she ran to the car and huddled outside the still-open door. "I just want you to know I . . . I believe you," she said.

"I know." He lifted his hands, traced her lower lip with a finger. "Go to Moss," he said. "Don't stay here by yourself."

She nodded. "I will."

Concern and trust emanated from her. He felt the urge to say something about the way she made him feel. He swallowed the impulse. He couldn't define the emotion. And thanks seemed so inadequate when what he felt was so overwhelming.

He wasn't sure what love was anymore. Was it the need to take care of someone? Or gratitude for her faith, even though he'd given her no valid foundation for it?

He recognized his gripping desire to touch her, hold her, make love to her. But that, by itself, wasn't love. He'd experienced that too many times when that was all he felt.

Was it love that had amassed this paralyzing lump of terror in his gut?

He couldn't love her. Loving meant losing. If he said he loved her, admitted it out loud, it would almost be like signing her death warrant.

All he knew was that this scraggly-looking, wet waif *was* everything right now. And if something happened to her—and if he didn't get out of this mess soon, something might—he wouldn't want to live.

"I'll be back as quickly as I can," he promised.

"We gotta go," the officer said, and Jonna backed slowly away.

The door slammed with a terse finality. The car moved out onto the highway and Sam twisted to gaze over his shoulder. Jonna looked forlorn, forsaken and fragile in the middle of the scattering male mob. Madden stood behind her, to one side; the FBI agent and the police chief flanked the other. He watched as they closed ranks, talking as they circled her and blocked her from his sight.

He realized what he was *really* up against. They absolutely believed he had killed three women, including his very own sister Denise. They were going to do their darnedest to make Jonna believe it, too. And believing it—that they'd caught their killer—they didn't think she was in any danger at all.

If Sam couldn't convince them otherwise—and very soon—there would be no one—no one in this world—here for Jonna when the killer came to visit again. And next time, he wouldn't kill one of her calves. Next time, Jonna would be the one to die.

Sam gazed down at his hands, staring at the ink smudges still staining his fingers. He felt soiled, inside and out. His lips were moving and he realized he was repeating a prayer again and again. "Please don't let her believe them." He said the words aloud. "Please don't allow her to let her defenses down."

"Barton?"

Sam lurched around hopefully. The sheriff stood on the other side of the steel bars.

Only the light in the small cell block had been turned on. In the evening's stormy gloom, Madden and his uniform blended into the shadows of the monotone-gray corridor.

As if reading Sam's mind, Madden swung and flipped the utilitarian switches by the door separating the jail from the rest of the county offices in the modern building. He approached Sam's cell again and the bars sliced the pleasantly plump man into thin portions.

"I promised Jonna I would bring you these," he said.

"She's here?" Sam looked past Madden, his weariness diminished, expecting to see her standing there.

"She headed for home."

"You didn't let her go home?" Madden stepped back, and Sam realized he had grabbed for the man and caught the cell door instead. "I'm sorry," he said abruptly and loosened his white-knuckled grip on the bars. "She didn't *really* go home?"

"I still have men there working. And she's just going to out to feed the horses. She's staying in town with Moss tonight," the sheriff said defensively.

Sam felt as if his whole body had been turned into a pressure cooker like the one his mother had used. He needed to vent steam. He felt an explosive mix of anger, frustration and desperation growing, rising out of control. And he had to cap it. He just couldn't afford to blow. It wouldn't help his situation at all.

"I'm fixing to call the Whitfield Café, ask them to send some supper over for all of us. Anything in particular you'd like?"

"I'm not hungry." Sam slumped on the side of the bunk, which was bolted to the floor. He was ready to immerse himself in the heavy books, and he opened the top one.

"Anything you *don't* particularly like?" Madden changed the question.

"I would kill for a cup of hot coffee and a cigarette," Sam said absently, then realized exactly what he had said. He glanced up, noted Madden's slack jaw and set the books aside. "Look, Madden, it's just an expression. A cup of coffee would be really nice."

Madden examined the toes of his shoes. "How about a nice hot beef sandwich with mashed potatoes and lots of gravy? It would take the chill off, maybe?"

Sam followed Madden's eyes to the small window above the bed. Night had set in and the sky continued to leak a steady drizzle. "That would be fine, Sheriff."

"Piece of pie for dessert?"

"That's generous, Sheriff Madden, but you might as well save the county funds. I couldn't eat it."

"I didn't know you smoked."

"I don't usually," Sam responded and settled with his yearbooks again.

"Uh, any particular brand?"

Sam couldn't prevent a wry smile. "Anything nonmenthol with a filter would be fine." The people here didn't seem to have a concept of how you were supposed to treat "bad" guys. They were *all* too trusting, and certain that if you ate regular meals and were kind to your fellow man, everything would be all right. That complacency was going to get Jonna killed.

He felt panic nearly choke him again.

"She'll be safe for a while," he told himself. The bright-haired, bright-eyed killer was gone. Jonna would surely be okay at least one more day. "Please, God, I can't be there. Please keep her safe."

Last night's storm was obviously a prelude, Jonna thought late the next afternoon, examining the gray-brown sky as she drove the nine miles home from Moss's to do the chores. Moss had wanted to come. Insisted. But she'd waited until he was called to the store for something. *If* there was trouble, the last thing she wanted to have to worry about was him having a heart attack.

She watched the storm build and brew as she took care of the horses, drove out to check the cattle tanks and put water in the giant pans she kept filled for the assortment of wild cats that had the run of the barn.

Madden's deputies hadn't been able to wash away the splotches of dried blood. No matter how she tried not to see, she could still read the stained message as she let herself into the house. Thank heavens it wasn't Magic, she thought, ridiculously relieved it didn't refer to a cat rather than a calf.

Another reason to know it wasn't Sam, she realized. If Sam had made this ungodly mess, he would have used Magic. He would have known killing her only pet was a much better way to get to her than killing one of her many, nameless farm animals.

She wondered without humor how Connors would like *that* reasoning. He sure hadn't agreed with the rest of her reasoning. "You believe everything he's told you?" Connors had asked when she'd taken the yearbooks by the jail last night.

"Not at first," she had answered, opening the outer flap of the top one and removing some papers. "Here. I brought these, too." She had shown him the faxes Sam's friend had sent. "These are the articles that helped Sam connect everything."

Connors had rolled an old-fashioned green leather office chair from behind a desk and invited Jonna to sit down. He'd eased himself onto the corner of Madden's desk, wriggling himself a cleared spot with his butt.

"So tell me *why* you think Barton isn't responsible for all this." His tone, his facial expression, the way his whole body curved down toward her, made it seem that he really wanted to understand.

"For one thing," she said, "he's had plenty of opportunity if that was his intention."

She interlocked her fingers, released them and did it all again. He'd made love to her. What better opportunity could he get? Her face grew warm as she thought of it. She focused complete attention on her fidgety hands.

"And that's all?"

"The first victim was his sister. He's still grieving for her. Why would Sam kill his own sister and cause himself so much pain? It just doesn't make sense."

Connors had leaned closer. "So you think we've arrested the wrong man?"

"Know," she asserted, looking directly into Connors's gray-blue eyes. "You should have seen the way Sam looked the day my house was vandalized and left in shambles. He was as shocked and surprised as I was. And upset with himself for not being there to stop it. People just can't fake reactions like that."

"I'm not surprised he convinced you," Connors said. "Psychopaths are notoriously good actors."

They'd already attached a name, a label to Sam. That was almost the worst thing so far. Jonna bolted from her chair.

Madden approached to calm her down and she held up her palm. "What about his sister? Why would he kill his own sister?"

"That's a bit tricky to explain, but it isn't unusual, either." Connors joined her and Madden in the center of the small room. "What people are the closest to you? Your family," he supplied before she could answer. "Who can make you feel and do things a stranger couldn't? Your family," he answered again. "Something happened between Barton and his sister. He killed her in a rage. It started this whole thing. She was the catalyst. He found out he liked killing."

"That's ridiculous." Tears filled Jonna's eyes, hazing her vision. She had promised herself she wouldn't get upset, wouldn't cry.

Connors lowered his voice patiently. "Sam has several colleagues in Texas who say he and his sister had a running battle in progress about her decision to move to California. It wasn't over, either. One of his previous girlfriend's told us he went out to Denise's awards presentation intending to convince her to come back to Texas with him."

"Sam didn't do any of this," she said stubbornly. The men exchanged another look. "And how about his relationship with me? It doesn't follow the pattern."

The agent agreed, perching again on the corner of Madden's desk. "But a psychopath is into power and control. You're fairly isolated. You may be the first subject he's had a chance to practice all that power and control on, to really terrorize."

"That doesn't make sense," she blurted.

"I heard you talking to Madden about pattern killings. You must have done your homework."

"Sam told me."

"Then he also told you pattern killings evolve?" He waited.

She stared at him mutely.

"You have to remember, we've just tied this together—"

"Then you need Sam's help. He figured it out a long time ago."

Connors ignored her interruption and went on. "We're only beginning to check out the lives of the victims immediately *prior* to their deaths. We may find a lot of similarities the further into this we get."

"And you plan to hold Sam in the meantime?"

"We have to, Jonna," Madden had said. "I'm not going to take any chances with you. You've got the award now—"

"So I'm on my own against the crazy that *really* wants to kill me."

"Jonna..."

Jonna had grabbed her purse off his desk and headed for the door. "Let me know when I can see Sam. And if you would be so kind as to get those yearbooks to him, I'd really appreciate it."

"Jonna—"

"You *will* give him the yearbooks, Rod?" Sheriff Madden had blanched as she pinned him with her best imitation of one of her father's commands.

He'd nodded. "And we'll still be watching your—"

"Don't bother," she broke in. "I'll be staying with Moss for the time being."

She'd left trembling. It hadn't stopped since. And instead of getting better, it had gotten worse when she'd gone by the jail this morning and Madden told her the name of the man Sam had identified.

"Quentin Kincaid," she murmured. The name, the face in the yearbook picture Madden showed her perfectly matched the voice indelibly etched in Jonna's memory from the telephone calls. Now, she had a face to complete her nightmares. And if he ever called again, she would visualize the smirky twist to his lips. Just thinking of him made her cringe.

With the chores done, Jonna walked slowly through the house, flipping on lights. For company, she turned on the TV loud in the living room—for people sounds—and to keep an eye and ear on the thunderstorm warning and tornado watch the weatherman had announced earlier.

She'd left her suitcase in the kitchen last night. She carried it upstairs and watched her hands shake as she unpacked it, stopping to stare at the drive and the farmhouse from time to time.

The house looked empty and isolated without Sam. Despite the "logic" Madden and Connors had tried to pound in, she would feel much, much safer with Sam there, right down the hill, than she did with him locked away.

An especially dark cloud hovered over the house. Maybe with the drapes closed, she could concentrate on getting some clothes packed to take back to Moss's. She got her sketching things. Maybe she could make a few rough preliminary drawings for the magazine. She couldn't just haunt the jail, hoping Madden would let her see Sam. And she couldn't spend the next few days wandering from room to room in Moss's small house.

Quentin Kincaid. Connors had merely said, "We investigate all leads." She prayed they were investigating him now. When they did, Sam would be free.

The phone rang and a glance at the clock said it was time to be on her way. She'd promised herself she wouldn't stay here longer than she had to to get things done.

"Hello," she said breathlessly on the second ring, anticipating the horror of Quentin's voice.

"Hi, Girlie. I didn't expect you there, but no one answered Moss's phone so I thought it was worth a try." Madden's voice was reassuring.

"I won't be here much longer," she confirmed, carrying the long corded phone to the window.

She parted the curtain. The sky, still holding on to its ominous fury, feigned an early dusk.

Madden cleared his throat. "I promised I'd keep you updated on the news," he said.

Jonna went very still. The corner of the drape drifted through her fingers and back into place. Somehow, she didn't think the news was going to be good.

"We received warrants from Colorado and California. We're officially booking Sam for murder," he finally said.

"No," she whispered.

"We've verified it all. He had access to the alumni information and the awards announcements before they were ever published," he went on. "He admitted to being in two out of three cities where the murders happened, *when* they happened," Madden emphasized. "And the fingerprints found in two of the victims' homes have been double-checked and positively ID'd as his. We're just waiting for the third. Sam doesn't have an alibi for that one, no proof he was where he said he was. The case is pretty solid, Jonna."

The news jabbed through Jonna's heart. Not Sam, she cried inside. Please, no, not Sam. He didn't do it. Sam didn't kill those women. And in a million years, he wouldn't have killed her.

"Madden?" His "what" was slow in coming. "Have you checked at all on Quentin Kincaid?"

"Agent Connors has several agents and every crime computer in the country looking for anything at all on the man." Madden was obviously relieved that was all she asked.

"Have they found anything?"

She heard him speak to someone with him. "Connors says we'll start getting reports back any time now."

"Thanks, Rod," she said sincerely. "And thanks for keeping me informed."

"You know you can ask me for just about anything." On the last three words, his voice was a shade harder than she'd ever heard it and she interpreted it to mean, don't ask for any favors for Sam. And Sam, in the eyes of Rodney Madden, county sheriff, had been tried and convicted. He was convinced they had arrested the right man, that Sam was a vicious murderer.

"If I stop by when I get to town, can I see him?" *Please, Madden, this one's for me.*

She heard his hesitation. "He needs to see a lawyer."

"I'll try to convince him if you let me. Just let me know," she said. "I'll be back at Moss's in a half hour or so."

He felt compelled to tell her going to Moss's was a precaution she didn't need to take now. The killer was in his jail. They said their goodbyes and Jonna hung up thoughtfully.

"You're a fool," she said aloud to the phone, but she didn't believe that either. As Moss had told her last night, "You know Sam. These guys don't. You've seen him with both your head *and* your heart. You have the most at stake," he'd finished his pep talk. "For everyone else, this is a game of fact and fantasy."

For once, she allowed herself to listen only to her heart. And her heart knew, knew beyond a shadow of a doubt, that Sam wasn't a killer.

Jonna grabbed a few more clothes, stuffing them in a duffel bag, then turned out the lights and made her way downstairs. She sat down at the kitchen table and picked up the phone to call her lawyer.

She was startled to find the line dead. Her heart started racing until she reminded herself this kind of weather *always* played havoc with the utilities. The wind had picked up. The rain and the thunder and lightning couldn't be far behind.

And she should be on her way before the elements quit playing around. She started to turn out lights and changed her mind. She wasn't leaving a dark house. And she wasn't coming back to one tomorrow.

Jonna swung her bag over one shoulder, and hung her purse from the other, unzipping the front pocket to find the keys as she opened the door.

She looked up and froze.

A man with frizzy blond hair stood waiting, as if he'd just rung the bell and expected her to fling it wide and invite him in. His thin lips stretched across largish teeth, forming a repulsive grin.

"Finally, we meet," Quentin Kincaid said.

Jonna knew her time had come.

CHAPTER FOURTEEN

Dolly will hate this one, Quentin thought. Jonna was beautiful, Dolly was plain. Jonna was successful, everything Dolly touched turned to mud. Jonna was graceful and shapely, Dolly was lumps and bumps, although she managed to convince herself—and her "friends"—that her bumps were in all the right places.

And he would totally enjoy his dear mama's bitter hatred.

Jonna Sanders was everything Dolly could never be. Yet exactly like her—a bitch who would use any man to get things she didn't deserve.

Jonna Sanders's eyes widened in fear. Then her nose lifted arrogantly and he knew she was also just like Denise Barton, a Miss Snooty-Tooty with her nose always in the air.

In college with him, dear, sweet Denise Barton had treated him like a pariah. She'd shunned working on any of the dual projects, even though they had both been constantly touted as the most talented students in the department.

And when she had been the recipient of the NAGA award instead of him, he'd known she wasn't above sleeping with every member of the committee who made the final selections.

It was *her* fault Conger-Fox Graphics had fired him. It was *her* fault Dolly had kicked him out of their apartment. "Prove you're not as worthless as your father," she'd admonished him, cutting off the allowance that was rightfully his. "Let's see you support yourself."

He *was* supporting himself, though dear Mama wouldn't think he was doing so well if she saw the way he lived. But he'd found both the job and the life-style suited him.

Now this bitch had lost him his position at G. Wells, one of the nation's largest clipping services. Where else could he keep in touch with so many fellow alums than through the trade journals he'd been paid to peruse and cut to pieces? Where else would he have found a prize like Jonna Sanders for *The Record?*

"You didn't appreciate my congratulations?" he asked, sweeping an arm toward the bloody letters she'd obviously tried to wash away. Quentin pooched out his lower lip and mimicked a disappointed pout. "I'm so hurt. I gave it my best college try."

He reached for the arm that hung loose over her purse. She let out a hoarse scream. He laughed. She couldn't even do that well. The purse and bag she carried crashed to the foyer floor.

He held up his hands, backing a step—only a step—away. "Oh, I'm sorry, dear Jonna Sanders, I didn't mean to frighten you." *Not much anyway.*

He put on his best leer, the one he'd learned so well from Dolly's lewd and lascivious friends. "But aren't you going to invite me in?" How well he remembered that phrase. They'd used it when they'd come to his bedroom door. He stepped forward into the entry, and she, trembling satisfactorily, cringed away.

"I was so hoping you would show me your brand-new award. Could I see it, Jonna Sanders?"

She blinked and he realized he was being very impolite. "Please?" he asked cordially.

She nodded carefully, never taking her eyes off him.

"Good. Where is it?" he asked, speaking as he would to a child. Her hand floated up and around, gesturing vaguely behind her.

"Where?" he asked, reaching for her arm again. That seemed to be the only thing that made her move.

She dodged again and said shakily, "Upstairs."

"Could you show me?"

She stared at him unblinkingly.

"Pretty, pretty please?" Damn, she was dim. It proved the only way she could have won anything was by buying it with the disgusting little "hiding place" between her legs.

"Come on," he said impatiently, and shoved her farther into the house. He stepped inside and closed the door behind him. "Show me, damn you!" he said, then gave her his most charming grin.

"I don't know what to think anymore," Sheriff Madden said, pulling up a folding chair outside Sam's cell. He handed Sam the report he'd just been faxed, ran a hand over his balding head and sat down. "You're right about one thing, this guy is strange."

"He's a killer," Sam said, realizing it was Quentin Kincaid's name emblazoned across the top of the page. "And he's still on the loose. And he's still after Jonna." He tried to sound calm, despite his mounting desperation. Sounding as feverishly insane as he felt would not help his cause.

"Read it," Madden said. "I'd really like a second opinion. Tell me what you think."

"What did Connors say?" Sam leaned over the paper to comply.

"He hasn't seen it. He's in Wichita filing some documents in the federal court." Madden looked away sheepishly and Sam knew the "documents" had something to do with him. "I probably shouldn't be showing these to you."

The report was a background summary sent by the San Francisco headquarters of the Bureau. Their massive computer hookups all over the country had pulled together an almost frighteningly thorough profile in an amazingly short period of time. Sam read, growing more horrified with every line.

Quentin Kincaid's father had died in a freak accident with a conveyor belt at the airport where he worked when Quentin was two. The offending airline had made a large cash settlement and—after Dolly's continual threats to pursue a suit anyway—the merry widow also received lifetime passes for the two on the airline. According to several family members, Dolly had considered the passes a pretty good exchange for her husband's life. She'd always wanted to travel and Quentin's father was a ne'er-do-well.

For the next several years, travel was just what she did, often leaving Quentin behind with "friends," until they were tired of being taken advantage of and were no longer friends.

When he was six, Dolly took him to San Francisco where, on encouragement from her most recent boyfriend, a real estate broker, she'd spent what was left of her settlement on an apartment building in a fashionable neighborhood. She and her son and a constant parade of new "friends" occupied the penthouse apartment. Renting the apartments below gave Dolly her livelihood.

Dolly had been an indulgent mother at times, sparing no expense to nurture Quentin's artistic talents, buying him lavish toys, dressing her young son like Little Lord Fauntleroy complete with "sweet little bow ties"—perhaps for longer than she should have. One former neighbor briefly described a major battle when an eleven-year-old Quentin refused to don the required garb.

On the surface, it looked as if Quentin had led a petted and pampered life, but several of Dolly's renters suspected it was more than a little difficult for the boy. Especially when he made the mistake of outgrowing his other, more important use to Dolly Kincaid. Many of the men Dolly had adorned her apartment with over the years had been overtly fascinated with young boys and Quentin no longer helped attract them. "Dolly just didn't appeal to normal guys," one neighbor was quoted. "But she couldn't stand not having a man around so she was inclined to take whatever she could get. After several drunks and beaters, she figured out that her poor little boy could be a very attractive asset to certain types. And they were almost always nice to *her*. Why wouldn't they be?"

Sam flipped the page to one of the attachments referred to and saw for himself that the current residence of at least two of Dolly's former live-ins seemed to support the speculation. They were residing in California prisons for certain crimes against juvenile males.

"Bizarre, huh?" Madden asked.

"That's not the word," Sam mumbled and shivered, squinting in the dim light.

Madden got up and switched on the lights and Sam took the papers to his bunk.

During Quentin's teen years, his mother railed against Quentin's lack of ambition and accused him of being "just like his father."

Somehow, he managed to win an art scholarship to North East Texas State where he'd done fairly well. There were no reports of trouble anyway, except that his peers reported that he was 'weird.'

"Denise was in his class," Sam pointed out to Madden.

"I know," the sheriff replied and shifted restlessly around on his chair. "But Jonna would have graduated two years before he enrolled at NET," he added.

"The other two would have been there a decade or two before he was," Sam mumbled as he continued reading the report.

Quentin hadn't blazed a trail of success in his chosen career as a commercial artist. Though he'd been hired and fired by most of the graphic arts and advertising firms in San Francisco, he was obviously talented—apparent by his nomination for the award Denise had won.

Madden had been watching Sam's progress through the report. "Do you happen to know what his alibi was the night your sister was killed?"

"His mother. Dolly Kincaid. She said he was with her, that they'd gone out to a late dinner after the awards ceremony before going home." Sam felt sick. He'd talked to her himself.

"Why would she lie?" Madden asked.

"Probably habit," Sam said, shaking his head at the sheriff's innocence. "With this kind of history, it can't be the first time she's been questioned by some authority or another. She's probably learned to say whatever she believes will lead to the fewest questions and the least amount of trouble." Sam leapt from the bed. "He *worked* with Denise." He began to pace. "How could they possibly miss all these connections when they investigated her death?"

"He'd been in Chicago nine months by the time Denise was killed," Madden answered impatiently, as if he'd puzzled over the question long enough to anticipate it from Sam. "She only worked in the same company for six weeks—in different departments—and that was almost two years before her death. Then they classified her murder as a bungled robbery, if you remember, no reason to check into distant past work associations."

Sam clamped his lips tightly. He wasn't going to mention the award again. It was insignificant—not the kind of thing someone would kill for. He hadn't tied it in as a motive until he'd sat in Barry's office and read about JoAnne from Connecticut and her death . . . it seemed like aeons ago.

Sam slowly handed back the report through the bars. "He's still loose," he said quietly.

Madden avoided his eyes, and a white line formed around his mouth. Sam felt sorry for the man but found little comfort in knowing the kindly sheriff was torn between his doubts and his responsibilities. Jonna was still at the bastard's mercy.

Madden's gray eyes finally met Sam's. "It's not a weekend. He's always killed on weekends. Why would he break the pattern now?"

Sam gulped back a protest. That was a pattern *he* hadn't seen and Madden had thought about this long and hard before he had come to get a second opinion from an accused murderer.

"Darn it all, Sam." The sheriff burst from the chair. "I don't know what to do."

"Let me out of here."

Madden's gaze pinned and analyzed Sam. "You're a hell of a mess," he finally said. "We aren't used to dealing with maniacs here, and now I've got two on my hands." He struggled with his uncertainties and Sam prayed.

Madden finally walked quickly to the door.

"What are you going to do?" Sam called.

"How the hell should I know? Wait, I guess," he contradicted himself. "We should be getting another report on what *this* maniac is doing now sometime soon." He waved the papers above his shoulder.

"It may be too late." Sam held his breath.

"Jonna's at Moss's. How would Kincaid find her there?" He opened the door, looked back at Sam and released an exaggerated sigh. "We've probably got several days before we really need to worry," he finished, offering logic he'd obviously been giving himself.

The heavy door thunked shut between them and stone-cold despair knotted Sam's stomach. *Probably.* The key word was probably. But what if they were wrong?

Jonna led Quentin upstairs, stumbling over a step or two as she tried to walk and watch him at the same time. He leered at her, prodding her from time to time. He didn't have a gun that she had noticed, but then her brain was just starting to function again. And it ran uncontrolled and rampant in all directions.

It flitted past prayers, for herself and one for Sam—please, God, let him come—then stuttered and tripped over on the realization that she loved Sam. She might never see him again, might never have the chance to make love to him and tell him. She didn't find any comfort in knowing she'd been right for once.

Oh God, would he survive without someone's love?

She cast a glance behind her as Quentin followed her to her office. He was as pale as his hair, emaciated. He looked weak. What kind of chance would she have if she ran?

As if reading her thoughts, he curled long cold fingers around the back of her neck and squeezed. She shivered and tried to resist his loathsome touch.

His grip tightened and he pushed her ahead of him. He was more powerful than he looked, she decided. He carefully stayed between her and the catwalk leading to the stairs.

Her gaze flicked quickly about the room while his focused on the small statuette she'd casually dropped on the center of her desk. Funny, how unimportant that little trophy from the Architectural Society of America had become. She lifted it, hefted it subtly, evaluating its potential as a weapon as she finally wiggled from his grasp.

She surprised him—and herself—by holding it out to him like an offering.

"You can have it if you want," she said and amazed herself again at how calm she sounded.

His pale face twisted and flamed a brilliant, furious red. "*You* are *my* prize." The fist holding the statuette swung.

Jonna ducked before she realized his aim wasn't directed at her. The statuette crashed on her desk, then flayed at her cherished blown glass castle. Glass exploded and flew randomly around the room and Quentin seemed totally caught up in a fury of destroying things.

Her wooden legs moved her quietly to the side door leading into her bedroom. Quentin didn't seem to notice, and his smashing and bashing didn't abate until she closed the door behind her.

Jonna heard a beat of total silence, then his heavy footsteps giving chase.

Jonna stopped long enough to grab and flip over the chaise longue behind her, then she ran.

She heard Quentin hit the door.

Her hand swept the dresser top as she passed, and she picked up the small lamp and tossed it in her wake. She slammed the bedroom door and thundered down the stairs.

A loud and angry expletive escaped him as she hit the bottom step. Two chairs from the dining room table. The coffee mug, the coffeepot at the edge of the counter, everything within reach flew behind her as she focused all her attention on the outside door. It helped her ignore his thrashing as he cursed and stumbled along ten feet or so behind her.

Her purse. The keys. She grabbed them from where they'd fallen by the door. She slammed both foyer doors and sprinted toward the garage.

She heard the door of the house close as she stepped into the garage. She was reaching over to lock the passenger door of the little truck when he lumbered in, his face contorted in fury.

Her hands shook so outrageously she almost couldn't get the key into the ignition. It finally rammed home and she glanced up to see him, three yards away and closing.

Her numb finger hit the garage door opener above her visor as her other hand released the emergency brake.

The wide door rumbled too slowly on its chains, gradually letting in the night. His foreboding grin invaded her side vision, inches from her face, separated only by a thin sliver of glass.

Bracing herself, forcing herself not to shrink away, she gasped back a sob and turned the key in the ignition. And didn't hear a thing.

Something tapped the the window beside her. She jumped, then cranked the key again. Tap. Tap. Again, the motor didn't do a thing. No chug, no churn. Just a tapping near her face.

A monstrous jag of lightning charged the sky, changing the early evening to daylight, and she saw something small and black and snakelike from the corner of her eye. *Don't look. Don't look* . . . but she had to.

Quentin stood propped against the roof of the pickup, his hand dangling a slender cord against her window. Its swinging connector cap rapped at the window, keeping a horrific, taunting beat.

He'd taken something out of her dependable little vehicle. He nodded jovially as the light of understanding dawned and she went limp.

The cab, still rocking in protest to her frantic entry, shuddered to a dejected stop. The movement triggered a memory and sobbing with hope, Jonna jammed the clutch and shifted into neutral. She'd never rolled the minitruck out of the garage, but once, she'd forgotten to leave it in gear and the slant of the garage floor had rolled the pickup into the garage door. She released the clutch now and prayed.

The pickup crawled an inch, then two. She threw herself back against the seat, helping and hoping with everything she could.

She glanced at Quentin as the pickup gained an almost imperceptible bit of speed.

Quentin's triumphant smirk turned to stunned dismay, then again to rage.

She shouldn't have looked. Stark, unremitting terror rendered her nearly catatonic. Confronting his face, so close to hers, jolted her back to shaking so desperately hard she almost couldn't think.

"Roll." She rocked. "Roll," she chanted, closing her eyes. She expected his hands to materialize somehow through the window and clamp around her throat. She felt permanent, burning scars where he'd touched her before.

The pickup rolled in earnest, as if in answer to her plea, coasting backward with zero control. The power steering, brakes—nothing worked without the engine. She urged all her energy to her hands and tugged at the steering wheel until her arms ached, turning the little vehicle by sheer will. If only she could get this sucker pointed down the hill...

The truck creaked almost to a stop as it finished its wide swing and she compressed the clutch. She released it again and the pickup started to roll, slowly, but this time, forward.

Please, God. As soon as she had a little momentum, she popped the clutch. Nothing.

She cast a frantic look around, desperate suddenly to see him. Quentin was nowhere in sight. Her hair flew in her eyes, almost blocking out the car sitting menacingly to the side of the garage.

He'd probably gone for that. For the first time in what seemed like hours, she breathed without aching to cry and felt a tremulous shred of hope.

A dull thud shook her little pickup. Her eyes jerked to the rearview mirror. The momentary respite from terror evaporated as if it had never been. He'd jumped into the bed and she was taking him with her on her escape.

Quentin's wild-eyed leer, his gleeful grin filled the view and seemed to radiate evil light into the cab, blocking out everything else.

Jonna popped the clutch simply because her knee was too weak to hold the pressure any longer. The little truck lurched over the crest of the hill. Nothing happened.

She popped it again and felt the hair on the back of her neck rising. She could almost feel his fetid breath.

Again she released the clutch, but with despair. She was past expecting anything this time. Whatever he'd taken from the engine must be crucial.

The little vehicle really moved now, increasing speed. It felt like a free-fall into the darkness, as if she'd hopped a roller coaster ride into hell. She pushed against the brake. It was nearly as stiff and uncooperative as the steering wheel she gripped uselessly.

She didn't have enough fright left to worry about what would happen when they reached the bottom of the hill. And even though everything had spun totally out of control, she was seeing it all in slow motion.

She glanced at the mirror, expecting Quentin's horrible eyes. Instead, she saw the small stepladder she'd used—only a week or so ago—as she painted Sam's house.

How strange. She now thought of it as Sam's house. She saw him. Felt his spirit. And if it was true that your life flashed before your eyes before your death, Sam must be the essence of hers. She felt him here, lending her strength.

Glass smashed. Pebbled glass showered her from behind. Cool night air crept under her skin. And Quentin's rage pressed on her neck.

The truck hurtled toward the cottonwood grove sheltering the big curve in the drive. Past thinking, almost past feeling, Jonna launched herself out the door. She rolled, not sure if the motion came from the impetus of the leap or conscious effort, and landed in the slight indent beside the drive. She watched, paralyzed, as the pickup crashed into the thick shelter belt with a thrashing, crunching sound.

Jonna wasn't sure how long she lay in the dead weeds fifty or so yards from Sam's house, stunned by her impact with the ground and dazed with terror. But she stayed where she was, aching and too afraid to even cry. Her lips quivered silently and she wondered vaguely if God would strike *her* dead for praying for Quentin's death.

She waited, waited, then finally eased herself onto her stomach. Slowly lifting her head, she searched the windswept night for a sign of movement.

"Okay, let's go." Madden brought the keys and was opening the door before Sam could get his feet off the bunk.

"Where?"

"Jonna's," Madden answered grimly.

Sam's heart stopped. "Has something happened?" he managed to say.

"Hell, I hope not."

Sam grabbed his shoes and practically had to run to catch Madden's plump, fast-moving figure.

The sheriff had his car running by the time Sam came around to the passenger side, and Madden's tires squealed as the car left the small parking lot behind the jail before Sam had closed the door. Madden—laid-back, easygoing Madden—was upset. And Sam couldn't choke out a word to find out why. His stomach churned and firmly clogged his constricted throat.

Madden muttered a string of expletives. That startled Sam out of his shock. The strongest language Sam had heard the man use was the three "hells" just minutes ago. "Eighteen months until retirement and I'm gonna get myself fired, letting one of the FBI's killers out of jail on no authority but mine." He swung an awestruck look in Sam's direction. "Do you have any idea how many murderers I've had in my jail in thirty-two years?" He didn't wait for Sam's reply. "None."

"Could we move it a little faster?" Sam said impatiently. He hated the feeling growing in his gut.

"Quentin Kincaid was fired from his job yesterday," Madden said. "For missing work Monday, the day of the calf thing," he reminded.

The feeling got worse. "What was his job?"

"He worked for a damn clipping service. Has for two and a half years. It's the longest he's held a job since he graduated, and he's been clipping items from trade journals the whole damn time."

"So, you expect him to show up at Jonna's? We're going to be waiting?" Why hadn't Madden brought his under-sheriff—or one of the deputies? Sam decided not to ask and press his luck.

"I got another report and tried contacting Connors—couldn't be found. I radioed the deputy on patrol—he's the other side of the county. He's meeting us there. I tried calling Jonna at Moss's—no answer."

Sam's spine stiffened, his skin began to crawl.

The sheriff's curses came in a rash again. "Gary went over there."

"You think Jonna's at the farm?"

"Don't know. She didn't answer her phone."

"And Quentin?" Sam's foot rammed against the right side of his floorboard.

"How the heck should I know?" Madden answered gruffly, and his knuckles showed white around the steering wheel.

"Could we hurry? Use the sirens and lights?"

Their speed picked up, but not enough. "I'm probably being far too suspicious," Madden said to himself.

"I don't want to tell you how to do your job, Sheriff, but isn't being suspicious part of it?"

"We have good people here."

"You're going to have a good but *dead* one if Kincaid finds Jonna before we do," Sam said between clenched teeth.

Madden stepped a little harder on the gas.

"Lights? Sirens?"

"Let's warn him we're coming so he'll hurry and kill her and get the hell out of there," Madden said wryly, shaking his head.

"You sound fairly certain he's there," Sam managed to say.

"I know, and that's what's so crazy." Madden slowed for a corner, then gassed it again, this time a little harder than was probably prudent. "I have no reason to think that."

"But?" Sam could tell there was a *but* there.

"I got that second fax. I started reading and about half-way through, I started shaking. I just keep seeing that poor little girl."

It took Sam a second to realize Madden was talking about Jonna.

"She's always been such a helpless little thing. Big John would kill me from the grave if I let anything happen to her."

The picture Madden painted of Jonna startled Sam. However Jonna struck him—and strike him, she did—

helpless wasn't how he would describe her. She was warm, too trusting, honest, intelligent, sexy, capable, generous—the words didn't quit coming. From the moment he'd seen her, on this subject at least, he'd treated her—and even told her she couldn't handle the truth—like a helpless, incapable child. And he'd been so determined to protect her, he'd put her at risk.

"I know it's ridiculous," Madden went on, "but this shaky feeling just won't quit."

On that subject, Sam had to agree. He hadn't quit shaking for three solid days. It was getting so bad now, he was afraid it would dislocate his ribs. And the horrible, devastating sense of dread weighed so heavily on him, he couldn't think.

"Did you check flights from Chicago to see if there is any record of Kincaid leaving there?" Sam rasped though he couldn't breathe.

"I thought about it for a second," Madden answered. "I didn't really want to know. That's when I came and got you. Made more sense to spend the time getting the hell out here."

"Thank you," Sam whispered, then begged, "Please hurry."

CHAPTER FIFTEEN

Jonna measured time by counting as far as her frazzled mind would allow. She hadn't seen a single sign of movement. Quentin must be seriously injured at the least. Heaven forbid, she still wished him dead.

She rose carefully and tossed out the idea of going down to check the mangled mess in the trees almost as quickly as it formed. Someone else could find him.

She tried to quell her permanent shivering. If she never saw that horrid face again, it would be too soon.

The wind moaned like an omen as she looked up toward her house. Every light blazed but the contemporary fortress on the hill looked cold, forbidding. And even if her legs could make it up there, the phone didn't work—whether by Quentin's hand or the worsening storm, she didn't know.

The farmhouse where she was raised looked a little more appealing, but nothing—absolutely nothing—looked inviting or warm, and Wedman's farm was four miles away. She didn't think she could make it there.

Stiff, bruised and casting feverish looks over her shoulders, Jonna headed for the old house. She stepped into the circle of yard not sheltered by trees and saw Sam's car sitting there. She limped hastily toward it. The best choice of all would be getting out of here. Find someone else to worry about and deal with this chaos. Find someone so she didn't have to be alone.

She wouldn't come back until every little reminder of this nightmare was gone.

And she knew exactly where she wanted to go. She longed more than anything for the security of Sam's arms. They could put her right in the cell with him and lock the door and throw away the—

Keys! Sam's car, of course, didn't have keys. She cursed his security consciousness, then remembered that one of the sheriff's men had brought it in from the end of the drive when they'd arrested him. The keys had probably been put with Sam's possessions at the jail.

Reluctantly, she turned toward Sam's house and prayed that his phone worked.

Her footsteps sounded hollow and ghostly as she crossed the ancient porch. Suddenly, the last thing on this earth she wanted to do was to go into any dark place alone. But she felt evil all around in the starless night. She hurried inside, sagging and practically falling back against the door, and she reached for the light.

Her groping fingers encountered a hand.

"What took you so long?" Quentin asked as he flipped the switch. Light flooded the room.

Jonna screamed as his face materialized inches from hers.

His malevolent laugh filled her bones, and he grabbed her arm, keeping her upright when her knees would have folded and thrown her to the floor.

Worst of all, she couldn't find strength to pull away from his cold, cold hands.

"You've been more fun than anyone."

His breath feathered her skin. She tried not to draw needed air into her lungs, repulsed by the thought that his breathing had contaminated it.

"It's going to be an honor, adding you to *The Record*, Jonna Sanders."

Disgust finally gave her the energy to pull away.

"Doesn't poor little Jonna Sanders like Quentin?"

Jonna felt her death draw near. Her brain refused to function.

"I might even let you see my collection." His grip tightened painfully on her upper arm. "Too bad I'm much smarter than you."

She thought he was baiting, playing with her until his eyes took on a distant glaze and he began to ramble. His hand opened, sliding slowly up her arm. As caressingly as a lover's, it crossed her shoulder and curved around her neck.

She shrank away. The doorknob jabbed her hip from behind and jarred a recent memory.

Her skin would surely melt from his odious touch, but she steeled herself, leaned into it, praying he would see the action as her yielding to his higher brilliance and power.

His wide mouth curved up at one end.

Jonna reached behind her, careful not to move any part of her body except that one forearm and hand. Her fingernail clicked clumsily against the metal knob. Her eyes felt bright and wide as she watched and waited for his reaction.

He kept right on talking.

Her mind couldn't decipher a word.

She squeezed the knob, twisted, held her breath, then yanked the door open as far as her body would allow.

Quentin's mouth gaped midword as he did exactly what she mentally begged him to do. He grabbed the door.

She crashed her body into it with every remaining ounce of strength.

Quentin's surprised howl of pain blended with a boom of thunder as Jonna rushed past him, stunning him just the way she'd surprised Sam the day she had thought he'd destroyed her house.

She rounded the stairwell, ran through the dining room, the kitchen and out the back door, refusing to let the memory of Sam catching her linger more than a second in her mind. Quentin would *not* catch her.

Hope rose as cool air blasted her face. Advantage Jonna, she thought as the wild night closed around her once again. This time, it felt comforting.

She didn't need to see the terrain. She *knew* the barren hills snuggling up close to her childhood home almost as well as she knew her name. Her feet felt like wings as she raced toward the dry creekbed a quarter of a mile beyond the barn.

Quentin emerged from the house behind her, blundering and banging and screaming in a mad mixture of rage and pain.

A bolt of lightning rent the sky and hung above her like some crazy neon directional arrow, and Quentin's otherworldly cry turned triumphant.

Another flash of lightning split the sky and a booming rumble of thunder fell through, bursting a cloud that held giant splats of cold rain.

Despair descended with the rain, trying to crush her reinstated hope. She refused it, shook it off, pushed it away. He'd seen the direction she had taken and there was nothing in this stark, open land to use for cover, but crazy, murderous Quentin Kincaid had to catch her, dammit. And he wasn't going to catch her—or kill her—easily.

She had too much to live for.

Sam and Sheriff Madden neared the long drive as a sprinkling of rain began to fall.

Madden pointed at the house on the hill. "Lit like a damn candle," he murmured. "What the hell is she doing still here?"

Sam's heart stopped. "She may have left them on intentionally," Sam offered, as much for comfort for himself as for the older man. "I don't think she's turned them off since he destroyed her house." He hoped—prayed—that was it. He wouldn't even consider what they might find if she *was* still here.

He felt Quentin Kincaid's loathsome presence as surely as he felt the approaching winter in this building, churning storm.

"Look."

"What?"

"That light wasn't on a second ago," Sam said quickly, pointing toward the farmhouse.

"You sure?" Madden's foot pressed the brake and they turned into the drive.

"Positive."

"Look there!" Madden aimed Sam's attention to a jumble of folded metal and broken trees. "Jonna's truck," he said unnecessarily. "Something's happened." Madden hit the gas and they were halfway up the drive and beside the smashed mess in seconds.

Sam was out and running to investigate before the car stopped. A bloodcurdling howl competed with the rolling thunder and froze him in his tracks.

"That wasn't Jonna," Madden said.

Sam changed course, started toward the noise. It mutated into a gleeful, horrendous chortle.

"Get back here, you idiot!" Madden yelled.

Fear in the sheriff's voice took the insult out of the order, but Sam hurried back anyway.

"Here." Madden met him halfway with his service revolver. "You may need this."

Sam shuddered. "You may, too."

"I've got a rifle in the car." He cocked his head in that direction as another streak of lightning slashed the night. "I'm gonna check this out—" he indicated the wreckage "—then head up there—" he lifted his head to stare at Jonna's house "—or follow you, depending on what I see or hear between now and then. You yell if you need help."

Sam nodded then charged again toward the farmhouse.

Jonna had almost reached the edge of the gully when she heard Quentin rapidly closing the distance between them. She hesitated, uncertain what she should do.

The cavity in the landscape was abrupt, a little deeper than she was tall. She had planned to use it for cover, running its length until it met the road. Should she risk getting into it now? With Quentin on her heels, she might be making her own trap.

The dry creekbed might also make a good fortress, she realized. There were rocks, dead tree limbs, lots of things she could pick up and pelt him with. Just let Quentin Kincaid try to come in after her.

Her body ached, a vicious stitch stabbed her side from the running. And the rain bore down, increasing in size, velocity and frequency with every drop.

She shivered. Her teeth chattered from cold, wet terror. But she was not going to let Sam's monster win.

Lightning silhouetted two figures against the sky as Sam rounded the corner of the house—male and female, maybe ten feet apart.

The Jonna shape paused, turned one way, then another. Her body vibrated with life and emotion, like a skilled and graceful dancer in a superbly choreographed ballet.

Her figure swayed and leaned against the slightly lighter backdrop of sky. Quentin's figure was tall and lean, and his movements were in many ways as graceful as hers, as he reached for her, reducing the distance between them to inches.

Sam's breath caught as Jonna's shape drifted elegantly away.

With Technicolor light and quadriphonic sound, Jonna performed a heartrending elusive lover's dance for Sam. But Quentin entered the exotic scene. And the accompaniment screeched sorely off-key.

Quentin reached for her, this time touching. And Jonna poised and balanced on the edge of some unseen abyss. Sam's heart felt as if it were being torn in two and dragged in pieces from between his ribs. His inanimate limbs came to life again.

The lightning died. Their shadows melded with the savage night. Sam cringed as a wounded cry ripped open the night. Then the wind whipped the sound away and Sam realized it came from him. And it was nothing more—or less—than Jonna's name.

Perched on the edge of the gully, Jonna felt Quentin's fingers grip her arm, then slip. A sob of relief escaped her and turned into a scream. Then she realized it wasn't hers. Someone else—Sam—was wailing her name.

All the emotion she'd been holding in poured through her soul and from her knees, her toes, her fingertips. She felt it overpower her, then escape from every centimeter of her skin.

She'd never imagined such horror existed. But it wasn't Quentin or her death that released the incapacitating terror. It was the sudden, sure knowledge that Sam loved her. She could hear it in her name. The sound echoed and reverberated around her and finally released her tears.

Now that she had found him, there could be no greater tragedy than never having the chance to tell him she loved him. He needed to hear it. He needed *her*.

Quentin's hands came at her again, brushing but missing their grasp on her neck.

She refused to die. She fought him off, twisting and turning toward where Sam had called for her.

Quentin lunged one more time.

"Sam?" she cried, wrenching aside as Quentin began to slide on the rain-slicked ground. She watched, paralyzed with disbelief, as he disappeared over the edge of the dropoff.

She heard a thud, an "oomph," as he hit bottom.

"Sam," she cried again, backing away as Quentin's vile hand clamped around her ankle. She sobbed as he tugged.

Her feet left the solid earth and he pulled her down, down into the dark hole with him. She grasped at the walls of the gully. She sought a stabilizing hold on the hard wet ground, the clumps of dried prairie grass—anything but Quentin—as she slithered and fell, feetfirst.

Quentin growled with triumph as she connected with the floor of the creekbed. She struggled as his hands encircled her throat.

Spreading herself flat against the angled wall, she scrambled, groped, strained away from his tightening fingers. His body pressed disgustingly against her, pinning her in place.

Her hand closed over a rough-edged stone. Her vision blurred. She raised the rock, aimed it shakily toward his head. It glanced off, barely scraping his forehead, so that she was stunned when his hands loosened momentarily.

He yowled, more from surprise than with the impact, and he renewed his assault on her neck.

Jonna's hand fell and immediately covered another rock. This one was rounder, heavier, a little easier to lift. She felt her consciousness waver, threaten to slip away.

Terror gave her one last burst of energy. This time, she swung wide, using the heaviness of the rock for momentum. She heard it thunk as it clipped him solidly on the side of the head.

His body jerked up, away from her. With her new-found mobility, she rammed her knee hard against his groin.

Quentin thrashed and fell against her. With a massive surge of strength fueled by revulsion, she thrust him aside and frantically searched for another rock. When her hands found a broken branch from some long-forgotten tree, she only used one smooth motion as she picked it up and struck.

The blow hit the back of his head, and the ancient wood shattered in her hands.

Quentin sagged against the side of the gully.

Sobbing, Jonna clambered out of his reach. The sob changed to a wail as her foot slipped and failed to find purchase on the slope. For every step up, she lost two as she slid back on the rain-slickened earth.

Quentin moaned and rustled, and her nerves screamed as a hand reached down through the rain.

"Jonna. Jonna?"

Sam's voice, the lifeline he extended just by reaching out to her suddenly seemed too far away as Quentin's hands clamped over her neck again, taking her air, casting a curtain of pain and dazzling bright spots between her and Sam. She tried to speak his name and the fingers tightened, rendering her weak and nearly senseless.

She heard a soft "oomph" as something dropped beside her. She felt Sam's presence as she'd never felt him before. A peaceful certainty that everything was going to be okay and a wave of blackness engulfed her at the same time. Suddenly, she didn't care. Sam was with her now.

She wasn't sure exactly how much time had passed when she realized Quentin's vile fingers were no longer on her. Gagging and gasping with the attempt to draw air into her oxygen-starved lungs consumed all her efforts as Quentin yowled again in frustrated pain. His animalistic snarl reverberated around her, then came to an abrupt end.

"Sam," she managed to croak as he touched her.

"Just a minute," he whispered. "I'll get you out of here in just a minute." She felt him leave her side and the wet and shadowy world gradually came back into focus.

Quentin lay on his side, staring blankly at her from the other side of the gully.

"Jonna?" Her drenched and muddy hair blocked her vision as she turned toward Sam's voice. He was above her again, his hand extended.

She grabbed it, hanging on for dear life as he lifted and pulled her up and out of danger, then folded and sheltered her against his heart.

She didn't know she was frozen until she felt his warmth. She didn't know her heart was still beating until she felt the pace of his. Suddenly, she wasn't sure that she *hadn't* died. This could very well be heaven—except for the violent rattling inside her head.

"Shh . . ." Sam stroked her, swayed her gently. And she realized the noise was the clatter of her teeth, her terrified sobs, maybe even her shaking bones.

"You bastard." Sam's other voice, his hard and hateful one, jolted her back to torrential reality. The arm that didn't hold her stretched over the deep scar in the earth. And his steady hand held a gun.

A streak of lightning revealed his target. Quentin. He looked even more deranged than he had earlier, but he'd lost his power over her and Jonna turned her remaining strength back to Sam.

Sam—the man she loved more than life itself. The man had already been nearly destroyed by the demon at the wrong end of the gun and he grew deathly still. She felt Sam's hatred curve his finger around the trigger.

"Don't," Jonna whispered and the now-gentle rain washed away all her fear—except for Sam.

Sam looked at her but she wasn't sure he saw her. "Sam, please, don't let *him* destroy you now."

Sam could taste the bitter revenge he'd hungered for, and Quentin Kincaid had earned the hell Sam wanted to send him to. But mud-caked, wonderfully *alive* Jonna, looked at Sam with absolute trust in her eyes and shamed him.

He'd betrayed her trust, never earned it. If it had been up to him, Quentin would have killed her.

Sam's arm tightened possessively around her. His finger twitched, and he focused back on the pathetically evil bastard sneering up at him.

Don't let him destroy you. Jonna's words reverberated in the air around him. Destroy him? The man already had. He'd calmly taken his sister's life. He'd tried to kill Jonna.

"Sam," she repeated softly. "We can't be like him. We can't."

Sam's warm tears mingled with the cold rain pelting his face. The bastard had robbed him of his soul. How could Quentin Kincaid destroy him any more than he already had?

"You did what you had to, Sam. The police are involved now. Let them have him. We don't have to kill him."

Sam could kill him, say it was in self-defense. He knew without question that Jonna would tell the authorities—if they asked—that he didn't have a choice, that he did it to save her. But Jonna had saved herself.

"He'll be here with us the rest of our lives if we kill him," she said.

Sweet, capable Jonna squeezed the hand he held tight about her shoulders, as if she could hear him think her name. He felt her strong, gentle love flowing to him, around him, quenching and drowning the hate.

He looked at Quentin, wanted him to die. But it wouldn't be for his sister now. Nothing could avenge Denise's death—or bring her back to life. The revenge would be for himself, nothing more than a payback for his having stolen Sam's tight control of his well-ordered life. He'd despised Quentin for making him feel powerless when he had every intention of saving the world.

Tension seeped away as he realized he couldn't save anyone but himself. The hand holding the gun dropped to his side.

Jonna sighed.

"God, I love you." He caught her so tightly to him he heard her gasp in pain. "I'm sorry."

"Oh, but it feels so good." She laughed, cried, murmured his name.

Quentin moved, and Sam waved the gun in the insane man's direction. "I wouldn't if I were you," he said, as sweeping strokes of red light painted the area around them ghoulish colors. "The sheriff's coming."

"Thank heavens," Jonna whispered. "How did you get here anyway?"

"Later." He bent to kiss her as a car door slammed behind them. "We've got too many things to do first." Live. Celebrate life.

"You two all right?" Madden heralded them.

"Will be as soon as you take this monster off our hands," Sam replied. "Oh, yes, we have lots to do," he repeated, nuzzling Jonna's ear.

Another of the sheriff's brigade started slowly across the rough pasture. "Quentin Kincaid, I presume?" Madden said, scowling at the vacant-eyed man.

"I'm not sure anyone is still home in there," Sam said as he set Jonna aside and helped Madden pull the shadow man from the ravine. A deputy and Connors disembarked from the newly arrived car. "He's all yours," Sam said as Madden clamped on handcuffs.

"Wait." Madden hollered as Jonna started to lead Sam away. "You can't leave. We've got to—"

"I'm wet. I'm cold," Jonna called. "You know where to find us."

"Tomorrow," Sam added.

"You can't... We can't..." Madden yelled after them.

Sam drew her as close as physically possible, given the circumstances. "You don't need me to protect you, Jonna—you're a very competent woman—"

She practically lit the night with her satisfied glow of pride.

"But if you'll let me stay, I promise, I'll keep you warm."

Her simple, secret smile warmed her eyes. "I'm counting on it." She sighed, stopping, turning in his arms. "Say it again," she urged. "Say you love me again, Sam."

He kissed her, holding her so tight even the rain couldn't get between them. "If it helps, I'll say it a hundred thousand times."

He said it.

"I love you, too, Sam."

"I know," he said. A peaceful feeling of awe mixed in with the genuine belief and genuine gratitude overwhelmed him. He kissed her again, this time with reverence.

"Now, let's get out of this storm." From the look in her eyes, this storm wouldn't be any stronger than the one building to be unleashed inside.

Neither looked back as they walked, wrapped in each other's arms, toward home.

EPILOGUE

Jonna smiled and waved as she turned the car into the drive. Coming from the opposite direction, Sheriff Madden waved back, put his turn signal on and followed her in.

It was fall again, exactly the kind of day it had been when Sam had first come. Jonna drove slowly, admiring the rich autumn colors of the trees along the lane, and watching for Ryan and Shelly, her hired man's two-and four-year-old kids. They were there, tanned and ripping and running across the yard of the old farmhouse, and Anita was sipping iced tea on the porch watching them. She lifted her hand toward her friend and felt a surge of happiness at the changes in her life in the last year. The biggest one came around the corner of the house from the direction of the barn.

This time she braked, and Sam sauntered up and opened the passenger door. She expected him to lean over and give her a kiss. Instead he threw his wide-brimmed cowboy hat into the back and got in.

"Through for the day?" she asked breathlessly as his lips brushed hers.

"For now," he murmured, drawing away reluctantly and flicking a thumb over his shoulder. "Looks like we've got company."

Madden honked as if in reply.

Sam closed the door and she restarted the procession to the top of the hill.

"Beautiful day," Madden called as he stepped out of his car.

"Oh, I don't know, Rod," Sam said, his hand protectively at Jonna's waist as he guided her toward the house. "I suppose it depends on what brought you here."

Madden faked disappointment as he followed them in without an invitation. "And I thought we'd become friends."

Sam laughed and pulled a chair out at the table. "Sit down, you old fool. What can I get you to drink?"

"Iced tea sounds good," he said, removing his hat and setting it beside him.

"You've got news about Quentin?" Jonna asked, impatiently sitting on her leg, leaning onto the table with her hands lightly clasped.

Madden shook his head. "No. And I don't think I will have any time soon. I don't think either of you will ever have to testify. Last time I talked to Agent Connors, he said Kincaid is more spaced out than the day they put him in that place for the criminally insane. The biggest reaction they've had from him was the day Dolly came to do her motherly duty by visiting him. He went berserk, tried to attack her, then immediately went into his zombie mode again as soon as they restrained him. I personally don't think that's going to change."

"So?" Sam set glasses down in front of both Jonna and the sheriff.

Madden hesitated, obviously pondering how to broach whatever subject he'd come to discuss. Jonna watched Sam lounge into the chair beside her and reached for his hand. It was so nice to be able to touch him whenever she wanted, to reach for him and know he would be there.

He smiled, told her all sorts of secret things with his eyes, then pulled her hand into his lap and idly twisted her wedding ring as he turned his attention back to Madden.

"You know I plan to retire in another six months," Rod said finally. "Elections are coming up soon and I've been thinking about my replacement for a long time. I hope I can convince you to run for county sheriff, Sam."

Sam laughed. "You're kidding. First you arrest me, now you want me to take your place?"

Madden fiddled with his hat sheepishly. "You know I wouldn't—"

"Oh, I know, Rod," Sam interrupted. "I'm just taken a little aback."

"You'd be good," Madden said. "I can't think of anyone who would be better than you. And you wouldn't have any trouble getting elected," Madden hurried on with his pitch. "I doubt anyone would even run against you if you threw your hat in the ring. You're pretty much a hero around here."

Jonna gazed at Sam, saw him quickly dampen the enthusiasm in his eyes. "What about Gary?" Sam referred to the undersheriff.

"Since that whole damn thing out here, he's gone nuts on me." Madden shook his head. "He doesn't want the job. He's been working day and night, taking some college classes at Emporia State, and Agent Connors is trying to help him get into the FBI academy. He's decided he likes *big* crime."

As if to contradict Jonna's earlier thoughts, Sam shook his head. "I've decided I kind of like farming, Sheriff," he said. Jonna squeezed his hand.

"Well it sure agrees with you *and* the farm," Madden said. "I couldn't help noticing when I came in, it's beginning to look as busy as it did when Big John was around— no offense," he added quickly, stealing Jonna a glance.

"None taken." She smiled. It would have taken a lot to offend her these days. "I was just going through the motions. I'm glad Sam has taken the responsibilities off my hands."

"So you think Sam running for sheriff would be a bad idea, too," he said glumly.

"Not at all. From what I've seen of how hard you work, Rod, I think Sam could probably do a bit of both if he wanted to—especially since we've hired another man. I think it's up to Sam."

Sam shook his head and Madden gulped down his tea.

"Let me think about it," Sam said, standing up and pretty much indicating that as far as he was concerned the talk was through. Madden didn't waste time with his leaving.

"So what did you think?" Jonna asked as soon as the sheriff was gone.

He drew her out of her chair, pulling her close, placing the gentlest of kisses against her brow. "Oh, Jonna. I haven't ever been as happy as I've been the past year with you. Why would we want to rock the boat? Mess around with things?"

"Because some of the changes have been so good," she whispered, trying to burrow even deeper against him so he wouldn't see the tears in her eyes. "I was just thinking about them on my way home. Do you know how lonely I was before you came? All that's changed."

"And we had to go through some bad to get to the good," he said, holding her tight.

"Do you know how much I love having friends just down the hill? And our anniversary is coming up in another six weeks. Oh, Sam, I've always loved this place, but this is how it's supposed to be, not lifeless like it was a year ago. My dad would be so proud of what you've done with it."

"I'm proud of it, too," he whispered, resting his cheek against the top of her head. "So how on earth would my being sheriff improve anything?"

"Maybe it wouldn't," she said. "I just think you should consider it. You always dreamed of saving the world. Maybe this is your chance."

"You think I can do that from Whitfield, Kansas?" He laughed.

She loved his laugh, she loved him, and the way his dark eyes sparkled and how he looked relaxed and at peace now most of the time. She loved the way he flexed and stretched when he was weary from hard work, as he was doing now.

She pushed him toward the couch in the living room and sat him down. "I think you can make it better. And right now, that's more important than it's ever been," she admonished him seriously.

"Oh?" he mocked her.

"Oh, yes," she said. "You wait right here, I'll show you why." She got her purse from the kitchen counter, dramatically opening it and withdrawing the picture. She savored the act of handing it to him as he drew her down onto his lap.

He frowned as he looked at the black-and-white picture that looked like a blob taken way out of focus.

"This is her head," she said, turning the picture right side up for him and outlining one of the more distinct shapes with her fingernail. "This is one of her arms—"

She got no further before he grabbed her, turning her around. "You're pregnant?"

She nodded. "And this is your first picture of your daughter," she said, holding it in front of his face again. "Isn't she wonderful?"

He laughed shakily. "She obviously takes after her father," he said, his eyes filling with tears. "I sure hope she gets as beautiful as her mom."

"Oh, Sam." She sighed and words were no longer necessary.

*   *   *   *   *

Dark secrets, dangerous desire...

Lovers
DARK AND
DANGEROUS

Three spine-tingling tales from the dark side of love.

This October, enter the world of shadowy romance as Silhouette presents the third in their annual tradition of thrilling love stories and chilling story lines. Written by three of Silhouette's top names:

LINDSAY McKENNA
LEE KARR
RACHEL LEE

Haunting a store near you this October.

Only from *Silhouette®*

...where passion lives.

JINGLE BELLS, WEDDING BELLS:
Silhouette's Christmas Collection for 1994

Christmas Wish List

*To beat the crowds at the malls and get the perfect present for *everyone,* even that snoopy Mrs. Smith next door!

*To get through the holiday parties without running my panty hose.

*To bake cookies, decorate the house and serve the perfect Christmas dinner—just like the women in all those magazines.

*To sit down, curl up and read my Silhouette Christmas stories!

Join *New York Times* bestselling author Nora Roberts, along with popular writers Barbara Boswell, Myrna Temte and Elizabeth August, as we celebrate the joys of Christmas—and the magic of marriage—with

JINGLE BELLS, WEDDING BELLS

Silhouette's Christmas Collection for 1994.

Welcome To The
Dark Side Of Love...

AVAILABLE THIS MONTH

#41 MEMORY'S LAMP—Marilyn Tracy

Sandy Rush's mind was no longer her own. In comforting a dying woman, Sandy's brain had somehow retained the murder victim's every memory. And one recollection, rife with terror, starred dashing archaeologist Cliff Broderick, who was quick to reach the crime scene—and now refused to leave Sandy's side. Sandy sensed that Cliff needed her, but why? She could think of only one motive behind his obvious interest, and now her troubled mind was reeling with doubt—and desire.

#42 BETWEEN DUSK AND DAWN—Val Daniels
Premiere

Jonna Sanders's peaceful world had erupted into a living nightmare. Eerie phone calls in the dead of night, unseen intruders and a mysterious yet sensuous stranger all added up to something weird. Sam Barton was battling his own demons, particularly the sinister serial killer who was plotting Jonna's destruction—a madman about whom Sam knew far too much....

COMING NEXT MONTH

#43 DARK, DARK MY LOVER'S EYES—Barbara Faith

When tutor Juliana Fleming accepted an assignment in Mexico, she had no idea the turn her life would take. Kico Vega—her solemn, needy student—immediately warmed to her presence, but Kico's father, Rafael, showed her nothing but contempt. Until he took Julie as his bride, ravishing her with his all-consuming desire—yet setting in motion Julie's worst nightmare.

#44 SLEEPING TIGERS—Sandra Dark

Someone didn't want Sabrina Glade to finish the biography she was ghostwriting—ever. First her subject mysteriously died. Then would-be heir Spencer Bradley emerged from obscurity, demanding that the book be stopped. Sabrina felt strangely attracted to the secretive Spencer, but then she began to wonder how far he would go to ensure that his family skeletons remained forever in the closet.

IT'S FREE! IT'S FUN! ENTER THE

☆ "Hooray for ☆ Hollywood" ☆

SWEEPSTAKES!

We're giving away prizes to celebrate the screening of four new romance movies on CBS TV this fall! Look for the movies on four Sunday afternoons in October. And be sure to return your Official Entry Coupons to try for a fabulous vacation in Hollywood!

☆ If you're the Grand Prize winner we'll fly you and your companion to Los Angeles for a 7-day/6-night vacation you'll never forget!

☆ You'll stay at the luxurious Regent Beverly Wilshire Hotel,* a prime location for celebrity spotting!

☆ You'll have time to visit Universal Studios,* stroll the Hollywood Walk of Fame, check out celebrities' footprints at Mann's Chinese Theater, ride a trolley to see the homes of the stars, and more!

☆ The prize includes a rental car for 7 days and $1,000.00 pocket money!

Someone's going to win this fabulous prize, and it might just be you! Remember, the more times you enter, the better your chances of winning!

ALSO Five hundred entrants will each receive SUNGLASSES OF THE STARS! Don't miss out. ENTER TODAY!

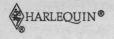 HARLEQUIN® 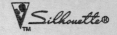 Silhouette®

The movie event of the season can be the reading event of the year!

Lights... The lights go on in October when CBS presents Harlequin/Silhouette Sunday Matinee Movies. These four movies are based on bestselling Harlequin and Silhouette novels.

Camera... As the cameras roll, be the first to read the original novels the movies are based on!

Action... Through this offer, you can have these books sent directly to you! Just fill in the order form below and you could be reading the books...before the movie!

48288-4	Treacherous Beauties by Cheryl Emerson		
		$3.99 U.S./$4.50 CAN.	☐
83305-9	Fantasy Man by Sharon Green		
		$3.99 U.S./$4.50 CAN.	☐
48289-2	A Change of Place by Tracy Sinclair		
		$3.99 U.S./$4.50CAN.	☐
83306-7	Another Woman by Margot Dalton		
		$3.99 U.S./$4.50 CAN.	☐

TOTAL AMOUNT	$
POSTAGE & HANDLING	$
($1.00 for one book, 50¢ for each additional)	
APPLICABLE TAXES*	$ _____
TOTAL PAYABLE	$ _____
(check or money order—please do not send cash)	

To order, complete this form and send it, along with a check or money order for the total above, payable to Harlequin Books, to: **In the U.S.:** 3010 Walden Avenue, P.O. Box 9047, Buffalo, NY 14269-9047; **In Canada:** P.O. Box 613, Fort Erie, Ontario, L2A 5X3.

Name: _____

Address: _____ City: _____

State/Prov.: _____ Zip/Postal Code: _____

*New York residents remit applicable sales taxes.
  Canadian residents remit applicable GST and provincial taxes.

CBSPR

"HOORAY FOR HOLLYWOOD" SWEEPSTAKES

HERE'S HOW THE SWEEPSTAKES WORKS

OFFICIAL RULES — NO PURCHASE NECESSARY

To enter, complete an Official Entry Form or hand print on a 3" x 5" card the words "HOORAY FOR HOLLYWOOD", your name and address and mail your entry in the pre-addressed envelope (if provided) or to: "Hooray for Hollywood" Sweepstakes, P.O. Box 9076, Buffalo, NY 14269-9076 or "Hooray for Hollywood" Sweepstakes, P.O. Box 637, Fort Erie, Ontario L2A 5X3. Entries must be sent via First Class Mail and be received no later than 12/31/94. No liability is assumed for lost, late or misdirected mail.

Winners will be selected in random drawings to be conducted no later than January 31, 1995 from all eligible entries received.

Grand Prize: A 7-day/6-night trip for 2 to Los Angeles, CA including round trip air transportation from commercial airport nearest winner's residence, accommodations at the Regent Beverly Wilshire Hotel, free rental car, and $1,000 spending money. (Approximate prize value which will vary dependent upon winner's residence: $5,400.00 U.S.); 500 Second Prizes: A pair of "Hollywood Star" sunglasses (prize value: $9.95 U.S. each). Winner selection is under the supervision of D.L. Blair, Inc., an independent judging organization, whose decisions are final. Grand Prize travelers must sign and return a release of liability prior to traveling. Trip must be taken by 2/1/96 and is subject to airline schedules and accommodations availability.

Sweepstakes offer is open to residents of the U.S. (except Puerto Rico) and Canada who are 18 years of age or older, except employees and immediate family members of Harlequin Enterprises, Ltd., its affiliates, subsidiaries, and all agencies, entities or persons connected with the use, marketing or conduct of this sweepstakes. All federal, state, provincial, municipal and local laws apply. Offer void wherever prohibited by law. Taxes and/or duties are the sole responsibility of the winners. Any litigation within the province of Quebec respecting the conduct and awarding of prizes may be submitted to the Regie des loteries et courses du Quebec. All prizes will be awarded; winners will be notified by mail. No substitution of prizes are permitted. Odds of winning are dependent upon the number of eligible entries received.

Potential grand prize winner must sign and return an Affidavit of Eligibility within 30 days of notification. In the event of non-compliance within this time period, prize may be awarded to an alternate winner. Prize notification returned as undeliverable may result in the awarding of prize to an alternate winner. By acceptance of their prize, winners consent to use of their names, photographs, or likenesses for purpose of advertising, trade and promotion on behalf of Harlequin Enterprises, Ltd., without further compensation unless prohibited by law. A Canadian winner must correctly answer an arithmetical skill-testing question in order to be awarded the prize.

For a list of winners (available after 2/28/95), send a separate stamped, self-addressed envelope to: Hooray for Hollywood Sweepstakes 3252 Winners, P.O. Box 4200, Blair, NE 68009.

CBSRLS

OFFICIAL ENTRY COUPON

"Hooray for Hollywood"
SWEEPSTAKES!

Yes, I'd love to win the Grand Prize — a vacation in Hollywood —
or one of 500 pairs of "sunglasses of the stars"! Please enter me
in the sweepstakes!

This entry must be received by December 31, 1994.
Winners will be notified by January 31, 1995.

Name _____

Address _____ Apt. _____

City _____

State/Prov. _____ Zip/Postal Code _____

Daytime phone number _____
(area code)

Mail all entries to: Hooray for Hollywood Sweepstakes,
P.O. Box 9076, Buffalo, NY 14269-9076.
In Canada, mail to: Hooray for Hollywood Sweepstakes,
P.O. Box 637, Fort Erie, ON L2A 5X3.

KCH

OFFICIAL ENTRY COUPON

"Hooray for Hollywood"
SWEEPSTAKES!

Yes, I'd love to win the Grand Prize — a vacation in Hollywood —
or one of 500 pairs of "sunglasses of the stars"! Please enter me
in the sweepstakes!

This entry must be received by December 31, 1994.
Winners will be notified by January 31, 1995.

Name _____

Address _____ Apt. _____

City _____

State/Prov. _____ Zip/Postal Code _____

Daytime phone number _____
(area code)

Mail all entries to: Hooray for Hollywood Sweepstakes,
P.O. Box 9076, Buffalo, NY 14269-9076.
In Canada, mail to: Hooray for Hollywood Sweepstakes,
P.O. Box 637, Fort Erie, ON L2A 5X3.

KCH